UNDERGROWTH

Also by Ellen King Rice

The EvoAngel (2016)

Lichenwald (2019)

PRAISE FOR *THE EVOANGEL*

'Compelling characters and plot with a little fungi thrown in! A FINALIST and highly recommended.' *The Wishing Shelf BookAwards*

"Melding together of science and a great thriller . . ."

"This is a great read and with such an unusual plot twist."

"A wonderful read!"

"A delightful page-turning thriller . . ."

"A totally engrossing read . . ."
On-line reviews

Dedicated to friends of nature, to fans of dogs,
and
to all people with hearts of courage and lives of resilience.

Cover by Damonza.com

Art by Duncan Sheffels.

Library of Congress Control Number: 2018904455

Paperback ISBN: 978-0-9969796-6-5
Epub ISBN: 978-0-9969796-7-2
Mobi ISBN: 978-0-9969796-8-9

UNDERGROWTH

By Ellen King Rice

A story of mushrooms in the woods
of the Pacific Northwest

www.ellenkingrice.com

The past is certain, the future obscure.
Thales of Miletus (c. 640 BCE – 546 BCE)

Chapter One

Saturday, April 22, 10 a.m.
Mason County, Washington

The dead man's body lay on the forest floor, just to the left of a magnificent shelf fungus. Dr. Oh's knees protested as he knelt to scrutinize the enormous *Bridgeoporus nobilissimus*. The pale-edged shelf fungus projected from a massive stump of western hemlock, *Tsuga heterophylla*. The fungus spanned approximately 1.5 meters, its rough surface congested with lichens, small ferns and forest litter.

The mushroom was an enormous specimen, even for *B. nobilissimus*. It easily weighed a hundred and thirty kilos. A specimen this big might be a record.

Dr. Oh knew his heart rate was up from its usual seventy-two beats per minute. This glorious specimen wasn't on the coastal side of the Olympic range. It was in south Mason County at a modest elevation, its longevity made possible by the superb protective landscape and the grove of surrounding trees.

This specimen existed because the cluster of ancient stumps created conditions that clearly suited the fungus. Dr. Oh looked at the tumbled slope above the stump. The jumble of logs, like so many pick-up sticks, signaled an unstable area. It would be dangerous to approach this bench of ground from above.

The steepness of the ravine below the stump and the thickness of the devil's club, *Oplopanax horridus,* and evergreen huckleberry, *Vaccinium ovatum*, at the gully bottom had kept out casual hikers.

Another important detail was the upright stance of the host stump. The *B. nobilissimus* required placement on a vertical tree or stump with an intact root system to survive. If the stump should slump horizontally, the fungus would fail.

Dr. Oh lifted his chin, proud of his ability to evaluate the biological details despite the adrenaline coursing through his system. He had made many discoveries in his fifty years as a professor of mycology and botany, but this was a particularly impressive organism. As an April drizzle fell through the trees, Dr. Oh's thin lips spread into a smile. He might be eighty-five, but he wasn't dead yet. He was out in the woods and still making discoveries.

He noted that his excitement momentarily overrode the twinges of complaint radiating from his knees — how fascinating that the mind could temporarily negate pain impulses. His physician, Dr. Park, had told him, "Keep the brain working with easy outings to learn new things."

He wondered what Dr. Park would say about today's hike. Finding a body next to a mycological beauty was surely not what Park had in mind when he'd suggested gentle excursions.

Dr. Oh turned his attention to the body. The dead man lay sprawled, face down, on the forest floor, flattening a mat of mosses. An oval of congealed blood pooled on a fallen leaf next to the man's crushed skull. The smooth, wooden handle of a tool protruded from the undergrowth nearby. A band of black electrical tape encircled the end of the handle.

The man's boots, daypack, rain pants and parka were unscratched and of high quality. A pristine camera lay in the duff with the door to the chip slot open. This had been a wealthy man.

Oh's eyes returned to the fungus. It really did look like a shelf protruding from the tree stump. Hikers had destroyed at least one large specimen of *Bridgeoporus nobilissimus* by jumping onto the organism. This species grew so very slowly.

He shook his head. How horrible to contemplate hundreds of years of growth destroyed in seconds.

"Ou-oo! Ou-oo-oo!" A haunting call floated through the woods.

Dr. Oh returned the cry, noting that both calls suitably mimicked the invasive barred owl, *Strix varia.*

The red of a jacket flickered through the understory as a hiker worked up the gully.

"Grandpa?"

"Up here," Dr. Oh called back. "Tread carefully, please."

Jasmine took her time coming up the slope. At eighteen his granddaughter had conquered the awkwardness of her earlier years and now picked her way up the ravine with the grace of a doe.

"Whoa, what a tree this was!" Jasmine grinned as she scrambled up to the bench of land where he knelt.

"There's more." He motioned her closer.

"A Fuzzy Sandozi?" Oh, my God. Look at it!"

Sudden tears blurred his vision for a moment. She understood. The scruffy fungus appeared magnificent to his granddaughter too. He sniffed and blinked. He'd become astonishingly sentimental of late.

Jasmine stepped around the edge of the stump and came to a stop next to her grandfather. She took in the size of the shelf fungus and then noticed the still body on the forest floor. "Holy shit."

Her grandfather did not admonish her. He stood and reached out to cup her elbow in his hand. "The man is dead. I believe this fungus is a particularly large specimen — possibly even a record."

"Do you think that guy was a mushroom hunter?"

Dr. Oh shook his head. "This species is not edible, medicinal or psychoactive. I don't see an obvious connection between the man and this fungus. However, recall what we saw on the road."

"Energy drink cans and candy wrappers."

"Yes. Lately men have been looking for *Acer macrophyllum.*"

"Fiddleback big-leaf maple. They are making money selling that stock wood to guitar makers." Jasmine stared down at the shelf fungus and then at the body.

"Yes. But there were no vehicles parked so I thought we would be alone in our exploration of this ravine." Dr. Oh studied the dead man for another moment. "Perhaps he photographed someone that did not want to be photographed." He paused before adding, "Do you know what I want to do?"

"Call the police?" she ventured.

"No." Dr. Oh took a deep breath and said, "I want to move the body."

Guard three things from your neighbor:
Your wife, your garden and your truffles. French proverb

Chapter Two

Saturday, April 22, 10 a.m.
Thurston County Fairgrounds, The Benoshek Building.

"TEOTWAWKI stands for 'The End of the World as We Know It.' Will you be ready?" Duane Dwerryhouse paused. With a blonde flat-top haircut and upper body muscles bulging under a camo T-shirt, Duane looked ready for war. At the rear of the seated crowd, his twenty-year-old niece stood and listened respectfully. Elspeth resisted the temptation to put her hands in her pockets or even flip her dark braid off her shoulder. Her uncle had no patience for sales help who looked bored.

No way would she check her cell phone. Not only would that earn her a hard eye from her uncle, it was also useless. She'd checked for messages six times during their set up hour. There was nothing from "her" professor.

Right. As if he was "hers."

Elspeth scanned the room. *It's got to be the earthquake show,* she thought. Today Duane's Survival Saturday Sale had drawn a mixed crowd. Earthquake details tended to mesmerize both urban and rural customers.

The couple in the expensive Arc'teryx jackets would be skeptical of the underground shelter plans but might bite on technology to protect cellphones and computers. She could sell them battery chargers and perhaps the gizmo to shelter electronics from an electromagnetic pulse. The device packaging promised protection from lightning, sun flares and nuclear explosions. She had her doubts on all three claims but, as Uncle Duane often said, her job was to sell, not to verify.

The large guys in jeans and flannel shirts were already devoted survivalists. They would have their home shelters, firearms collection and bug out bags — but their minds and wallets could be led to the "Without rule of Law" situations. The WROL anxious usually bought pocket copies of the Constitution and the shell holders for ammunition trading.

Elspeth knew the home-schooling mothers escaping their children for the morning would be the best buyers of the day. Each of the women had already been given a "survival-shopping checklist." The ladies usually departed with headlamps, water purification pumps, freeze-dried foods and a coupon for the online shop, all expressions of profound love and anxiety.

The Boy Scouts were easy. Knives and fire starter.

The stoner dude and his girlfriend might drop a twenty on a mushroom field guide.

Elspeth's beloved eighteen-year-old cousin, Carmen, brought down the meeting room lights and Duane thumbed the slide show clicker. *The Cascadia Fault* flashed on the screen in a neon green font. Elspeth grinned. *Right again.*

Duane said, "We're waiting for the biggest earthquake in U.S. history to arrive on our doorstep. The U.S. Government tells us there will be a margin rupture quake of 8.7 to 9.2 on the Richter scale as the Juan de Fuca Plate slides under the North American Plate. We'll be without power for weeks. Hundreds of people will die, thousands will be unprepared."

Elspeth checked the audience. No snickers. Good. She resisted the temptation to check her cell phone. She could get away with a check now that the lights were off but she hadn't felt the buzz of an incoming call. She stifled a sigh and focused on her uncle.

Duane continued, "An earthquake begins with a high frequency wave. Your dog may start to bark. Next comes the seismic waves and then the big shake begins. In a major rupture in our area, we may have as many as one million buildings collapse. That would include hospitals, schools and fire stations. Then the water hits."

Duane brought up a video clip of the 2011 Japanese quake. "The 9.0 Tohoku earthquake lasted four minutes. Minutes later a tsunami wave hit coastal towns." The screen filled with footage of an ocean of black water spilling over retaining walls, submerging buildings and easily tossing about boats and cars.

"Eighteen thousand people lost their lives in the Tohoku earthquake and a nuclear power plant went into meltdown."

Duane brought up a geological map of Washington State. "In our area, the slippage of the Juan de Fuca plate will cause the ground to immediately drop by six feet and then jump thirty feet or more to the west. Water in the Sound and the ocean will slosh and two giant tsunamis will move east and west. Everything west of I-5 will be disrupted."

He changed to a photo from a 2016 Italian quake showing acres of flattened buildings. Duane said, "If you survive, you can expect to be without power for three months or more. It will be a year or more before you can expect piped-in water. FEMA projections tell us that there will be a million displaced people and another two and half million people who will lack food or water."

Despite the gloom of the darkened room Elspeth managed to catch Carmen's eye. The cousins exchanged a smile and a wink. They should sell out of the portable solar panels for sure. Duane allotted a bonus when they sold a big-ticket item.

Uncle Duane usually ended a slide show with a 'how-to' demonstration, but with the home school mothers in attendance, Uncle Duane wouldn't demonstrate any of his hand-to-hand combat tips. Upset ladies asked questions. They didn't spend money. As a pulse of warm air fanned her face, Elspeth smiled again. Water filtration. Whenever a venue was well heated, people became thirsty. Disaster video clips and parched clients meant strong sales in water filtration units. Maybe she should offer Dr. and Dr. Arc'teryx jackets the deluxe Big Berkey water filtration unit.

Today's demo would no doubt be the pocket water filtration straw, suitable for backpacking and emergency kits.

Elspeth felt her phone vibrate in her jeans pocket. She fished out the phone and smiled at the number. *Yeah! It's the professor!*

The wise adapt themselves to circumstances,
as water molds to the pitcher.
Chinese proverb

Chapter Three

Saturday, 10:10 a.m.
Thurston County Fairgrounds

Elspeth slipped out the rear exit door. She threw a glance at the raindrops bouncing off the sidewalk before taking a position under the roof overhang of the building. She leaned against the wall and tapped her beautiful rose gold phone. She loved this phone. She held the phone up and chirped, "Hey Professor! "

"I am not a professor yet," a young male voice growled. "And I never will be if I screw up this proposal."

Elspeth winced. "Sorry, boss," she said. "What do I need to fix?" This was her life in the gig economy. Translating dictated files into word documents paid the cell phone bill, barely.

Nico's deep voice rumbled. "There's a whole section missing," he told her. "It's where I talk about the history of phenotypically cryptic fungi. It lays the groundwork for why we need to acquire funding for field units that can do rapid DNA analysis."

"Oh. Right. I remember you said you were going to insert some background stuff to justify the big money ask."

Nico sighed. "In a nutshell, yes. The historical section is missing."

"I haven't gotten that section yet." Elspeth frowned, thinking. She asked, "Are you sure it was in the file? I went through it twice."

There was a pause.

"Shit! It's on my phone!" Nico blew out a second 'shit'. "Elspeth, I'm so sorry. I forgot. I didn't narrate that section at the computer. I went for a walk and recorded it."

Elspeth smiled at the change in Nico's tone. The grumpy man had evaporated and a sweet, frustrated graduate student remained. She pictured him leaning his forehead against a wall or scowling out a window. Either way, her mental picture included his halo of black curls and the exquisite long lashes that framed a pair of glorious olive green eyes.

She said, "No worries. Send me the file and I'll transcribe."

"I need to pay you too."

"That'd be great. Can you stop by?" Mentally she thought, *And I'll bat my own weenie eyelashes at you,* she thought.

Out loud she added, "I'm working for Uncle Duane until mid-afternoon. I'm housesitting so I have to go feed a cat. You could meet me there about four —— but it has to be quick. I'm bussing tables from five to nine. I'll go back to the house to spend the night with the cat. I can have that section over to you by midnight, latest."

"How many jobs do you have?"

"You don't want to know. I try not to think about it." Elspeth said with a laugh. She looked up to see her cousin Carmen limping out the exit door. The same drop in barometric pressure that brought rain also aggravated Carmen's aches. She had to be hurting to limp like that.

Elspeth said, "Nico, I gotta go. I'll text you the address where I'm staying. Don't freak out. We'll get it right." Elspeth tapped off the phone and smiled at her cousin.

"How's the phone?" Carmen asked.

"Absolutely beautiful. I love it. Are you sure you don't want it?"

"No. Mom gave it to you. My phone suits me. It's not that old."

"Well it's about the nicest thing I've ever gotten from anyone, ever."

"Everything else okay?" Carmen asked.

"Sure. The grad student's stuff needs a tweak. I'm good."

"He's not a problem, is he?" Carmen's dark eyes scanned Elspeth's face.

"Nico? Nah! Uber nerd. The worst he does is grumble at me in polysyllabic dismay. He's actually very sweet. I like him." Elspeth leaned against the exit door and closed her eyes. Her morning caffeine buzz chose this moment to evaporate and she went from perky to exhausted in seconds.

"What kind of tweak?"

"Huh?" Elspeth blinked.

"What kind of tweaking is this guy doing?"

"He's writing a proposal for graduate school project funding. He's clean!"

"Good. You're falling asleep on your feet," Carmen scolded. "You're working too hard."

"I've got to save two thousand dollars before fall term begins," Elspeth countered. "And I promised Uncle Duane that I'd earn it all legally."

Carmen nodded. "Right. No selling magic mushrooms."

"Which makes paying for school damn near impossible. There aren't enough hours in the day."

"Nico. He pays well?"

"He pays great! He's gone through enough transcribers to appreciate that I know a fungus from a ficus. He's actually onto something interesting. He wants to adapt the FBI's rapid DNA machine into a portable mycological field unit. If he could take a sample of a fungus in the wild and identify it on the spot, that could be huge."

"Ooh, breakthrough science! Cool. You're going to have to tell me all about it after the show. Any big money for you when he gets his field mushroom machinery?"

Elspeth threw an arm around her cousin's shoulders and squeezed gently. "Big Money? Nah. Which means that I need to get my butt inside and start selling, right?"

"Actually I came out to tell you that those guys just walked in. Bearded Creep, Smoking Creep, Red Cap Creep and Weasel Face Creep. Do you want to skip out? Dad and I can handle the sales."

"No. Thanks. All they do is stare. Big losers." Elspeth snorted. She kept her face calm as she dropped her arm back to her side. She looked down and smiled before using the toe of her sneaker to move aside chips of the landscaping bark where she stood. "Look. Little brown mushrooms."

Carmen bent over to study the cluster of small domes. "Poisonous or psychoactive?"

"Either is possible. Little brown mushrooms are diverse. They could be completely benign. We'd need to take a cap and leave it on a sheet of paper or glass to get a spore print and then use a field guide to key it out to the genus. These little brown jobs can be difficult to key out to the species level."

"Think a kid might eat these?"

"I hope not. We could kick them over but there's a whole mycelium system underground. There'll be more mushrooms in a few days."

Carmen straightened and winced. "You are using my love of biology to distract me from my mission. My mission is to ascertain if you are weirded out by the skeezy creeps that are part of our customer base this morning. I don't like how they look at you."

"Hey, sales opportunity." She did not want to burden Carmen—or Uncle Duane—with her unease. With Aunt Yera in hospice, they had enough to handle. Elspeth took a breath. She'd keep near others. She'd manage. Her brain bubbled with all her looming challenges. Typing text for

12

Nico. A cat that wasn't eating. Aunt Yera. Money. Ye Gods. Money. And now creepy stalkers at her workplace.

She put on a bold smile and said, "I'll bet you I can sell the Creepy Four two hundred dollars worth."

"Make it three and I'll be impressed." Carmen sketched a wave and limped toward the showroom door.

Elspeth felt tears prickling as she watched her cousin's lurching walk. *Other girls have healthy bodies,* she thought. *Other girls have college funds. Other girls don't have family members dying so young. What the hell did we ever do to deserve all this?*

Elspeth sucked her cheeks in and bit down to bring in a burst of pain. The Dwerryhouses would overcome. *We're tough. We're strong.* Of course she knew that other girls had to contend with a stalker.

She was just special. She had four.

The Ravine,
Mason County, Washington

"No. No way. We are *not* moving the body." Jasmine Oh crossed her arms and stared at her grandfather. "Haven't you ever watched a detective show? Moving the body is — bad juju — and worse science, and you know it. We do not move the body." A scattering of raindrops hammered down as if to emphasize her words.

"Yes, yes. I hear your concerns. But this," Dr. Oh gestured at the shelf fungus, "is a special specimen. We must protect it. It is hundreds of years old and one large, clumsy policeman could destroy it."

"So we don't get a large, clumsy policeman." Jasmine uncrossed her arms and moved closer to her grandfather. "There's a deputy from the Sheriff's office who came to my political science class to talk about search and seizure rules. He seemed pretty sharp. Let me give him a call."

"You have his number?" Dr. Oh's eyebrows lowered to a straight, disapproving line.

"I have my cell phone and that can get me the Mason County Sheriff's office. Come on, I'll get a better signal on the road." Jasmine kept her tone brisk. There was no need to mention to Grandfather that the deputy she had in mind had broad shoulders, long legs and a tight tush.

Dr. Oh said, "I suppose I should cover the man with my jacket."

"I don't think that's wise. We're not supposed to touch or move anything."

"I already checked him to see if he was dead."

"I mean other than that. We shouldn't touch the camera either." Jasmine stood and carefully stepped up the slope to skirt the tree stump. As her face came near the vertical stump she could pick out lichens in three shapes and at least four mosses in brown streaks, emerald green lumps and light green fuzzy clumps. She stretched out a hand to move a branch and peered downhill at the tool handle projecting from the fern fronds. "Looks like it might be a hammer. We should leave that where it is too."

Her grandfather sighed.

Jasmine studied her grandfather. His color wasn't good. There was an undertone of deep yellow flushing his skin. He suddenly looked very old.

"Let's go back to the car," she said. "I'll make the call and we'll make some tea."

It worried her when he did not object.

14

"Lust is a sharp spur to vice." Saint Ambrose

Chapter Four

1550 Deer Fern Lane,
Olympia, Washington

Richard Adam Sutherland adjusted the focus on his binoculars. His watery blue eyes observed his wife of two decades pruning the barberry bushes in the far corner of the back yard. Twenty-five years his junior, she was a shapely woman of forty-five whose soft cloud of hair had grayed early. Lucinda Sutherland pruned bushes the same way she did everything. First she had studied the barberry row and then she moved in with a clinical precision.

He knew the garden clippers would be razor sharp. Lucinda's purple smock, her floppy gardening hat and her lavender gardening gloves did not fool him. His dear wife had the heart of a raptor. She had the eyes of a raptor too, so he'd best be careful.

Richard rolled his wheelchair back from the upstairs window. His morning oxycodone had taken effect. He had popped a Cialis after breakfast and he now felt rather wonderful. As his age-spotted hands gripped the wheels of the chair, he smirked. He was grateful to Lucinda. He truly was. Her work made his hobbies possible. Of course, his status made her nature socially acceptable.

Theirs was a gracious home. These days so many academics never secured tenure. His career had, blessedly, begun early enough that tenure had been typical and retirement benefits were significant. His timing had been excellent.

His lanky form did not fit well in the wheelchair. His feet were too long for the footrests, so each turn of the chair had to be calculated. Many other sorts of calculations were things of the past. He was no longer a lady's man feasting on the herds of co-eds who so charmingly crowded university walks and lawns. No matter. There were other avenues to the young.

In retirement, he found he had an abundant appetite for youth. Nymphs in computer photo images and video clips did not recoil from his sagging right eye. The ravages that oculopharyngeal muscular dystrophy had inflicted on his body did not hamper his enjoyment of pursuing forbidden fruit in the online world.

The betrayal of his body was a daily hardship. It was, he had concluded, due to his maternal grandmother, a French Canadian of Montreal. The handsome old girl had passed down to him a defective gene that contained too many repeats of a particular codon. The nucleotide triplet of Guanine, Cytosine, and Guanine was supposed to be present in a string of ten copies, each instructing the creation of the amino acid alanine. Alas, for Grand-mére and himself, the gene had expanded to a dozen copies, resulting in an alanine buildup in some muscle cells. His cells could not clear the alanine clumps and, as a result, certain muscles were dying. His right eyelid drooped. His tongue and throat muscles were atrophying.

His mind and his penis were fine.

Richard rolled up to his computer. He unzipped his trousers and typed in the name of his website, *Trail Cameras for Young Vixens*. He glanced at his watch. He should have twenty minutes. His hands hovered over the keyboard as he thought through his options. He smiled and typed in his password, *Papa Wolf 1*. He would watch Emily.

11 a.m.
Mason County Sheriff's Office

Deputy Don McRae stuck his head over the edge of the wall to his supervisor's cubicle, his long legs making the process easy. "Yo. Boss. I just got a call on a dead body. It's an hour's drive and a quarter mile hike into the woods. Want in?" The tall young deputy was a redhead with dancing gray eyes that were failing to look casual.

Detective Rodger Raposo looked up from his cluttered desk. He had three reports to write, a dozen phone calls to return, and two earmarked wedding magazines that he had promised Brooke he would review on his lunch break. Raposo didn't hesitate. "A dead body? Yeah, I'm in."

Raposo stood up, the creases in his rumpled khakis mirroring the creases in his rumpled face. With a deep voice that resembled the low growl of a bloodhound, he said, "I need to stop by my locker for boots."

"You'll want gloves too. The caller said there's a patch of devil's club."

"Devil's club. I hate that stuff. The thorns make me itch for days. Who called in the body?"

"A young woman — and she asked for me by name." McRae couldn't hold back smile.

Raposo studied his deputy. "Your broken heart seems to have mended."

"Wasn't broken. A little squished. I lost out to a good guy."*

"There is that. You got a wagon lined up?"

"Ambulance will be there about two. That should give us enough time to process the scene. The young lady says there's a head injury and, get this, a hammer."

---

*The EvoAngel - A mushroom thriller set in Olympia

Raposo's eyebrows snapped down. "The body is a quarter mile into the woods and it's death by *hammer*?"

Deputy McRae answered with a palms up 'who knows'. "So she says — and there's a humongous fungus. We're supposed to be tiptoeing in. A rare species. She said so about six times."

"The dead fellow's a mushroom picker?"

McRae rotated his hands up and open. "Not clear. The caller is going to wait at the roadside and guide us in."

Detective Raposo rolled his eyes. "Okay. Just another day at the office." He reached under his desk and pulled out a faded red daypack. He transferred items from his blazer pockets and double-checked he had his phone, pens and a Rite in the Rain notebook. He leaned over this paperwork pile and plucked out a pair of vinyl gloves from an open box. He added a water bottle and looked around. "Okay. What am I forgetting?"

McRae grinned. "You want me to bring the wedding magazines for the ride?"

"It'd be such a shame if you tripped into that devil's club," Raposo said.

"Yes, boss."

An empty cart rattles loudly.
Korean proverb

Chapter Five

Saturday, Noon.
Thurston County Fairgrounds

"You'll love it." Elspeth knew to keep up the positive chatter as she ran the customer's card through the card reader. A sale wasn't a sale until the charge went through. "It's top of the line."

"I really hadn't planned to spend two hundred dollars on a water filter," said the woman, holding her purchase. "But after hearing about that Cascadia fault, well, it seems smart to have."

"We recommend you have a clean bucket in the garage marked 'Water only' for fetching what you'll put through the filter," Elspeth said.

"That's a good idea. Thanks!"

The beep on the card reader finalized the transaction and Elspeth offered the tablet for the shopper's signature. As the woman swiped her finger around the screen, Elspeth surveyed the room. Most of the crowd had shopped and melted away. Unfortunately, the creepy four lingered.

Weaponry was a standard part of the survivalist community. Elspeth rarely gave a second glance to a sheath knife or a holster pistol. But these men made Elspeth uneasy. Their leather knife sheaths had the abrasions and shine that came from everyday use. The straight blade knife handles were wood with a distinctive metal end cap.

Elspeth knew the knife brand. Uncle Duane considered it a most excellent product line and had considered stocking it before concluding it was too expensive for the bulk of his customers.

The Creepy Four were wearing twelve-dollar jeans and carrying six hundred dollar knives.

The eldest of the four was a broad man who towered over the other customers. His iron-gray beard draped down in a greasy tangle over a flannel shirt that strained to fit over a wide barrel of stomach. Graybeard stared at Elspeth from across the room and kept his eyes on her as he made a comment to the youngest and smallest man of his group, a whip thin male of about twenty whose narrow face made Elspeth think of a weasel. Weasel Face laughed at the old man's comment as he, too, kept his eyes on Elspeth.

Elspeth forced a smile for the next customer who purchased a pair of whistles and a solar powered flashlight. She could hear Carmen at the next table finalizing a sale on a bucket of freeze-dried foods. Uncle Duane stood nearby, chatting with a man with dark clipped hair in a polo shirt and khaki slacks who also wore an Olympia Police Department badge clipped to his belt next to a holster holding a short-nosed pistol. He was smiling as Duane's hands mimed casting with a fishing rod.

The policeman's presence steadied Elspeth's nerves. He had stopped by to survey products for his department and clearly Uncle Duane was turning on the charm in hopes of reeling in a big buyer.

Elspeth swallowed as the other two creepies moved to her checkout stand. The middle-aged grimy man and the young grimy man in front of her were likely the son and grandson of Graybeard. As the pair came closer she could see acne scars under the grizzle of unshaven cheeks and crowded, stained teeth. The middle-aged man's shirt sleeves and cuffs were streaked with dark brown that might be dried blood. The nails on his right hand and the crease between the first two fingers gleamed yellow from past cigarettes.

His twenty-something son unnerved Elspeth more than the other three. He wore a filthy red baseball cap over long, unwashed blonde hair. He stared at her face, then her chest and then raised his eyes to her face once more. There was an intimacy in his raised eyebrow that sent frissons of alarm down the back of her neck. Red Cap wasn't quite as narrow-faced as the weasel looking young man across the room but he had the same feral air.

Elspeth had an unsettling sensation of familiarity. She had seen Red Cap elsewhere. Queasily she considered that it might have been at a bonfire where she had once marketed magic mushrooms.

Tobacco Fingers and Red Cap exchanged a knowing look.

"Dad!" Carmen called.

Uncle Duane's head swiveled and took in Carmen's head tilt and the two men at Elspeth's station. Duane began moving across the room with the policeman following.

Tobacco Fingers threw down a stack of hand-warming packets in front of Elspeth. He said, "Ring them up, darling."

There was nothing to do but to start scanning the bar codes and begin dumping the product into the complementary sack marked "3D Survival." Elspeth didn't bother to smile or speak. She was relieved when Uncle Duane arrived to stand in front of her table.

Red Cap eyed Elspeth and said to Tobacco Fingers, "I've got a good eye, don't I? Nice. Real nice. I do like a bite of prime rib."

Elspeth couldn't help it. She blushed. She tried to speed up the scanning of the packets. Her hands betrayed her with their trembling. *Nothing's going to happen*, she thought. *I'll get through this and they will be gone.* The customers remaining after these two were a young Scout and his father. At Carmen's table there was only a muscular young man in a black Harley Davidson T-shirt. *Two more sales after this one and we're done.*

Tobacco Fingers smiled at Elspeth. He pulled a large roll of money out of his front jeans pocket and slipped a rubber band off the roll. He pursed his lips in a kiss towards Elspeth. He turned to Duane and said, "How much wampum for the little squaw?"

Duane's left fist came arcing up and through the space occupied by Tobacco Fingers' chin.

The man went backwards like a felled tree. The wad of bills stayed clutched in his hand as the back of his head whapped down on the linoleum.

Young Red Cap shouted, "Hey" as Graybeard and Young Weasel started across the room. The old man had his hand on his knife handle as he eyed Duane who had already taken position in front of the table, shielding Elspeth.

The off duty officer shouted, "Olympia Police! Stand down!"

Elspeth watched in horror as the next man in line yanked his young Scout into a protective embrace. Out of the edge of her perception Carmen was frozen in place even as the young man in the Harley Davidson shirt moved in front of Carmen in a blockading move.

The policeman took charge. "Let's not escalate this situation. Russell, take your hand off that knife handle. Now." The officer threw a look at the red-capped son. "That goes for you, too, Troy."

The enormous old man opened his fingers and slowly moved his hands away from his sides. His grandson did the same.

"Smart choice, gentlemen," the officer said. "Ricky Lee," he said to the man on the floor, "You know me. I'm Sergeant Martinez with the Olympia Police Department. I strongly advise you to get up slowly."

Duane stood with his hands fisted but lowered. He said, "You *gentlemen* need to leave. Now."

The man on the floor rolled to his left and came up slowly, holding his face with one hand and his wad of money in the other. "He hit me! That's assault."

"And the young lady can have you hauled into court on a sexual harassment charge and maybe a hate crime charge too. You want that mess on your record?" Sergeant Martinez asked. He added, "I'm on my way home. I'll be really cranky if I have to drive back into town to spend the afternoon booking people into jail. Seems to me that you and your family leaving right about now could solve a lot of problems."

Tobacco Fingers, now known to Elspeth as Ricky Lee, scowled at Duane. After a long moment of silence he turned to his family and said, "We're done. Let's go."

The men left with the metal door loudly clanging shut behind them.

Duane looked at Elspeth who gave him a weak smile. Duane turned his attention to the small Scout who was snuggled up to his father's hip. Both watched Duane with careful eyes in pale faces.

Duane went to the Scout and knelt down on one knee. "My name is Duane and I just screwed up."

Elspeth felt a lump well up in her throat. Tears prickled at her uncle's kind tone.

"I'm Michael. This is my Dad."

"Michael Senior, Nice to meet you, Duane."

On her left, Elspeth saw Carmen swallow hard before summoning a smile for her customer. The young man looked concerned even as Carmen regained pace with her sales patter.

Duane was still with the Scout. Duane said, "I should have let my friend, Sergeant Martinez handle that problem. Hitting customers is, well, not real smart. And I didn't give Elspeth a chance to deal with it. She handles herself really well and now she's gonna be mad at me that I had to go stick my manly oar into it. I'm sorry if that chin jab stuff got you worried."

Michael's eyes shone with delight. "That was amazing. You totally clocked him."

Duane shook his head. "That's what I'm afraid of. That you might think it was awesome. Let's call it 'short-term effective.'"

Elspeth smiled. Her uncle was always effective.

Michael said, "My mom's part Makah. No one should call a woman a squaw. What you did was *awesome*."

Michael Senior said, "Don't worry. I'll talk to him about some other tools to have in the crisis management toolbox."

Duane stood up. "That'd be great. Here, take this." Duane reached across to a display rack and pulled off a Buck knife in a plastic shell. He handed the packaged knife to Michael Junior. "This is on the house. The knife you were about to buy is a Swiss Army knife with a wine bottle corkscrew. Don't waste energy carrying something you don't need. This knife is better for whittling and the stuff you're gonna be doing. Safer too, because it has a locking blade."

Michael Junior looked up at his father, who gave a smile of approval. "Thanks!" Michael breathed. "This is uber awesome."

Elspeth smiled too. She knew what Duane would say next.

Duane put on a rocky face and said, "No taking this to school. Not even by accident or 'accident on purpose.' School principals' got no leeway when it comes to a Buck knife. I'll be real sad if I hear you get in trouble that way."

Michael nodded. "I know." He threw his arms around Duane's middle and hugged hard. "Thanks. It's a cool knife."

Duane awkwardly patted Michael's shoulder. "All right, then."

As the Scout and his father made their way out the door, Elspeth exhaled in relief.

Carmen's muscular customer paid for his purchases. Her cousin's face brightened as the young man spoke again.

At least Carmen was having a good afternoon.

Elspeth reached under the table for a box that would hold the goods from the table display. Sergeant Martinez offered to help, saying, "Let me take down the rack. I've got some time to kill."

"Thanks. And thanks for helping us."

"No problem."

Duane began boxing up product. He spoke to Sergeant Martinez. "Who were those guys?"

"The Fickham family. The old man is Russell. His son is Ricky Lee. The two grandsons are Troy and Tate. Troy was the one in the red ball cap. They're shake rats."

"Shake rats?" Elspeth asked.

"Guys making a living out of the woods. They find old cedar stumps or downed logs and turn them into cedar shakes. They'll also cut big-leaf maple, not always legally, and anything else that can make a buck. The family, is, ah, known to law enforcement. They also specialize in liberating catalytic converters from cars and chainsaws from unsecured garages."

"I thought they might be mushroom collectors," Elspeth said.

Sergeant Martinez eyed Elspeth. "Maybe. I'm not sure they're smart enough to be safe pickers. Please don't eat any mushrooms those guys are selling. Not unless you really know mushrooms."

"Not a problem! I wouldn't eat anything touched by those guys!"

Carmen's customer left and she came limping over to help with the packing.

Sergeant Martinez said, "Normally I'd say those two young guys are mostly bluster. That big old man, however, is dangerous. He lives just over the county line on Kamilche peninsula and he's been a problem in Mason County for years. He has another son named Henry who is seriously scary because Henry's actually smart. Henry's into drugs, weapons, explosives — If a buck can be made, Henry will give it a go. Except prostitution. Apparently Henry doesn't go there."

"What does Henry look like?" Duane asked.

"He's one of those guys that can fade into a crowd. Medium height, medium build, brown hair, black eyes. You'd notice the eyes, Duane. Very alert."

Duane looked at Carmen and Elspeth. "Doesn't ring any bells for me." The young women agreed.

Sergeant Martinez asked, "Have these other guys been bothering you before?"

"They've been here at the last two shows. I sold one of them a flashlight on clearance." Elspeth replied. "They haven't been big buyers."

Carmen said, "They've been watching Elspeth. Every time they're here."

"You two tell me next time that happens," Duane grumbled. "We'll make a plan."

"Okay." Elspeth knew she should tell Uncle Duane where she might have met Troy Fickham, but Sergeant Martinez was still nearby. It could wait. The sergeant began slotting canisters of freeze-dried apricots into a storage box.

She said, "I can do that, Sergeant Martinez."

"Call me Marty. I don't mind helping out. My wife and daughters are hosting a baby shower and I sure as heck don't want to go home just yet. Pregnant ladies make me nervous and there's about twenty of them at the house."

Duane laughed. "Rather take on four ugly men than mom hormones?"

"Any day, bro. Any day."

Elspeth stretched to take down a sales banner. Her magic mushroom sales were in the past. She would just have to make sure her history stayed out of sight. She sighed as she thought of the work ahead. She would help with product packaging, inventory, and reviewing receipts before assisting with loading, transporting and unloading the show remains. Uncle Duane would be particular when they reached the storage unit. There would be no hasty flinging of goods onto the racks of shelving while he was around. And she still had a full day of work after the show goods were stored.

She sighed again. She did miss the all cash, no tax economy of selling psychoactive mushrooms.

"I know that look," Carmen called. "You're thinking of mushie sales."

Elspeth flashed her cousin a weary smile. "Only thinking," she said.

The Sutherland Home
1550 Deer Fern Lane

Lucinda Sutherland closed the clippers and slid the fastener to hold the blades shut. She dropped the clippers into her gardening basket and stripped off her garden gloves. She had given Richard plenty of time to indulge in his sordid little hobby. It was time to get on with her list for the day.

She glanced down the row of trimmed shrubs with approval. It was so important to tackle garden tasks in April. There were simply too many days of rain and if she left trimming and weeding until the sunnier days of mid-May, her work would double. Plants grew in the western Washington spring with astonishing speed, despite the cool temperatures.

Lucinda studied the long garden border and identified places where she could plant clumps of *Violas*. She would have to hunt for the lavender-faced violets as so many of the garden centers stocked the native yellow violas instead. She smiled. It could be amusing to thrust a bouquet of violas under Richard's nose. The ionone compounds the flowers produced could temporarily deaden the senses.

She needed all of Richard dead.

She wasn't completely on top of things. She threw a glance at the back door to the garage. It would be best to clean out the Mercedes next. She would put the pill bottles in to soak so she could peel the labels off after lunch. Peeling labels was somewhat tedious and she disliked the citrus scented glue solvents but it had to be done. She needed to have an assortment of prescription bottle sizes on hand. The new venture had to be professional.

The other important task for the day was to review the photos from the newly arrived memory chip. That would take some time.

She'd heat soup for lunch. With Richard's swallowing challenges, half her life seemed to be soup. If she was going to have the time to review photos, Richard had to nap. That could be arranged. She had an extensive pharmaceutical collection.

Lucinda checked her watch. Richard had taken his morning dose of oxycodone at nine. Xanax at noon wasn't wise, although it certainly would take care of her problems.

A trio of mushrooms caught her eye as she moved to the back door to the garage. The *Amanitas* were back. These were the only wild mushrooms she knew, courtesy of a neighbor who had identified them for her by pointing out the pale blotches spotting the tan caps and the ring of tissue dangling like a skirt from each stem. He had pushed back one tall mushroom to show her the egg-shaped base buried in the soil. "It's the combination that we should notice. This base, the stem skirt, the white gills, the cap blotches combined are all signals we have an *Amanita*," he had said.

"How do they taste?" she'd wondered.

"Oh, tasty but quite possibly poisonous," the neighbor had replied.

"Are they deadly then?" She made sure no eagerness marred her tone.

"Well . . . I'm sure these are *Amanitas*. There are a number of species in the genus. Being early spring, I'm guessing *Amanita pantherina* group, which certainly could be fatal to a puppy or small child. To an adult? I don't know. I certainly would not eat one. The King of Bohemia, Charles the Fourth died from eating the wrong mushrooms, you know. Be careful. These do look like an *Amanita pantherina*."

The neighbor had wandered off to finish his walk, leaving Lucinda with a treasured tidbit. Something deadly sat at her back door.

She had, of course, researched poisonous *Amanitas* after that conversation and had concluded that mushroom poisoning was too slow, too inexact, and too likely to be picked up by the physicians of Northwest emergency rooms.

The poisonous varieties of *Amanita* contained a ring of eight amino acids that caused the liver cells of humans to burst open. Although the symptoms might not appear for a day after ingestion, it was common for any patient in an emergency room who presented with mysterious cramping and diarrhea to be asked if wild mushrooms had been recently consumed.

Richard's difficulty in swallowing added to her assessment that death by *Amanita* was not a feasible path.

Still, it was heartening to see the *Amanitas* this spring morning. Their presence filled her with hope.

"My dear if you could give me a cup of tea to clear my muddle of a head." Charles Dickens in Mrs. Lirriper's Legacy.

Chapter Six

Saturday, Noon.
Mason County, Washington

J asmine said, "Grandpa, I think we should have some tea." A rain shower had swept in as they had walked out of the woods, leaving the air cool and laden with moisture. They were back at the family car they had parked at the bottom of the ravine.

"Yes. That would be wise." Dr. Oh was breathing hard.

Jasmine opened the passenger door and said, "Please sit down. It would be good practice for me to make the tea."

Dr. Oh's eyes regained a twinkle. "That is such a nice way of saying that I am old."

"You are old. And I do need the practice." She didn't like her grandfather's color. Finding a Fuzzy Sandozi and a dead man was a lot of action for an eighty-five-year-old man. Her grandfather's lips were tinged with blue. She saw a tremor in his fingers as he fumbled with raising the zipper tab on his jacket. He managed to open the bottom of his jacket before carefully sitting down in the car's front passenger seat.

Jasmine opened the trunk of the car. She pulled out a storage bin and removed a tiny backpacking stove and a pot.

A stiff breeze rushed down the road, chilling the midday air. The skies were gray blue and promised more rain. It was hypothermia weather.

Jasmine dumped half a water bottle's worth of water into the cook pot and lit the stove. She would double sugar the tea. As she waited for the water to boil, she agonized over her grandfather's worries. She'd never hear the end of it if that big fungus became damaged.

The stove roared under the pot as Jasmine unpacked tea bags, sugar, and mugs from the car bin. She called up to her grandfather. "It may take awhile for the deputies to find us. We could collect some mosses after tea. I know a student who is looking for tardigrades."

"Tardy grades? Like academic marks?"

"Tardigrades. They are these teeny animals with eight little legs that live in mosses and lichens. They're really cute when magnified."

"I should know this. Why have I never heard of these?"

Jasmine shrugged. "Maybe because you like plants more than animals?" Her grandfather's memory was definitely spotty and slipping. One of the first things he had ever put out for her to see with a microscope had been one of the "moss piglets."

She set tea bags into the pot of hot water and turned off the stove. She tacked back to the topic of tardigrades in a way that she knew he would enjoy, saying, "The tardigrades may be specialized to the moss or lichen they inhabit. With so many moss and lichen species out here, there may be lots of undiscovered species of tardigrades."

"Ah. So your friend might have the honor of naming a species."

"That would be cool." Jasmine unpacked sandwiches from her daypack and took a sandwich and a cup of tea to her grandfather. She nudged his mind along by asking, "How hard is it to go through the naming process?"

"Oh, it's work." He accepted the cup of tea with a nod of thanks as Jasmine laid the sandwich on the dashboard of the car.

Dr. Oh slurped the sweet tea and said, "The first step is to make sure that no one else has already described and named what you have found. That alone can take months of research — made easier now with the Internet. In a typical year we are seeing about 18,000 new species named and about half of each year's list are insects."

"That many? Wow."

"I agree. Wow." Dr. Oh slurped more tea and then picked up the sandwich.

Jasmine watched closely as he took a bite. His color was already improving.

After a moment he swallowed and said, "Tell me more, please."

Jasmine beamed a smile. "Tardigrades are very interesting physiologically. They can dry up into a static state and stay dehydrated for years. Then if they get wet again, boom, they come back to life."

"Ah! Of course!" Dr. Oh beamed. "This is cryptobiosis! These are the animals that got shot into space, yes?"

"Yes. Some were put into space by the Russians. The tardigrades went dormant and some were later revived."

"Water bears or moss piglets. That's the names I know." Dr. Oh chewed on the next bite of his sandwich. "Genus *Milnesium*. Yes. Very interesting animals. We can see them with the microscope easily."

Jasmine was pleased to see her grandfather's memory and color were returning. She knew he was worried about the big polypore and suspected that the dead body had unnerved him more than he was willing to admit. It certainly had unnerved her. It was best to stick with taxonomy until the deputies arrived. She said, "Say my friend looks and no one else has reported on what she's found. Then what?"

"Then she writes a highly detailed description for publication that is accurate and, hopefully, exciting or intriguing. We scientists," Dr. Oh deadpanned, "are drama queens."

"You've done this many times," Jasmine countered. "You're not the theatrical sort."

"You would be surprised. My description of a golden spearwort was lyrical in the extreme. I crafted a hundred words just describing the lustrous petals. A good taxonomist is a poet. It helps to justify our oddities."

Jasmine snorted. "All right then." She finished her tea and asked, "We're supposed to submit our ideas for a biological research project in class on Monday. I'm not totally sure what I want to do just yet — but would it be alright to bring the tardigrade girl over to use one of your microscopes? Her name is Carmen."

"Of course. I could show her my photographic slides of mosses and liverworts."

"Ah, how many slides?"

"I have several hundred on mosses and their associated substrates. If you like, I can discuss the modern botanical clues to past geology and current acidity." Dr. Oh drained his tea mug, energized at the lecture prospect.

"Grandpa, that'd be a lot of slides."

"There is a lot to know! Our woods are full of life. Much has been made of the canopy layer in recent years, but there is so much going on in our undergrowth! We must delve into the diversity to understand the communities."

"Right. I'll warn her." Jasmine tilted her head, collecting a sound. "Grandpa, Do you hear that?"

"What?"

"It sounded like a click. From down the road. I heard it a moment ago as well."

Dr. Oh swiveled his head about. "Sorry. I'm not hearing it, but your hearing has always been better than mine. I think I'm hearing a vehicle."

"Yeah. A car."

Jasmine put her hand out to take the tea mug from her grandfather. She heard the click again. "I think someone may have a trail camera out here," she said.

Tardigrade

Saturday, 3:45 p.m.
1553 Painted Fern Court, Olympia, Washington

A double cheeseburger and a cup of coffee made life worth living. Elspeth gulped down the last bite of the burger and tossed the wrapper onto the passenger side floorboard of her ancient Honda Civic. The car was a mess. She really should take ten minutes and clean out the worst of this month's trash.

Elspeth checked her watch. Almost four. As usual, it had taken longer than she liked to get the products counted, packed up, transported and unloaded to Uncle Duane's storage locker. She was bone-deep grateful for the help of Danny, the storage compound attendant, who had rapidly flung bins onto shelves. Without his help there wouldn't have been time to race through the drive-through window at the McDonald's on Harrison Avenue.

She'd left her uncle and Carmen with a hug, knowing that they would go to spend an hour with her aunt. She was glad she could plead the cat-sitting job as a reason not to go along to the hospice. Now, re-fueled, she would stop and feed the cat and meet with Nico before changing into her restaurant uniform

Elspeth turned right into the upscale Cedar Hills subdivision. Double storied mini-mansions on quarter-acre lots lined each side of the woodland themed streets. Elspeth passed Sword Fern, Lady Fern and Deer Fern before turning into Painted Fern Court. This cul-de-sac hosted single story ramblers for seniors. Mrs. Lowenstein's home was at the top of the loop, a taupe-colored model with a manicured lawn that led to a wild backyard. A scruffy pair of sixty-foot madrone trees leaned over the side of the house, leaving their mark on the lawn via an abundance of large, leathery leaves scattered across the ground.

The leaves. Elspeth sighed as she drove closer to the home.

Mrs. Lowenstein had left directions for the madrone leaves to be raked up regularly. She had said, "The trees have a fungal infection. That's why so many of the leaves are black and ugly looking. My neighbor is afraid that his rhodies are going to be infected, which is silly. It's not a rhody fungus at all. Still, I'd appreciate it if you'd keep the leaves tidied up. I don't want him after me to cut the trees. They're Northwest natives and I just adore them."

There just hadn't been time in the last several days to keep the lawn up to Mrs. Lowenstein's standards.

As she rounded the final curve, the sight of Nico Pavlopoulos distracted Elspeth from the thought of raking leaves. He was lounging against a cherry red Jeep parked in the driveway, a frown on his face.

Elspeth registered Nico's broad chest and curly hair with a happy flip in her stomach. His green sweatshirt asked, "Got Mushrooms?" under a cartoon of porcinis.

As Elspeth emerged from her car, Nico called, "I thought you were cat-sitting here."

From the interior of the house came a round of frantic barking.

"Oh no!" Elspeth gasped. "She didn't!"

Elspeth reached into her daypack for Mrs. Lowenstein's keys and ran for the front door. "Mrs. L has a flakey niece with a dog." Elspeth jammed the key in the lock where it promptly stuck. "I was told that Mitzi might try to get in on my pet-sitting but I'm supposed to say "No." The barking from inside reached a hysterical pace as Elspeth swore and jiggled the key.

"Let me." Nico reached in.

"Careful. The dog is right there."

"Noted." Nico closed his hand over hers, sending a ripple of thrill up Elspeth arms. Tragically there was no time to enjoy it. The key turned.

Elspeth had barely moved the door an inch before a long doggy nose wedged into the opening crack. As soon as the door opened further a large red dog came barreling out.

"Grab her!" Elspeth shouted as she scrabbled her fingers down the dog's back.

Nico seized the dog in a headlock and dropped to the ground. He wound his fingers through the dog's collar and said, "Got her!"

That was, at best, an optimistic statement. The Irish setter wiggled, danced, shoved, pulled and barked continuously. Nico hung on gamely with one hand as he freed his belt from his jeans with the other.

"Get over here," he said. "Fast."

Elspeth flung herself down next to Nico and tried to reach out a soothing hand to the dog.

"Just grab her collar and hang on," Nico directed. "I'll thread the belt through her collar and that'll give us a leash."

As soon as the belt was attached, the dog reared back and thrashed like a large red fish. Nico scrambled to his feet and pulled the dog toward a budding azalea bush. The dog surged forward and squatted to pee.

Elspeth staggered to her feet. "That poor dog. I haven't been here since before dawn this morning."

"You think she's been inside all day?" Nico asked. "You may have a mess inside. A dog like this can destroy a lot."

Elspeth's eyes widened. "Mr. Midnight!" Elspeth ran to the door of the house. She pushed the door open while Nico worked to control the dancing dog at the end of the makeshift leash.

The living room was a sea of ruin. Sofa stuffing erupted through long gashes in the cushions. Foam bits covered the carpet. A stinking brown mound of dog shit sat like a melted brownie in the walkway to the kitchen. A bookshelf lay overturned, spilling books of all sizes onto the floor. A bound journal had been chewed into a soggy mass of leather and pulp and an uprooted houseplant had been shredded into long strands of green slime. The glass was shattered in a framed photo of a long ago girls' softball team. The room stank of dog.

Elspeth surveyed the wreckage of Mrs. Lowenstein's travel mementoes. An embroidered souvenir pillow showing a Hong Kong junk on blue waters was ripped in half. Fortunately a baseball-sized bronze statue of Buddha seemed unharmed as it rested sideways on the carpet.

A longhaired black cat crouched on top of a tall china cabinet. He surveyed Elspeth with deeply irked yellow eyes.

"Mr. Midnight! Here, kitty, kitty," Elspeth cooed.

The front door bounced open and the red dog surged in, towing Nico.

Mr. Midnight hissed and backed away from the edge of the china cabinet, hunching into a ball of fur.

Nico closed the door and let go of the belt end. The red dog sprang free and began to rocket around the living room. Nico said, "She really needs to go for a run."

"I haven't got time," Elspeth wailed. "I'm due at The Azul Kitchen in half an hour!" She dodged the dog and made her way to the kitchen where a lake of urine stood between her and the counter where there was a leash, a bag of dog kibble and a dog bowl. A sheet of notepaper protruded from under the kibble bag.

Nico navigated to join her in the kitchen. So did the red dog, who reared up and put her paws on the edge of the counter with a happy lashing of her tail. She barked enthusiastically.

"I'll bet she hasn't been fed," Nico grumbled. He tore open the kibble bag and filled the dog bowl. The setter leapt up onto Nico. He planted a firm knee in her chest. "Down!"

he ordered. As soon as the setter's front feet hit the floor Nico set down the bowl. The dog leapt at the kibble and began to eat, nosing the dish across the floor like a hockey puck in play.

Elspeth read the note out loud in a whiny, sarcastic falsetto. "Dear Aunt B, I know you said that now wasn't convenient, but I got a fabulous invite to a party in ARUBA!!! I'm sure it will work out with your cat and pet sitter because Zoom is such a love. I should be back the day after your boat docks. Love, love, love Mitzi."

Nico looked down at the big setter who was now licking the bowl clean. "The dog's name is Zoom?"

The dog looked up and gave a gentle wave of her tail.

"Sounds right," Elspeth said sourly.

"When is Aunt B due back?"

Elspeth blinked back tears. "Not for two more weeks."

Nico stepped around the urine pooled on the linoleum and reached the kitchen sink. He lifted open the window over the sink, letting in a blessed spurt of fresh air. He started tearing off sheets of paper toweling and began tossing them over the urine pond. Zoom came bounding over to check out this new game.

"Elspeth?"

"Yeah?"

"You need reinforcements."

"Laws are spider webs through which the big flies pass and the little ones get caught." Honore de Balzac (1799-1850)

Chapter Seven

Saturday, 4 p.m.
The Lowenstein Home

I haven't got reinforcements. I have to handle this myself." Elspeth looked up at the kitchen clock. "In fifteen minutes I need to be out of here."

"You can't leave Zoom here like this."

Elspeth blinked back tears. "I can't afford to put her in a proper boarding kennel. Not for two weeks."

"How about your family? They got a yard?"

Elspeth shook her head. "My Aunt Yera is in hospice. My uncle and my cousin are over there now. I can't saddle them with a giant dog."

Zoom was nosing the empty dog bowl across the linoleum. She looked up at the word 'dog.' She came, in a rush, to join them. Zoom hit the remainder of the urine pool, lost traction and slammed into the kitchen cabinets. She rebounded with a scrabble of toenails seeking purchase on the slick floor before righting herself to launch again at Nico's chest.

"Down!" he commanded.

Zoom dropped into a sit and gazed up at him adoringly.

"She seems to like you," Elspeth said.

"And I like her." Nico scratched Zoom behind one ear and the dog leaned into him. "But my mother's best show spaniel is about to whelp. Mom would kill me if I brought doggy bedlam home."

Elspeth heartstrings parted with a ping. Nico was out of her orbit. Nico was from good people. Show dog people.

People who could afford to buy their son a Jeep and graduate school.

"How about your parents?" he asked.

There was no hiding who she was. She cleared her throat and said, "My cousin and my uncle are my family. My father died three years ago. He suffered from Huntington's disease like my Aunt Yera. It's a disease that can affect the mind. My dad ended his life by leaping off an overpass into rush hour traffic on I-5. A family in a van died too. You may have heard about it on the news." It seemed that everyone in the state had.

"Wow. Yeah. I did. I'm so sorry."

Elspeth swallowed hard. She said, "He'd been ill for years. He was angry all the time, so I can't say I have the greatest memories of my dad."

She looked down at the floor and said, ""Look, I haven't got much time, so let me lay this out fast. My life was a mess and it got worse. My mom remarried and moved to Florida. I don't like her new husband, although, to be fair, I haven't given him much of a chance. At the time I thought that I could be cool and that I could handle myself. I got into some stuff and . . . ended up serving five months in prison."

Nico stared at her. "You were *in prison?*"

"I had a little home garden business with some friends to grow psychoactive mushrooms. We sold locally and on-line. The money was great. I worked like crazy and learned a ton. Then we got busted."

Nico exhaled. Zoom scooted her rear so she sat on his feet. Nico looked down at the dog and stroked her head.

Elspeth blinked back tears. He had to think she was horrible. She brought her chin up and said, "I'll never trust law enforcement again. You wouldn't believe how awful they were to all of us. All over some mushrooms that anybody can find growing in their lawn."

"Except that if you don't know what you're doing, you can pick *Galerina marginata* instead of *Psilocybe stuntzii* and then you're dead."

"There's that," Elspeth admitted. "Actually we were dealing in *Psilocybe cubensis* which isn't found around here. We were growing 'shrooms in big plastic tubs. " She wiped her eyes and exhaled. "We were good at it."

"You did this inside?"

"Yeah. A basement bedroom. My job was to mix a nutritional substrate, sterilize it in jars, add in some *cubensis* spawn and then transfer the jar mix to another substrate once the mycelium infiltrated through the jar. Every couple of weeks we'd have a new crop of mushrooms to sell. It's important to have clean techniques. I did screw up on one thing — which ended up being a good thing once we got busted."

"How big a crime is selling whoo-whoo mushrooms?"

"Psilocybin is a Schedule One drug like heroin — which I didn't know. I was charged with a Class C felony. We actually weren't in trouble for selling the spores by mail because the spores don't have psilocybin — but you have to grow mushrooms to get the spores." Elspeth allowed herself a sour grin. "We actually lucked out because we had some mold problems. We were experimenting with some new bulk growing techniques. I was trying a different second stage substrate and I contaminated and then over-watered. It was disgusting."

Elspeth tilted her head to one side as she recalled how close she had sailed to disaster. She said, "I had just cleaned out ten tubs of gross mushrooms and slimey goo. I had the tubs out back drying when the DEA showed up. Drug charges are by weight and fresh mushrooms can weigh a lot. If the feds had ever checked our compost pile, I would have been in jail forever."

Nico laughed. "Is the compost pile still there?"

Elspeth smiled. "I heard some very motivated elderly Dead Head friends came over with a bucket loader and a truck that very night. They scraped the heap down to bare dirt and disappeared. I am so grateful to them!"

"Probably made good compost?"

"Maybe!" Elspeth sobered. "Nico, I want you to know I don't think I hurt anyone. We only sold to people who contacted us."

"Still illegal, Elspeth."

"I know. Uncle Duane sees it that way too. I get it. I promised him that I'm done with any law breaking. I owe him. When I walked out of prison, he was there, waiting for me with a job offer."

She sniffed back more emerging tears. "He helped me get going in a new direction. I'm working real jobs and I'm going to get my degree even if it takes me a thousand years." She had to wipe her eyes. There. It was out.

She said, "Right now I don't need to associate with old friends and I don't have new friends. I have family in pain and . . . that's it."

"It does seem kinda harsh that you got jail for a first time offense."

"Oh, I was so stupid. I did everything wrong. I didn't get an attorney and I was too embarrassed to call my mom. I thought if I just turned on the tears and told some sob story about my dad killing himself, they would cave and let me go. I kept talking and they kept taking notes. I hung myself."

"Did the others go to prison too?"

Elspeth sniffed. "No. One made a deal. Another was out of town and I heard he just kept going south. Last I heard he was in Mexico." She looked down at the floor and said, "I had a few sketchy friends from that time who I don't need in my life again — and my high school friends who are good people shouldn't get bothered by an ex-con."

Nico frowned, "I checked you out before hiring you. There was no criminal record . . . "

Elspeth grabbed the paper towel roll from Nico and began pulling off toweling. Her humiliation was about to be complete. She might as well have it all out while mopping up dog urine. "My name is Dwerryhouse now," she said.

She knelt down and spread out the paper towels. "My father was a Spaniard with a hyphenated last name. 'Meso-Landa'."

"Oh man, that's right. That was on the news after he jumped."

"And every Internet troll in the universe had fun with it." Elspeth stood up and carried the sodden paper towels to the kitchen garbage bin. "It was unbelievable what people said on-line. Like I said, my dad had been an angry guy for years. A few people had crossed him and that made 'Meso-Landa' a howling, hilarious joke for them. There was no point in trying to explain that the disease can distort a person's personality. "

She dunked the sodden wad into the trash and added, "Uncle Duane said if I wanted to be a Dwerryhouse and start over on a new path then he'd take me to the courthouse and pay for the name change or he'd give me two hundred dollars for counseling and respect my choice."

She added, "It meant a lot when Uncle Duane said I could be a Dwerryhouse. He's proud of his name."

A lump sat in her throat that felt the size of a grapefruit. Nico had to think she was beyond appalling. She was a convicted criminal with a family burdened with suicide, illness and grief and her name had been the butt of thousands of on-line jokes.

"Uncle Duane is giving me a roof and a chance even as his hands are so full with my aunt's dying. My aunt. God. My Aunt Yera? She's in the middle of dying and she knows it, but she gave me her phone. My smart phone is really her phone but she wanted me to have it."

Elspeth swallowed hard. "My cousin Carmen is still recovering from a rough year too. I can't ask more of them. They don't need a dog in the house." She looked up at the clock again. "I need to get changed and get to The Azul Kitchen." She exhaled with a sigh. "The dog is going to have to wait here until I get back. Hopefully she won't do any more damage."

Nico fondled Zoom's long ear. "You have been through a lot."

"Yeah."

"I'm feeling like my life is cushier than I knew."

Elspeth tried a laugh. "Yeah. Funny that."

"If you'll trust me with the key, I'll take Zoom on a long run. I can pick up a chew bone for her too. That will give us some time to think about options." He added, "Before you go, take some pictures of the living room and send them to Mrs. Lowenstein. She needs to know what's happening."

"Good idea."

"I'll pick up the foam bits when we get back from the run."

"That's really nice of you. I'll be back a bit after nine. I can walk her again and then I should be able to get your stuff typed after that. I can email you the file by midnight for sure."

No doubt Nico would send her a last check and ghost. Elspeth squared her shoulders. She didn't know what she would do with Zoom, but a crisis postponed would have to do for now.

Saturday, 4 p.m.
Mason County Sheriff's Office

"The young lady seemed happy to see you," Detective Raposo observed as he tapped on his computer. "I'm sure you could call her if you find you have more questions."

Deputy Don McRae leaned against the doorframe of Raposo's office and folded his arms across his chest. "Ms. Oh is eighteen years old," McRae said carefully. "I checked her driver's license."

"Eighteen is an adult."

"Not in my book." McRae shrugged. "Very cute. Very smart. Too young."

"I suppose you're right. Any luck finding a name for our body?"

McRae shook his head. "No missing persons match. Poor quality fingerprints from the first try. The morgue says they'll get better prints in the morning."

"So we have an Asian male, probable mid-thirties, medium build, no wallet, nice camera, no storage chip and no fingerprints yet . . ."

"American made clothes and boots. New. From REI."

"Hmm. How about you check the Olympia store tomorrow to see if a clerk remembers him?"

"Okay."

Raposo flipped through his field notebook and then scrolled through the photos on his cell phone. "And where the hell did that hammer come from?" He scowled up at McRae. "Don't go saying 'the murderer'."

"No sir. The initials are interesting."

"RAS. Scratched in the head a long time ago. That may not help us. Could have been sold at a yard sale."

"Do you think the big fungus is part of this?" McRae asked.

Raposo shook his head. "Dr. Oh said it's not a mushroom that makes money or makes somebody high. No commercial value at all."

"Is this is a crime of passion?" McRae asked.

"In my experience a pissed off lover usually marks, stomps or smashes more."

McRae's eyes narrowed. "So what we've got is someone very cold?"

"A business transaction gone bad?" Raposo looked up from the computer. "Go up the ravine to transact a deal and someone decides to cut their losses? Maybe." He shook his head. "Doesn't feel like a meth deal."

"Opioids?"

"Why not meet in town? Or near town? Why go way out in the sticks?" Raposo mused.

"You think there's something at that location?"

Raposo smiled. "We know there is. A hell of a big mushroom lives there."

McRae uncrossed his arms and straightened up to his full height. "So now we want to know what else lives or is stored near a big shelf fungi?"

"That, sir, is an interesting question."

One person with a belief is equal to a force of
ninety-nine who have only interests.
John Stuart Mills (1806 - 1873)

Chapter Eight

4 p.m
The Oh home

D r. Oh knew how to get his way. Upon arriving home, he had submitted to Jasmine's insistence that he rest. He bargained with her that having his feet up in a recliner in the family media room was sufficient. He was firm that he would not be harassed into a lie-down in his bedroom where he knew he would fall asleep. He had thinking to do.

First he had to own the embarrassment of forgetting what a tardigrade was. He needed to acknowledge the brain block before he could address it. His brain synapses around the topic of tardigrades had clearly become fouled with amyloid plaques. Amyloids, he knew, were simply an assortment of proteins folded together. The beta amyloid form was sheer trash that should be cleared out of the brain by the janitorial microglial cells. Unfortunately, the garbage clearing slowed down after age forty. After a couple of decades of slowing service, the janitorial cells became poisoned by the trash heaps and turned into a lattice work of tangles that not only blocked synapses, they also destroyed the brain cells on either side of the synapse.

His sleep regime, diet and exercise were designed to the minimize beta amyloid buildup and construction of protein tangles.

Clearly he was not doing enough. He'd had numerous lapses of late. Fortunately it was almost always possible to construct new synapses.

He could navigate around the tangles and the garbage piles by building more cognitive reserves. He needed to build his alternative connections on tardigrades and pay attention to the other brain freezes that were causing his family to look at him in alarm.

It took new material to build new synapses. He couldn't stay in his comfortable collection of topics. That was irritating. He liked what he liked.

But staying on familiar mental roads was not an option. It was time for some Daniel Boone style frontier work. He would need to think about tardigrades in a new way. The tardigrades were outliers in the world of biology, so he should be able to learn a few new things about them. He should use his on-line journals to search for the most recent information.

With the thought of professional journals, his mind jumped to the shelf fungus. How should he document the *Bridgeoporus nobilissimus*? His name was known well enough that he had an assortment of journal outlets for a short note. Dr. Oh mulled this choice. It wasn't the drafting of the article that made him reluctant. It was the time it would take for an editor to respond and for the piece to be peer reviewed. Everyone was so busy these days. Even a short article could take months to appear. He would have to summon the energy to guide the piece forward, like the Border Collie herding sheep he'd watched on that Animal Planet documentary.

He was too old and too tired to be a Border Collie of mycological records. Furthermore, documenting the existence of a specimen would be doing something he had done many times before. Innovation was the key to brain health.

It would be easiest to simply post the find on mushroomobserver.org. He could follow up with some specifics on location in an email to a handful of mycologists that he trusted.

Trust. Yes. That was a concern for mycologists. They were such a secretive lot. As were the orchidists. Black markets for rare species and much habitat destruction from fumble-footed and often ignorant competitors elicited hiding and hoarding behaviors. He acknowledged himself as cautious and cryptic. Jasmine had been correct. It would have been very wrong to move that poor man's body to shield the fungus.

Ah, his mind was wandering again.

Next on his agenda, the young student friend of Jasmine's interested in tardigrades. He should not insist the student sit through one of his slide shows. Jasmine was correct again. No one sat through slide shows anymore. It was all Powerpoint shows and YouTube videos. He knew how to make a Powerpoint show. YouTube filming seemed daunting although Jasmine might point him in the right direction. The important thing was to get all of his photographic slides digitized. Well, perhaps not *all* of his slides. He had thousands.

He should review his slides and digitize those that would support this next lecture. It should be a good performance. An outstanding show. The culmination of a lifetime of study. He should connect diversity in tardigrades to the diversity of life forms in the neighboring woods. Not just the mosses. The trees, the shrubs, the vines, the ferns, the fungi — all combined to make communities. He would call the talk "Saving the Earth through Understanding Botanical and Mycological Associations." Yes. That was an alluring title. No. A better one was "The *Real* World Wide Web!"

He would lecture from the ground up, starting with mycorrhiza, *myco* meaning fungi, *rhiza* meaning root. When he had explained to Jasmine that ecto-mycorrhizzal fungi sheathed plant roots, she had replied, "Like a condom?"

Had he known what a condom was when he was eighteen? He recalled that part of the allure of botany had been all the lush female parts described so vividly in his textbooks. He was in another era now. He could not afford to be a prude. He must meet the students of today on their ground. Perhaps he should take a page from Lady Gaga and wear something outrageous. Could he be a dancing toadstool?

Dr. Oh snorted. Not bloody likely.

His mind was wandering again! The important part was communicating that the sheathing fungus expanded the surface area of roots. With a fungal partner, the absorption rate of nutrients and water could increase by a thousand fold. In healthy ecosystems, there were miles of fungal filaments in each tablespoon of soil, with each slender strand releasing digestive enzymes to break down the soil into nutrients.

He was tired of seeing so much landscaping that consisted of a few bushes plopped down in a sea of cedar mulch. Plants and animals lived in communities!

There were common mycorrhizal networks that connected plants to one another. The fungal partners shifted water and nutrients from areas of high resources to areas of low availability. It was the ultimate in Communism, of course, which is perhaps why it had been so slow to be understood by western scientists. Unlike human politics, however, this form of Communism worked.

Dr. Oh closed his eyes, working through the word choices for a section of this lecture.

He settled on, "Yes, there are malingers and parasites. One mycorrhizal cheater in the northwest woods is *Monotropa uniflora*, the lovely Indian pipe or 'corpse plant'. The small white perennial feeds on a *Russula* fungus, which in turn receives its nutrients from nearby trees."

"The *Real* World Wide Web!"— ah, that was a delightful title — had to be taught. Even young children should understand it.

Finding the Fuzzy Sandozi had triggered a new clarity in his mind of how the woods should be understood. Dr. Oh settled a bit deeper into the recliner

Delivering a dazzling lecture would be a reassuring exercise for both him and Jasmine.

Her generation was so clever and yet so different. He needed to think outside the documentary box. Could he do a TED talk?

"YouTube, first," he decided as his eyelids fluttered. "Then I must figure out this Snapchat, Twitter and Instagram." His mind added, "What about 4chan?" Fungal condoms would appeal, he thought. So much biology was rooted in abundant sex. He would sleep. Then he would learn about broadcasting on YouTube. Perhaps he could do an Ask Me Anything on Reddit. Root condoms made of fungi. That was the ticket.

As sleep edged in to close down his thinking, Dr. Oh smiled. He was old. He wasn't dead yet.

Saturday, 4 p.m.
Evergreen Path Hospice, Olympia

Carmen watched her mother twitch. Her mother's body looked so slender and frail in the wide hospice bed. Her mother exhaled with a minor snore and seemed to fall asleep. Carmen relaxed. Today there was no agitation, no terrified eyes, no fury and confusion. The end was near.

Carmen stood up as quietly as she could and waggled two fingers in a walking motion. Her father nodded. Duane would sit with his wife while Carmen went for a breath of air.

As she exited the hospice room, Carmen nearly bumped into a heavy blonde nursing aide. "Hey, Lexi," Carmen whispered. "I'm headed out for some air. Join me?"

Her friend nodded. "You bet!"

Moments later the two young women stood next to a tall rhododendron at the rear parking lot of the hospice building. They shared a cigarette.

Carmen blew out a cloud of smoke and handed the cigarette to Lexi. "God. What a day."

"No kidding." Her friend gave her a sideways glance. "How's the withdrawal going?"

Carmen groaned. "About as you predicted. I am really cranky and I ache. It's like having the worst PMS ever along with the flu and a bad case of homicidal tendencies."

"You've been on powerful drugs. Well advertised for pain relief. Unfortunately, they can be harsh on some people."

"How long until I start losing this weight?"

Lexi shook her head. "It will be slow. Gabapentin works by minimizing nerve transmissions, which is great as long if there are no side effects. That's why the doctors prescribe it — but it is also minimizing the signals our stomachs are sending that says 'I'm full.' I'm in week five of titrating off and I still feel like I'm starving all the time. And that's just one side effect."

"Side effects. Oh yeah. Like I want to kill my doctor."

"I didn't hear that. The wind is in my ears."

"Oh, I already told him. My Dad was right there too. We all agreed that I'm going to get off this stuff and then I'm never taking anything more than a vitamin."

"My body is a temple. That's the new me. How's your mom?"

"You know. At the end."

"I'm so sorry. Huntington's is a horrible end. I should be in there for you. Mouthing off got me moved." Lexi inhaled.

"Now I've got all 350 pounds of the raging Mr. Krepski." She exhaled. "Only you didn't hear me say that."

Carmen winked as she took the cigarette back. "Didn't hear a word." She waved at the empty parking lot. "Heavy traffic noise out here."

Lexi snorted and waited for Carmen's drag. Then she took the cigarette back.

Carmen asked, "What did you mouth off about?"

Lexi sucked on the cigarette and held the smoke a moment before letting a stream of smoke seep out. She said, "Ever hear of Medicare fraud?"

Carmen shook her head. "Not really."

"A facility like this has people arriving and departing all the time. Bills go to Medicare or Medicaid. It's easy for an administrator to pad the patient lists with made up names. Ghost patients. Medicare gets billed, the bill gets paid and, whoosh, the ghost patient disappears. It happens more than you might think. Sometimes there are medications and durable goods for the ghosts too."

She grimaced. "Silly me, I see a list of patients on an administrator's clipboard at the nursing station. I know we don't have anybody by those names so I'm goofing with Monica who is counting the dinner trays. I point at the clipboard and go "whoo-whoo." Monica was laughing and saying stuff like "Oh, no, more ghosts are haunting us!"

Lexi took another drag on the cigarette. "Then I looked up and there was Mrs. Sutherland, the head admin, standing right there." Lexi shook her head. "She's frightening. We don't call her 'Lucinda.' It's always 'Mrs. Sutherland.' She looked at me with her unblinking eyes and said that my job did not include rubbernecking her paperwork. Next thing I know Monica is let go and I've got the job of getting Mr. Krepski on a bedpan."

Lexi sighed. "Maybe I'm overthinking her. Her husband has a debilitating condition and it's got to be exhausting to run this place and take care of him too."

"Car coming," Carmen said as a dark Mercedes turned into the parking lot.

"Shit! That's Mrs. Sutherland!" Lexi dropped the cigarette and ground the butt with her toe.

"You go! I'm too slow."

"Okay. See ya." Lexi scurried up the walk and disappeared into the building.

Carmen picked up the cigarette butt and made her way to a trashcan at the edge of the landscaping. The lady in the Mercedes parked and triangulated to meet Carmen at the door.

"Good afternoon," the woman said.

"Hi." Carmen replied.

"You're Mrs. Dwerryhouse's daughter, aren't you?"

"Ah. Yeah."

"A friend of Lexi's too?"

"We just . . . talk a little bit now and then. Girl stuff." Carmen relaxed her face. Her round cheeks did 'stupid' great.

"I see."

"I, ah, should get back to my mother." Carmen said.

"Let me get the door for you."

Carmen inwardly writhed. It was humiliating when older adults helped her. There was nothing to do but limp through the opening as fast as she could with her best "Thank you" thrown out.

"Are you healing?" Mrs. Sutherland asked as they moved down the corridor.

God, that's a new way to be asked, 'what's wrong with you?' Carmen thought. *I haven't been hit with that one before.* She summoned a cheery tone and replied, "Every day is a new opportunity for growth!"

Mrs. Sutherland narrowed her eyes, clearly picking up on the hint of sarcasm.

Carmen didn't care. Her limp was her business.

Lucinda Sutherland pressed on. "I know Huntington's disease is so terribly frightening. Please let me know how I can help."

Carmen's eyes flashed. "How kind of you."

Mrs. Sutherland arched an eyebrow. "Any time."

They came to a cross corridor and Mrs. Sutherland reached out to put her hand on Carmen's upper arm.

Carmen stiffened. She felt goose bumps prickle up her spine. She lowered her eyebrows and turned to face Mrs. Sutherland.

Mrs. Sutherland said, "Lexi has a habit of gossiping. Sometimes she talks too much." She peered into Carmen's face, as if seeking a sign of agreement.

"I wouldn't know about that," Carmen said. "She's been extremely kind to my mother and me."

"That's good." Mrs. Sutherland dropped her hand. "I hope your mother has a good evening."

"Thank you. I shouldn't keep you. I know you have *so* many patients to think about." Carmen turned and shuffled down the hall, thinking *Take that!*

Lucinda Sutherland watched Carmen limp away. She pulled the keys out of her handbag and opened the door labeled Billing Office.

She set her handbag down behind her desk. She'd hoped that she could ignore Lexi's intrusion with the patient list, but if Lexi was talking about the patient list, well, that was dangerous. There could be no threats to her income streams.

Lucinda rubbed her temples. She shouldn't have left the damn clipboard unattended. There were just too many details to manage at the moment. She really did need to shut down the extra billing. Medicare fraud worked best as an occasional pop-up activity. She risked being caught if she fed too long at the Medicare trough.

Her official work here was demanding too. Richard's needs were draining her at home. She wasn't sure she had the energy for the most exciting prospect of all. Her next venture could be so wonderfully lucrative.

Altogether, these projects were too much for one woman to manage. She didn't need the additional worry of what Lexi knew or what Lexi was saying.

She would call Henry. He had such a way of slicing through problems.

"Fall seven times, stand up eight."
Japanese proverb

Chapter Nine

Saturday, 7 p.m.
The Dwerryhouse Home
4828 Rogers Street NW, Olympia

"Homolog," Carmen muttered. She and Duane were home from the hospice. She was working on her college research project at the kitchen table. The Dwerryhouse home was a 1940's bungalow with scarred wooden floors, coved doorways and a pale yellow exterior that needed a new coat of paint. Duane called it "HQ" but Elspeth and Carmen called their home "The Dwerry Dell."

"Similar structures that come from a shared ancestor. Giraffes and humans both have seven cervical vertebrae. Dogs and cats have a similar pelvis and that leads us to . . ." She closed her eyes. "To 'Paralogs', which are genes that are duplicated and the duplications can go spinning off into new directions." She had her laptop open on the dining room table and was making notes on scratch paper. She added an arrow from "homolog" to "paralog."

Carmen sipped her energy drink. It was caffeine, B vitamins and too much sugar. She needed all three. There was much to be done before her Monday biology class.

"How's it going?" her father asked. He pulled out a chair from the dining room table and sat down next to Carmen.

"Slowly." Carmen sighed. "We know that Huntington's disease starts when a long repeated sequence of DNA grows even longer because of an error."

"Dr. Park said it was like a copy machine that went nuts and made a hundred copies instead of ten," Duane said.

"Yeah. It's a repeated sequence. Several illnesses have this condition. In Huntington's the cell mechanism gets confused. It's supposed to make a protein that directs a bunch of cell trafficking. You get a nutcase traffic cop directing traffic and it gets ugly."

"Tell me your idea again, honey."

"I barely have the chemistry, Dad, but what I'm learning is that when a carbon atom has three hydrogens attached it is called a 'methyl' group."

"Like the methyl cigarettes you're not supposed to be smoking?"

"No. Those are menthol — flavored with eucalyptus — and I'm quitting."

"Good! So what the hell is the methyl group doing?"

"It's acting like a wine cork. There are four kinds of nucleotides that make up the DNA ladder. Only four. Adenine, Cytosine, Guanine and Thymine. Remember, we talked about this before."

"C, A, G and T," her father recited.

"Good job! Methyls need a spot where a C is sitting next to a G. That's when a methyl group can pop in there, attach to the Cytosine and bring the copying machinery to a slamming halt."

"I'm getting it," Duane said.

"Here's where it gets hairy. Huntington's disease is a tri-nucleotide disease. When you get three nucleotides together that are a little instruction book that's called a 'codon.'"

"Codon," Duane mumbled.

"Right. We're looking for CAG codons that are repeated to look like CAGCAGCAG and even more. If a person has more than 36 of the CAG units in a row, then a mutant protein is manufactured. That's the bad traffic cop."

"So we gotta stop the machinery before it reads past number 36."

"Right. We need a wine cork before 36. Methylation won't work on a single CAG because we need the C to be next to G — but what I'm seeing is that if you stick codons together you get CAGCAG and then there is a G and C together where one codon ends and the next begins — which should be able to take a methyl wine cork to stop the manufacture of the mutant protein."

Duane beamed. "I got that! We're cramming in something to stop the machinery. Your old man is not totally stupid!" He sat back in the chair and asked, "And you learned all this from Elspeth?"

"No. I'm figuring this out as I go. Elspeth is the one who told me that certain mushrooms provide methyl groups that can be taken up by human DNA. Medicinal mushrooms have been in use for centuries. It's only been in the last thirty years that we have begun to understand how a fungus works to change a sick body. One path is through contributing methyl groups."

"So we're looking for a mushroom-made methyl group. One that will stop this particular repetition. How hard is that part?"

"For me, shades of impossible. I'll take organic chemistry next term but even then I won't know enough. There are thousands of different species of mushrooms. Right now I'm just trying to sketch out the idea in theory. I want to get it laid out and evaluated theoretically, then I can start asking mushroom people to suggest some candidate species to research."

Carmen added, "The guy that Elspeth is keyboarding for, Nico, is developing a machine that'll help identify fungal species in the field but even that idea is in design." Carmen sighed. "The other thing I can do now is learn more about medicinal mushrooms that are already in use – and I can dig into horizontal gene transfer."

Duane put his hands up to his head and massaged his temples. Wearily he asked, "Horizontal gene transfer?"

"When one species borrows a big chunk of DNA from another species. My second idea to stop Huntington's would be to borrow a healthy section of DNA from another person or another species."

"So when you figure out this 'DNA borrowing' am I going to wake up with the head of a monkey or the ass of a mule?"

"Maybe." Carmen grinned at her dad. "For Biology 102 all I have to do is a team paper on how the topic could be researched. I can use a little moss creature called the tardigrade as an example because they live around here and some species of tardigrades may have some borrowed DNA. That would be a much easier project to design and I've already got a couple other students interested in it."

"Who's on your team?"

"No one's committed yet. It is supposed to be a group project, and, as usual, all of us are now up against a Monday deadline and we're finally talking to each other. I'm hoping to corral two other students."

"Your own fire team!"

"Something like that. There's a really sharp girl named Jasmine who I'd like to work with. She knows a lot of biology — and another kid named Taz." Carmen frowned. "Dad, you need to know that Taz prefers the pronoun 'Zay'. That's important."

"Huh?"

"It sounds like "Zay" but it's spelled X then E. Do you know what intersex is?"

Duane snorted. "A kick ass athlete. But what the hell is a pronoun?"

Carmen laughed. "Dad. You gotta be nice." Carmen's face took on a stern look. She said, "With Taz, we don't say 'she' is on my team or 'he', we say 'xe.' And instead of "her book' we say 'xyr' book. Can you do that?"

"Does Taz care if I eat left-handed?"

"Surely not."

"Does Taz care how I wipe my arse ?"

"Please don't ask."

"No one could ever force me to be right-handed, although a couple teachers tried. I figure I need to let other people be as God made them. If Taz can help figure out how to constipate the Huntington's codons, Xe and everybody else in the damn alphabet are welcome here and I'll call them whatever the hell they want to be called."

"Thanks, Dad."

Duane stood up. "Sounds like you have work to do." He frowned. "I wish you were up at the University of Washington. You deserve to be there."

"Dad, we discussed this already." Carmen held up a hand and ticked off the reasons on her fingers. "The community college has some high quality classes. I'm helping out the business. I've gotten off the opioids and I'm working on the neuropathy pills. I'm near Mom and I still have a couple surgeries to go. I'm earning credits and it's saving us dorm costs." She leveled a stern look at him. "I'm in the right place for now."

He bent over and kissed his daughter's head. He said, "I am so proud of you."

"Dwerryhouses don't quit. Not even when we are getting our rears kicked," Carmen said, with a smile.

"That's right. We find the right mushroom and cram it down the maw of the enemy."

Carmen grinned. "I think that would be a great video game, Dad."

"It'd be even greater if I could get my hands on the enemy. I need to kill something — DNA, tri-new-cleo whatevers, menthol methyl group, horizontal whats-it. Something."

Carmen sipped the last of her drink. "I know the feeling. I'll see what I can find for you."

Saturday, 9:20 p.m.
The Dwerry Dell

Carmen finished posting her research concepts a little after nine. Jasmine Oh was on line and agreed to join Carmen's project, offering the comment, "DNA methylation and horizontal gene transfer may be a reach for us. However, my grandfather has some microscopes including one with a camera so we could collect and document some of the local tardigrades."

"From moss?" Carmen typed back.

"Or lichens. We could collect an assortment of botanicals too and see where we find tardigrades. At least we'd have one piece that we could demonstrate."

"Super. Talk to you tomorrow."

"Okay. 'Night"

Carmen yawned and stretched. She checked her phone. No messages. Her heart sank. The guy in the Harley Davidson T-shirt had introduced himself as 'Jed' and had asked for her number. That didn't mean he would call. Jed. Jed with muscles. Like he would call now. Right.

He probably just wanted some coupons for survival gear. Carmen sighed. A guy with muscles like that wouldn't want her tired, fat, lame self. Tears prickled and she blinked them back. Whatever. She didn't have time for a guy anyway.

Caffeine still jazzed her system. Sleep would be impossible. Her father, however, was stretched out on the sofa and snoring. Carmen pushed back from the table quietly. Her father needed the rest.

Carmen rinsed out her drink can and decided that she wouldn't balance one more aluminum can on top of the recyclables basket. She'd take the basket out to the big bin in the garage.

Duane roused as she pulled the kitchen door open. She called, "Just me, Dad. I'm taking out the recycling."

Carmen limped out with the bin.

A skinny man popped out of the shadows of the garage, causing Carmen to jump back with an awkward hop.

"Elspeth? That you?" he asked.

"No! I'm her cousin. Who the hell are you?" Carmen kept her voice down. The man was some sort of anorexic hippy with toast brown shoulder length hair and a long face. His dark eyes looked out under puppy-like eyelashes, inviting a friendly response.

He used his looks to disarm. "I'm Pete — but my friends call me Liberty."

"Right. As in Liberty Caps, the mushrooms?"

He smiled, flashing a deep dimple. "Yeah! Elspeth talk about me?"

"A little bit. She's done with selling you know. She's working her butt off to get into school and she's completely out of the mushroom business."

"I know. I've got a little job for her. Pay is good. Can you get her for me?"

Carmen eyed him. "What sort of job?"

"Just picking up a trail camera. Totally legal."

"So why aren't you doing it?"

"I have, ah, other commitments." He made it sound like he was a business executive who just happened to be wearing a pilled fleece jacket and ripped jeans.

Carmen set the bin of cans down and leaned against the side of the house. She crossed her arms across her chest. "What sort of commitments?"

"Business. Look, I need to get this camera picked up and I thought Elspeth would like the job. It's a really valuable camera. It's got, ah, pictures of wildlife. I'd pay, ah,a hundred, cash."

"This isn't about drugs, or magic mushies? Not at all?" Carmen's eyes drilled into Liberty's.

"Shit no! Who are you? Elspeth's parole officer?"

"No. I'm her cousin and I don't want her back into stupid stuff. A hundred for picking up a camera?"

"This is legit," Liberty protested. "Can I talk to her?"

"She's not here, but I know where she is. Let me leave a note for my Dad and you can follow me over to Elspeth's."

"Ah. I got dropped off. I don't have a license right now," Liberty said. "But if you give me her address I can catch an Uber."

Carmen eyed him. She didn't think he'd be a problem in the car. Not only did she outweigh him by forty pounds, she also knew how to give a powerful neck jab to a passenger from the driver's seat.

She said, "I'll drive. I want to be standing there when the details get sorted out. This needs to be a completely up and up deal."

"Ah. Absolutely. No problems, I swear."

"The guest of the tortoise has mushrooms for supper."
Zambian proverb

Chapter Ten

Saturday, 9:30 p.m.
The Oh Home

Jasmine amused herself by poking around the Internet to learn more about DNA repeats. Was Carmen really thinking their team could find a breakthrough on Huntington's disease? Her ideas were interesting. Execution would be daunting to impossible.

It was nice to be part of something real. Why not a project by "Dwerryhouse and Oh"?

She smiled as she recalled Carmen's suggestion for a third team member. Taz Candelaria. Taz was probably the smartest of the three of them and would, no doubt, be lead scientist on their research report. "Candelaria, Dwerryhouse and Oh. In your dreams, girl," she snorted, entering another search term.

Jasmine scrolled through an educational website. A human being consisted of approximately thirty-seven trillion cells, each with five to six feet of DNA. The math was staggering. Five feet multiplied by thirty-seven trillion cells equaled one hundred eighty-five trillion feet of DNA per human. Jasmine's fingers flew over the computer keyboard's numerical keys. Dividing by the number of feet of DNA by five thousand two hundred and eighty, she saw the result was thirty-five billion miles of DNA per person.

She rubbed her eyes. That was a lot of DNA. She knew most DNA sat dormant, wound up in histone spools in storage. Each type of cell in the human body had its own library selection of DNA in use and away in storage. Thirty-five billion miles of DNA was a hunky dunky huge, huge amount of DNA to choose from.

Carmen was telling her that fungi could add a methyl group and cause a section of DNA replication to stop. No wonder mushrooms were a popular research topic among naturopaths.

What would bring spooled DNA out of storage? Could mushrooms do that as well? Jasmine scrolled through an article on DNA methylation and histone storage. The alphabet soup of compound names was indecipherable. In addition to billions of miles of DNA, each living thing had millions of astonishingly complex biochemical actions happening simultaneously.

How did a scientist ever target a specific drug or mushroom to a specific section of DNA?

What about the disease that Carmen's mother was fighting? Her searching took her to the Stanford site on Huntington's disease. It told her all the cells in the human body produced the huntingtin protein. However an altered form of the protein could muck up the cells of the brain by adding garbage-y bits that could not be cleared and by making the cells extra-sensitive to the neurotransmitter glutamate.

Jasmine checked the wall clock. She should go wake up her grandfather from his nap in the recliner. He would be stiff if he slept there all night.

He'd want something to eat. Jasmine's stomach growled. Mushrooms and DNA would have to wait.

The Azul Kitchen parking lot

Troy Fickham slouched in the driver's seat of his worn sedan. The car had once been a light tan with a cream interior. Now the exterior of the car wore a decade's worth of road grime and the seats were stained, scratched and yellowed. The passenger foot well stank of wet boots and mildew.

The passenger seat functioned as Troy's workbench and office. He had a cheap laptop open on top of a jumble of papers and tools.

The GPS tracker his grandfather had installed on Elspeth's Civic at the fairgrounds worked. His grandfather had noticed the "3D Survival Gear" window sticker and thought the old red Civic might belong to one of the girls. His grandfather, being the lowlife bastard he was, had a shaved Honda key on his key ring. He'd sent Troy to fetch the electronic unit from the family Suburban while Tate kept a look out for anyone emerging from the building. Once Troy had the device in hand, it had taken under a minute to open the Civic, plug the broadcasting device into the OBDII port under the dash and relock the vehicle. His father, Ricky Lee, had delivered a vicious kick to one of the tires before grinning at Troy.

The next step was to activate the online account that recorded and shared the car's location.

Troy smirked. His grandfather was a cheap old bastard, except for technology, guns, knives and tools. Troy now knew where to find his woman. He'd have her first and then he'd see if his father, his brother or his grandfather wanted a turn. If the girl held up, then they might just keep her through the summer. His grandfather said the hunting was the best part. He disagreed. The lust part was to his liking.

He watched as Elspeth emerged from the staff entrance of the restaurant. She pulled her hood up and trekked through the drizzle to her car while holding a restaurant to-go box. She opened the car and slid in, the dome light illuminating her dark hair when she shoved back the hood of the jacket.

Troy waited to start his car. There was no hurry.

As Elspeth started her car, Troy thumbed his cell phone. He brought up the tracking app and smiled when Elspeth's Civic showed up as a bright blue dot. He watched the dot as Elspeth reversed the car. The dot hovered as she changed gears and then the dot slowly traversed the screen as Elspeth drove across the parking lot and turned onto Harrison Avenue.

Troy smiled as he started his car. He'd see where she was living. He'd keep an eye out for that flat-topped uncle of hers, but if Elspeth was living alone, then tonight might just be the night to get to know her better.

The Lowenstein Neighborhood

Elspeth turned her car into the Cedar Hills subdivision, weary from her day. Her calves ached and her lower back threatened to spasm. She tried to visualize how many bussed tables equaled a semester of college tuition and gave up when her mental math reached the thousands.

Her system jolted alert when she turned the curve onto Painted Fern Court and saw Nico's Jeep sitting in Mrs. Lowenstein's driveway. Of course! Nico had taken the key. Now he had to be here to transfer Zoom and the house key back to her.

She smoothed her hair and dug a breath mint out of the depths of her bag. No matter how hopeless the situation, a Dwerryhouse carried herself with some dignity.

Sighing at her surely short-lived bubble of hope, Elspeth shouldered the bag and slid out of the car. Her foot crunched on a leathery madrone leaf, reminding her of the raking task that really should happen soon.

Elspeth heard Zoom's happy barks from inside the house and Nico's deep "Shush, girl!" as she came up the walkway to the front door. Elspeth smiled and opened the door. Zoom pranced on the tile entryway, tail wagging.

The dog could not restrain her happiness at seeing Elspeth. Zoom bounded around the Lowenstein living room, completing two circuits before plunking her bottom down next to the sofa where Nico sat, carefully scratching the ears of Mr. Midnight. The cat eyed Elspeth with a blend of distain and tension radiating from his bright yellow eyes.

Nico kept up Mr. Midnight's ear rub with his right hand as he reached out with his left hand to massage Zoom's closest ear.

"Wow. Domestic tranquility," Elspeth said. "And I love what you've done with the place." She glanced around the restored living room. "What did you do with all the stuffing bits?"

"I stuffed them back into the sofa cushions and then turned them rip side down. I also filled a couple vacuum bags." Nico smiled up at Elspeth. "Zoom and I ran eight miles and then we ate tuna fish sandwiches in the kitchen. That smelled interesting enough that Mr. Midnight joined us."

"It doesn't even smell doggy anymore."

"Baking soda. Stay out of the kitchen for a bit. I ran the mop around a few minutes ago and it still needs to dry. The window is open so it shouldn't take too long."

"You are amazing."

"How was the restaurant?"

"Busy." Elspeth sank down on the sofa next to Nico and said, "I can't believe how calm Zoom is. She's like a completely different dog."

"Exercise and competent leadership," Nico grinned. "You can thank my mom. We talked about Zoom and she said that if we can get five to ten miles of running in every day, then Zoom should be a lot easier to handle."

"Five to ten *miles*?"

"Yep. A minimum of two hours of movement each day, taking care not to get her overheated and most of it should be trails which are easier on bones. Oh, and my mom's bitch had her puppies. Three girls and a boy."

"Hey, congrats Uncle Nico!"

"Thanks. It means we can take Zoom to visit. You and Zoom are invited to lunch tomorrow, if you're free."

Elspeth's exhaustion fled. She sat up straight. "I'm invited to your parents' house? Really?"

"Yeah. She wants to meet you. Dad too but Mom really does."

"Oh." Elspeth was still processing the lunch invitation when the doorbell chimed.

Zoom leapt up and began barking.

Nico slid his fingers around her collar and gave Elspeth a nod. "Got her."

Elspeth peered through the sidelight window and then opened the door. "Carmen!"

Carmen stepped inside the house and raised her eyebrows as she took in Nico and Zoom. Mr. Midnight leapt off the couch and disappeared down the hall. Carmen jerked a thumb at the person following her and said, "This guy says he's your buddy."

"Ah, Hi ya Elspeth," Liberty wiggled his fingers in a hello and followed Carmen into the living room.

"Liberty!" Elspeth frowned. "I don't know what you're selling but I'm out. O-U-T."

"It's a camera pickup," Liberty protested. "Completely legal. My car's going to be in the shop so I thought you'd like to earn some bucks."

Carmen swung around. "You said you didn't have a license. What is this?"

Liberty's eyes darted around the living room. He noticed Nico and said, "Hey."

Nico let go of Zoom, who bounded over to sniff Liberty. Nico nodded and acknowledgement and said, "I'm Nico."

"Liberty."

"Great. Nico, I'm Carmen, Elspeth's cousin. Now we all know each other, what the hell is going on? I thought you were feeding a cat here." Carmen turned to Elspeth who put up both hands in semi-surrender.

"I am housesitting and you already know I'm taking transcription for Nico." Elspeth's eyes flashed. "Take it easy."

Carmen sighed. "Sorry. I'm not myself."

"I know." Elspeth smiled at her cousin. "You are stressed and doped."

Carmen nodded. Then she jerked her head at Liberty. "Was it a mistake to bring this guy over?"

Elspeth crossed her arms and stared at the thin man standing awkwardly in the middle of Mrs. Lowenstein's living room. "You have one chance to tell the truth before I call the cops and start telling them stories."

Liberty's confidence returned as he laughed. "You're a jailbird, Els. You're not calling any cops."

Nico stood up. His voice was steady as he said, "Elspeth might not feel comfortable calling them. I, however, have no reservations."

Liberty tried to look fierce. He couldn't sustain the look. He said, "I got into a little trouble. I was trying to help my grandmother."

"Oh, right. Your grandmother." Elspeth rolled her eyes.

"No! Seriously." Liberty jammed his hands into his jeans pockets. "I know you got reason not to believe me, but I'm on to something really special. I just ran into a little trouble."

Outside the house, Troy Fickham made his way down the side of the house, past a bedroom window to the back yard where he could see into the kitchen and past the counter to the living room.

He sidled up to the open kitchen window.

In the pool where you least expect it, will be a fish.
Ovid (43 BC-17 AD)

Chapter Eleven

Saturday, 9:45 p.m.
The Lowenstein Home

"I was helping my Granny out." Liberty sat on the sofa caressing Zoom's long ears. "She's kinda out of her mind, so, hey, why not?"

"Why not what?" Elspeth asked from her perch next to Nico on the sofa.

"Well, ah, I gave her some 'srooms." Liberty said. "A small dose. Not much at all."

"You gave *your Granny* psychoactive mushrooms?" Carmen's nostrils flared. "Were you out of your mind?"

Liberty laughed. "A little." He quickly added, "I love my Granny. I do. She's not herself anymore. She gets mad. She doesn't know where she is — well, she didn't — so, ah "

Carmen stomped across the living room and leaned down into Liberty's face. "You are scum! Total scum!"

"Ease off, Carmen," Elspeth pleaded. "Let's hear him out." She turned to Liberty. "Where is your grandmother now?"

"She's back at my aunt's place. I just had her for a weekend. And," he turned towards Carmen, "She was better after the 'shrooms. Seriously. She was smiling and happy and, get this, she knew who she was. She knew who I was. It was beautiful."

Elspeth looked over to Nico. "Is that possible?"

Nico shrugged. "Who knows? Maybe? I mean we know there are medicinal mushrooms and we know psychoactive mushrooms affect the brain. I think we could ask my parents."

Liberty grinned. "Old Deadheads, huh?"

"No," Nico replied. "Emergency room doctors. They sometimes treat people who are having their kidneys implode after eating poisonous fungi."

"Oh." Liberty slumped back in the sofa. Zoom pressed forward and offered his hand a lick.

"What does this have to do with the job for Elspeth?" Carmen asked.

"I was thinking maybe I had this cure. You know. For Alzheimer's?"

Nico groaned. "Go on," he said.

"I contacted this pharmaceutical rep. I told him I had this awesome new mushroom that could clear up, ah, amyloid plaques." Liberty leaned forward, intent now on selling an idea. "That's what fucks up the brain in Alzheimer's. I read a bunch about it online. The brain cells get all mucked up and the old person can't think straight. Man, it's, like, tragic."

Liberty straightened and weighted his words with a sudden passion. "No one has a medication that can clean out the brain cell gunk. No one. The best they've got is stuff to slow down more damage. There was a guy who discovered penicillin by accident, so maybe my granny and me found something big."

Defiantly, he added, "I called this guy at Gentcon Pharmaceuticals. I told him I had a good thing that he should see."

"You were wanting to make some money," Carmen said.

"Totally! Do you have any idea how many old people have Alzheimer's? It's like millions."

Nico looked over at Elspeth. "At least he has that much right."

"Yeah. I do. " Liberty frowned. "Hey, I can take my business elsewhere, you know."

Elspeth said, "Please, just tell us the rest. Don't pay any attention to these guys." She held up a hand to forestall an outburst from Carmen. "Let's get to the end here."

Liberty pressed on. "So I called and got talking and this pharma rep was all excited. He kept talking about how many species of mushrooms are, 'unknown to science.' I figured I had better show him something, ah, interesting — so I tell him to meet me out at this gully I know."

"I'm not following," Nico said.

"I am," Carmen said grimly. "Standard sales technique. People like to think they are getting something exotic and limited. The pharmaceutical rep would not be impressed by standard magic mushies growing in a plastic bin in somebody's back bedroom."

"Yeah!" Liberty agreed. "It should be really wild shit. Romantic and organic! I don't have a driver's license or a car right now so I called a buddy to drop me off and then I get thinking."

Liberty said, "So this mushroom idea is worth millions of dollars. I've got to have some proof that it was my idea, right?" Liberty held his hands up.

Nico said, "You might run into some troubles collecting royalties. I'll grant you that."

"So I've got some stuff at the house that I found. At a yard sale. Yeah. So I'm thinking there's a trail camera. I look, and, yeah, there is. I look it up on the Internet and figure out how to set it up."

"Because you had . . lost . . the instruction book, of course," murmured Carmen.

"Right."

Elspeth motioned him on.

"So when my buddy shows up, I take the trail camera. When we get up into the woods, he drops me off and I set up the camera. That way I can prove it, right?"

"Prove what?" Nico asked.

"Prove that it was me that met with the pharma guy. That this cure to Alzheimer's was my idea!"

"Right." Nico rolled his eyes Elspeth reached out and grabbed Nico's kneecap with a strong squeeze that generated a wince. He got the message and refrained from explaining some of the details of pharmaceutical licenses.

Liberty continued. "I texted the pharma guy and he says he's almost there." Liberty came to a halt.

"And?" Elspeth leaned forward.

"I needed to take a dump," Liberty whispered.

"Seriously?" Carmen asked.

"Yeah. I, ah, went into the woods." Liberty closed his eyes and reached up to wearily rub his face. "Okay. I'm in trouble. A little bit of trouble."

"Why am I not surprised?" Carmen said.

Elspeth leaned in and patted Liberty's knee. Zoom licked his hand. Elspeth said, "Liberty, tell me. I'll help if I can."

Over her head Nico and Carmen exchanged incredulous looks. Elspeth ignored them. "I know what it's like being up a creek. Go ahead and tell us and we'll figure something out."

Liberty exhaled. "That'd be great, Elspeth. I was squatting there, pants around my ankles and I can see down to the road. This nice car pulls up to the mile marker. I'm, ah, not in a professional-looking position."

Outside the kitchen window, Troy Fickham put his hand up to his mouth and bit down on a knuckle to keep from laughing. He knew Liberty. The Mason-Thurston County informal cash economies were robust and interconnected. Liberty sold magic mushrooms and Troy sold liberated chainsaws and firearms of dubious origins. Their customer bases had overlapped for years. In fact, it had been at Liberty's bonfire where Troy had first seen Elspeth. Liberty was a good businessman, except for when he wasn't.

Inside, Liberty said, "It's the pharma guy and he has someone with him. They get out. I know the second guy.

He's a seriously bad dude. The two guys look around a minute. Then they go up the gully."

Liberty swallowed. "I finish up and I'm standing there thinking. I'm not sure what to think. It's not a good scene. It's making me nervous." He sniffed and stared down at Zoom who looked back up at Liberty with adoring eyes.

He said, "I waited. Kinda a long time because I didn't know what to do. Then the scary guy comes out of the woods. He gets in the nice car and drives off. I, ah, stood there. I waited a long time more. I finally get some nerve up and go up the gully."

Liberty looked at Elspeth. He said, "The pharma guy was dead on the ground. Had his brains bashed in. I booked it. I ran out of the gully and down the road and then I bushwhacked down to another road and thumbed a ride on a logging truck. I forgot to get the camera. I don't have a car and I need to get that camera out of the woods. It has, like, evidence, on it. Maybe even a picture of me." Liberty stared at the floor. "Okay. I was messing with the camera a lot. I know it has some pictures of me."

"And you want Elspeth to go get it?" Nico was outraged.

"I think we should," Carmen said.

"What?" Nico and Elspeth shouted together.

"I was online with another biology student tonight. Her name is Jasmine Oh. She said she and her grandfather were up a ravine in the woods looking for spring mushrooms this afternoon and they came across a body. Head bashed in. They spent the afternoon with the sheriff's deputies as they processed the scene. I'll bet it was the same guy. The cops should get the pictures."

"So let's call the deputies!" Nico said.

"No." Elspeth shook her head. "No police. But if we can pick up the camera and delete Liberty's pictures, maybe we can mail in the rest anonymously."

Outside the open kitchen window, Troy Fickham was listening avidly. He moved closer to the window and peered in. The next words from Liberty shocked him.

"The police will want this guy," Liberty said. "He's a big time fentanyl dealer. His name is Henry Fickham."

Troy gasped. He stepped back into a pile of madrone leaves that crackled under his weight.

Inside the house, Zoom alerted to the sound and then to the face at the window. She let off a torrent of barking and galloped into the kitchen. Nico yelled, "Hey!"

Troy ran. Lust was forgotten. He had to warn his uncle.

For they sow the wind and they reap the whirlwind.
Hosea 8:7

Chapter Twelve

Saturday, 10 p.m.
The Lowenstein Home

Troy ran to his car. He yanked open the car door and flung himself inside and then inserted the ignition key with shaking fingers. The car's engine roared to life and Troy jammed the transmission knob into drive as Nico came running into the street with Elspeth. Troy ignored their cries of "Hey!" and "Stop!"

His heart rate soared as he took the curve too fast. The car fishtailed and settled as Troy brought the vehicle under control. He steered around a pizza delivery car and made himself ease off the accelerator.

Troy turned onto Evergreen Parkway and sped through two roundabouts before turning onto Mud Bay Road. He knew where he could go. He gunned the car down a hill and finally slowed to turn into a rough lane that led behind an abandoned bakery.

Troy's fingers were shaking as he tapped on his cell phone. He failed at entering the passcode. He was about to make a second effort when Liberty's story returned to his mind. Liberty's mushrooms might be worth millions of dollars.

Troy set the phone down. He needed to think about this. His ragged breathing began to ease into a smoother rhythm.

The easiest thing would be to call Uncle Henry and tell him about the trail camera. Then it would be Henry's problem and his uncle would owe him a favor. That could work.

It could work even better if he went to get the pictures from that trail camera. He would have something on his uncle and on Liberty. That might get him some of the millions Liberty was going to be making.

Liberty's story made perfect sense.

Troy sat back and stared at the raindrops running down the windshield. His heart rate began to settle as he watched the crash of the raindrops. He had a tracking device on Elspeth's car. He knew where she was staying. He knew the restaurant where she worked. He could wait. She would go fetch the camera and then he could get the pictures from her. His brother could help with breaking into the house and restraining her.

Uncle Henry could be contacted later, once the pictures were in hand.

Troy smiled. That was a better plan. He'd get Elspeth. He'd have his fun. This project Liberty had going bore some watching. He could do that too. Troy re-pocketed the cell phone and leaned over to open the glove compartment. It was time for a little celebratory smoke.

At the Lowenstein home

Nico had his arm around Elspeth, trying to understand her concerns. "Who was that guy?"

Carmen answered. "He's one of the Fickham family who have been hanging around our shows. He watches Elspeth's every move. Today his creepy father called Elspeth a squaw and offered money for her. My dad punched him and they left in a huff."

"God. Oh, God." Liberty rocked back and forth on the sofa. "Troy will be telling Henry. I'm dead. I am so dead."

"Stop it!" Carmen barked. "We'll think of something."

Liberty stopped rocking long enough to say, "You don't know the Fickhams."

"Fill me in," Nico commanded.

Carmen folded her arms and said, "We learned about these guys from Sergeant Martinez of the Olympia Police Department." She recited, "Old Man Russell Fickham. In his seventies. Six-foot-four. Three-hundred-fifty pounds. Beard. Hard eyes. His son, Ricky Lee Fickham. About forty-five. Five foot ten. Must weigh Two-twenty. Smokes. Incompetent jerk but scary too. Troy Fickham. Next generation. About twenty, maybe a little older. Six feet. Skinny. Red ball cap. Dirty long hair. Last is the little brother. Tate Fickham. Five-foot-ten. Also skinny. Really narrow face."

Elspeth took up the description. "Backwoods guys. Bad teeth. Flannel shirts. Cheap jeans. Expensive knives."

Nico turned to Liberty, "And you know them?"

"Yeah. Yeah. Mostly just Troy. He, ah, had an outlet for some stuff I picked up." Liberty moistened his lips and added, "It was an antique revolver. I, ah, got it and didn't know what to do with it. Seemed kinda dangerous to put it on Craigslist."

"Right," Nico said. "Is Troy a magic mushroom guy?"

"No. More a weed, boilermaker and guns kind of guy."

"What's a boilermaker?" Nico asked.

"Shot of whiskey chased by a beer," Elspeth said. "A fast drunk."

"And this Troy, the one in the red ball cap. He has a crush on you?" Nico asked Elspeth.

She shuddered. "I guess so." She reached out to fondle Zoom's ears. "Good thing I didn't get around to raking up those madrone leaves."

"You should leave the leaves," Nico said. "Natural alarm bells."

Liberty said, "I'm going to need more than leaves to survive after Troy tells his uncle that I saw him." His eyes

82

darted around the room as if already seeking a hiding place. "He's gonna kill me."

Elspeth took a trembling breath. "No. We're going to figure out some alternatives. Liberty, is there somebody out of town that you can go visit?"

"Ah. My brother is down in Eureka, California. He, ah, has a small business there."

Elspeth sighed. "Let me guess. Magic Mushies for the Humboldt College kids?"

"Yeah."

"Right. Can you go hang with him?"

"I don't have a car."

Carmen pulled out her cell phone. "Let's check the bus schedule. I think there's a midnight bus going south. I can get you to the station. I can also take you to your place to pick up some clothes."

"Ah, actually, I don't care about clothes but I want to pick up some of my, ah, business materials."

Carmen rolled her eyes. "Why am I not surprised?"

Elspeth said, "Tell me where the camera is and I'll go get it. I can delete any pictures of you and mail the rest into the police."

"You should go in daylight," Liberty said. "You won't find it tonight."

"All right. I'll go at dawn." Her voice wavered. Elspeth rallied and said more forcefully, "I can get it. I could go . . . "

Nico interrupted. "What about this Troy? I don't like the idea of him knowing that you are staying here."

Carmen eyed Nico. "Come on, big boy. Think. Who scared off Troy tonight? Zoom and?"

Comprehension bloomed on Nico's face. "I'll stay with you. We'll go get the camera and tomorrow we can work on the notes together. Zoom and I will go with you."

Elspeth turned into Nico's shoulder and burst into tears of relief. He gingerly put an arm around her shoulders and gently pulled her into a hug.

"I'll be your reinforcement for as long as you need me," he said.

Elspeth wiped her eyes and sniffed. "Thank you. That means a lot. I think I should send another text to Mrs. Lowenstein and tell her that I have a stalker. God, she's going to be really worried about her house now."

"No. She'll be glad she can count on you to keep her updated," Nico said. He rubbed her shoulder. "You sent her pictures of the living room. Did she respond?"

Elspeth nodded. "I didn't get a chance to tell you that. She'll pay me some extra for keeping Zoom and she said she'd deal with her niece. I'm not sure what that means exactly."

Nico lowered his eyebrows and said, "Hopefully something about finding Zoom a better owner." He turned to Liberty. "Anything else we need to know?"

"Ah, no." Liberty stroked Zoom's ears and then turned sorrowful eyes on Elspeth. "I'm sorry, Elspeth. I heard Troy Fickham liked you. I didn't know he was, ah, stalking you."

Elspeth used the back of her hand to rub her dripping nose. "He was at your spring bonfire last year, wasn't he?"

"Yeah. Then you, ah, went away, and he thought that was cool."

"Great. He adores me because I'm a jailbird."

"Ah. Yeah."

Tears plopped down onto Elspeth's lap. "Nico. You don't want to take me to your parents. My life is a disaster. I'm broke and I'm never going to finish school at this rate."

"Shh." Nico stroked her hair. "You are amazing. This is not your fault."

Carmen turned to Liberty and asked, "What about the other Fickhams? Were they at the bonfire?"

Liberty stared at Elspeth. "Man. I dunno. Can you remember?"

She hiccupped and sniffed, then said, "I wasn't there that long. It seemed like a pretty young crowd."

Liberty nodded. "I think I would have remembered if Henry was there. He's got those eyes. He's a nasty dude." Liberty paused. "The old man is really scary too. I know the old man wasn't there. Maybe Tate was? I can't remember. It was a crowded night. We were celebrating the end of truffle deliveries and everybody was happy." He looked up and said, "You watch yourself, Elspeth. I don't know who else might be working with him."

"I'll be careful." Elspeth rubbed her eyes and sniffed again. "For a state capital, somehow Olympia can be a surprisingly small town."

Nico nodded. "We all need to be careful."

The Sutherland Home
10 p.m.

Lucinda Sutherland sat up from her naked sprawl in front of the fireplace. "I am so glad you came over," she said.

Henry Fickham ran a hand up her leg. "You sounded so exhausted."

"I have been. Taking care of Richard, the Medicare lists, the online videos, and now the new business – all on top of my administrative duties – it has just been insane. It was so stupid of me to put that clipboard down where an aide could see it. That's exactly the sort of error that will sink us."

"You're making me feel guilty," Henry said. He sat up and stroked her thigh. "I shouldn't have pushed the new business details on to you. It was too soon."

"Oh, darling," Lucinda reached out to cup Henry's cheek. "It is going to be so wonderful. I can't tell you how excited I am. Running just one online business sounds like heaven. And we'll be doing such a service. There are just so many old people. They really are in the way."

"You won't miss the videos?" Henry leaned in to plant a kiss under her ear.

She shook her head emphatically and said, "Good heavens, no. That has been Richard's passion. I just monetized it." She tapped his hand, signaling him to stop his exploration. She knew Lexi would be off at 11 p.m.

She said, "I need to go."

Henry caressed her face. "You can do this."

She smiled. "Oh, yes. Your idea is brilliant. I can get a scalpel and gloves from the supply room. All I need to do is make a small slice in the bottom of a chocolate and slide in the carfentanil tablet."

"Get a mask to wear too. They use this stuff on elephants. It's really potent."

"Why is there a market for a drug this strong?"

Henry slid his hand up under her breast. "It's supposed to be a big high but it's too dangerous. That tablet is the last of my supply and I'm not handling any more after this. I am strictly in fentanyl from here on out. The fentanyl is challenging to handle too. You don't want even a speck of powder to fall on your skin. We'll have to make sure we use the pill press with a laboratory hood."

"We'll be careful." Lucinda said. She caressed Henry's cheek. "That's just one of the things I so love about you. You are so careful and professional. If everyone took care of details the way you do, then the world would be such a better place."

Henry took her hand and kissed her palm. "You have worked so hard. You're a survivor." He kissed her palm again. "A survivor with such class."

She smiled up at him and then shifted to reach for her lavender panties. "You should go."

"You're giving it to her tonight, right?"

"Yes."

"It'd be fun to sit in the parking lot and watch her try and drive home. I like watching troubles disappear." Henry said. "But tonight it wouldn't be smart. I'll go back to my place and work on our contacts list. I want to suss out some of the bottom feeding attorneys in town. I'll talk to you later."

"The pill press should be delivered tomorrow. The pill bottles are done. I'm almost finished with this week's photos and videos too."

"Good. I'm glad to be out of delivering to druggies. The fentanyl for grannies will work so much better for us." Henry ran his hand up her waist to rest beneath her breasts. "You're incredible."

Lucinda lowered her eyes. She gasped when Henry tweaked her nipple. Only Henry had ever been able to make her feel honored by a touch.

Henry ran his thumb around her aureola. He said, "I need a few more tools. Mind if I raid your garage?"

"Not a problem," Lucinda breathed. "Take what you need."

"Richard won't notice?" Henry replaced his thumb with his mouth. He nursed her teat and sent Lucinda into her third orgasm of the night. She bucked and clawed his shoulders before giving way to an exhausted collapse.

Lucinda rallied to smile up at Henry. She gestured to the nearby sofa where her husband lay snoring with his back to the fireplace. "He's totally stoned. He wouldn't notice an army arriving. Take whatever tools you like."

Henry moved in to nuzzle her face. "It is so nice to have some quality tools," he said. "Nice balance makes a difference." He gave her a deep-throated kiss and said, "Go have fun with chocolates."

"All right." Lucinda smiled. "I bet she'll eat the whole box."

Four minutes later Richard Sutherland quit his snoring act. He felt confident that Henry and Lucinda had departed. He was amused to find that feigning sleep next to the lovers had given him an erection. He adjusted a pillow and snuggled deeper into the sofa cushions while thinking about Lucinda. This lover was taking her to new levels of cold creativity. He would be wise to be careful.

"Equo ne credite, Teucri!" – *Do not trust the horse, Trojans!*
The priest Laocoon, as reported by Virgil c. 29 BCE

Chapter Thirteen

Saturday, 10:50 p.m.
Evergreen Path Hospice, Olympia

Lexi slid out of Mr. Krepski's room as quietly as she could. He was asleep and that was a Godsend. Many evenings he was at his most challenging just as the shift was ending.

She pulled the sliding door shut and turned to see Mrs. Sutherland approaching from the administrator's wing. What was she doing here at this time of night?

"Lexi!"

A cheerful wave? Had zombies eaten Sutherland's brain and replaced it with some sort of soul? Lexi stuck on a smile and tried to look happy about seeing an administrator late at night just ten minutes from the end of her shift.

"How is Mr. Krepski this evening?" Lucinda Sutherland asked.

"Sleeping. His medication change seems to be helping him," Lexi answered.

"Great. I owe you an apology."

"Me?"

"Yes. I completely forgot that you had that back strain last fall. We should have never put you with a patient as large as Mr. Krepski. I came in tonight to work on the roster and I see that we can make some changes. Ramon can help Mr. Krepski and we'll put you back with Mrs. Dwerryhouse. I believe the Dwerryhouse family appreciates your work."

"Wow. That would be super." Not only was it good news, it made sense. Mr. Krepski preferred a male nurse.

He'd said so repeatedly. It was about time he had what he wanted.

"I also wanted to say 'Thank you' for all your hard work." Lucinda held up a small gold-foiled box. "It's a quartet of bonbons. Just a little treat."

"Thanks so much!" Lexi's smile was genuine this time.

Lucinda smiled back and said, "See you tomorrow."

West of Olympia

Carmen Dwerryhouse sat at the wheel of her car trying to stay calm. She checked her phone. No messages. No Jed. As Carmen waited in her car in a rutted driveway next to an open pasture, Liberty was inside a moss-roofed mobile home packing his gear. He was taking his time. Carmen recalled what Elspeth had said about psychoactive mushrooms and Schedule One drugs. She knew that spores and grow kits were not illegal because a spore never contained psilocybin — but any amount of psilocybin containing mushrooms could trigger an arrest.

Carmen had heard enough about growing mushrooms to understand why Liberty wanted his jars of mycelia. As a spore from a mushroom began growing, it had to compete with molds and bacteria. A grower had to provide a sterile beginning to be a successful businessman. He would pack canning jars with tapered rims with a growing medium like rye grain. The next step was heat sterilization. That, Carmen knew, was absolutely crucial.

Capped jars of sterile growing medium would have small holes punched into the metal tops. This is where a spore syringe would be inserted. Each jar would receive several syringes worth of spores. The spores would begin to sprout and eventually the fungus would infiltrate the entire jar, consuming the growth medium.

That was only the first step in growing mushrooms. Once the jars were filled with mycelium, the grower would tap the jar contents out and set the congealed tower onto a bed of moist perlite in a plastic tub.

Carmen knew that the mycelium needed the right moisture content and daily venting of carbon dioxide. Elspeth had described mushroom growing as "dairy farming." Details were important. So was cleanliness.

Elspeth's inexperience had saved her. She had contaminated her mycelia, resulting in the growth of a mysterious stinking mold. She had hauled the mess to the compost pile just hours before the DEA had busted her operation.

Carmen jumped as a dark shape loomed up out of the darkness. It was a black cow coming over to the fence to study her. She could see some other dark forms in the pasture. She counted them. Fifteen cows.

Liberty was sure taking his time.

Carmen drummed her fingers on the wheel of the car. Liberty did not seem like the sort of person who would be intensely clean or hardworking. Elspeth, yes. Liberty, no. He seemed an odd fit for the meticulous work of mushroom production.

One thing Carmen knew for sure was that her father would kill her if she got busted for magic mushrooms while driving Liberty and his stash to the bus station. She squirmed.

No. Dad wouldn't kill her. He'd be disappointed. That would be so much worse.

As if on cue, her cell phone chimed the arrival of a text. It was her father. "Where are you?"

She typed back, "Giving ride to friend to bus. Home soon."

Duane responded, "Elspeth Okay?"

Thinking of Nico's plan to stay the night to 'protect' her cousin, Carmen smiled and typed, "She's fine."

Carmen had no more sent the message than her phone chirped with an incoming call. Lexi.

"Lexi! Hey!"

"Hey yourself. You won't believe this."

"Good news?"

"Yes! I'm going to be the evening nurse for your mom starting tomorrow."

"Oh, super!"

"And you won't believe this. Mrs. Sutherland also gave me a box of chocolates."

Carmen laughed. "A bribe to keep quiet?"

"Maybe. She has to know that institutional Medicare fraud is hard to prove. Even if I did call a hotline, I don't have the paperwork. She's smart. I'll bet whatever I saw is under lock and key or shredded by now. I've got suspicions, but no proof. Now I have chocolates and a better patient. Yeah. It's a buyoff. "

"You going to call that hotline anyway?" Carmen asked.

"I'm thinking about it. The ripoffs aren't going away by themselves and even in a small facility like this one, we're talking tens of thousands of dollars."

"How can I help?" Carmen asked.

"I'm not sure. Let me think about it. I'll call you tomorrow."

Carmen felt better after talking with Lexi. She checked the time. 11:20. If Liberty was going to make the midnight bus, it was time to get going. She left the car and made her way up the weedy walkway to the mobile home. The sound of a video game came through the thin walls. Carmen climbed three slippery steps and opened the door. Liberty sat on a sofa with a game controller in his hand, muttering as a racecar buzzed around a television screen race track. "Outta my way!" he swore.

"Liberty!" Carmen shouted.

He looked up.

"Are we going to the bus?"

"Ah. Yeah. Let me finish this level."

Carmen limped over to the wall outlet and pulled the plug. "We're going now."

"I was almost done!"

"I've been waiting half an hour in a cold car. Get moving or the hell with you."

Liberty threw the game controller down on the sofa and grabbed up a daypack. "Okay!"

"That's it? No mycelia jars?"

Liberty had the grace to look a bit sheepish. "Naw. I'm not a grower. I got my laptop with my mailing list. I'm good to go."

"Why all the mystique? Why tell me you have to pack up product?"

Liberty looked at the floor and shrugged.

Carmen answered her own questions. "Because being enigmatic helps sales." She rolled her eyes. "You sell by being quirky and cryptic. The mysterious man of mushrooms."

Liberty shrugged again, this time with a small smile brightening his face.

"Ugghh!" Carmen growled as she checked her cell phone. 11:24. She would have to hustle to get Liberty on the bus. "Get your butt in the car," she said as she stomped out.

A few minutes later Liberty and Carmen were in the car bumping down the long rutted driveway while the dark shapes of the cattle in the pasture appeared and disappeared in the mist. Carmen's cell phone buzzed. She drove with one hand as she pulled the phone out of her rear pocket. She handed the phone to Liberty. "Answer that, will you?" She needed both hands on the wheel for the next bumpy stretch.

"Ah. Hello?" Liberty listened and said, "She's with me but we're headed into town. I can tell her you called." A pause. "Okay." He tapped the phone off.

Carmen navigated a shallow pond of water covering the road ruts and gratefully turned onto a paved road. "Who was it?"

"Huh?"

"Who called?"

"Jed? He said Jed. Or Jeb? He's, ah, going to bed. He'll try you again sometime."

Carmen clutched the steering wheel. Her father was right. Sometimes a person just needed a chance to throttle someone.

The Fickhams' compound, Kamilche Peninsula

Russell Fickham stroked his beard and sent crumbs flying. He reached for another corn chip and said, "That survival man made you look a fool."

His son, Ricky Lee, frowned. He leaned back to swing up the footrest of a drab green recliner. He popped open a can of beer and said, "Surprised me, that's all. I could take him."

Russell's matching recliner was loveseat wide. The tufted arms were streaked with black and gray stains. Russell wiped his chip scooping hand on the fabric and then tapped on a computer tablet screen. "You can't let this lie, Ricky Lee."

"Yeah." Ricky Lee sipped his beer. He missed Karla. His life had gone to hell when she got sick.

He stared at the window where a branch of Indian plum came out of the darkness to tap at the glass with each gust of wind from the night's rainsqualls. He'd met Karla at the Mason County Fair when Troy was seven and Tate about five. The boys had been squirrelly while waiting for a fried elephant ear and she had scolded them but with a twinkle in her eyes. She got them distracted and talking. Before long the line had moved up and they had their food. Troy had invited

Karla to sit with them and she did. Six months later she and Ricky Lee had moved into a double-wide trailer near the Shelton airport and life had been bliss.

Ricky Lee sipped his beer and remembered. The money had been good. He drove a truck and she waited tables. The boys zigzagged through school but Karla kept after them to stay out of trouble.

Then her back started hurting.

A few months later they learned the phrase "ovarian cancer" at the same time they learned that her health insurance wasn't worth shit.

She died the following March. Medical bills overran his life. The boys were wild. He drank too much and three DUI's meant he was out of the truck driving business.

Troy quit high school his junior year. Tate didn't make through tenth grade. They'd had no choice but to move back in with the old man.

Ricky Lee had forgotten how much he had hated his father. Russell was one mean sonnafabitch. In the last three years Tate and Troy looked more and more to Russell. They were getting nastier by the day.

He sipped his beer. He was nasty too. He was proud of some of it. Ricky Lee thought of Karla again. She had been good people.

What the hell had come over him to offer money for that sales girl? His beer tasted flat. It was cheap for sure. He knew why he'd offered money. He was trying to be the Big Man in front of Troy. That had blown up. Stupid. He was broke, drunk and stupid.

And his father wouldn't let it lie. Russell said, "You need to fix this. That man disrespected you."

Ricky Lee scowled. "Don't know his name."

"Internet says here that the 3D Survival Company is run by a Duane Dwerryhouse. Gives an address. Near Division Street."

"Troy's the one who wants the girl."

Russell nodded. "And he should have her. She's a handsome thing." He loaded another chip with guacamole, ate it and added, "You've got two sons. What about the other girl?"

"The fat one?"

"Yeah."

"She has a limp."

"Tate that particular?"

Ricky Lee smiled. "I doubt it."

Russell wiped his hand again and tapped on the tablet. "Troy and me put a tracker in the girl's Civic. He's checking out where she is tonight. We'll drive by the 3D business address tomorrow. Then we can make a plan so you can get even."

"You thinking we'd pick up the girls and bring them out here?"

Russell grunted. "You got a better idea?" He scooped up another towering blob of guacamole and said, "Out here no one hears any screaming. If anyone ever did, we'd just say we've got a loose peacock. Gawd, those birds are screamers."

"Yessir. They are." There was never danger in agreeing with his old man. Ricky Lee added, "It's been a while."

"We've been busy. I ain't had the urge." Russell's large belly rocked with a low laugh. "Seein' Troy with the urge gets me the urge. Funny that way."

Ricky Lee's frowned as he recalled his father's past tendencies to join in on other people's parties. He said, "Troy gets his girl, he gets her first." He could do that much for his son.

Russell slanted a look at Ricky Lee. "Sure thing. Now if Tate don't want the fat one, do you care much what I do?"

"Nah. Just give Troy some space." Ricky Lee settled back in the recliner and sipped on his beer. He thought of the

G40 Glock pistol he had snugged up under the seat of his car. Next time he met Duane Dwerryhouse, he'd be ready.

Strobilurus trullisatus

97

Clear conscience never fears midnight knocking.
Chinese proverb

Chapter Fourteen

Saturday, 11:30 p.m.
Mrs. Lowenstein's House, Midnight

Nico sat on Mrs. Lowenstein's floral brocade sofa knowing he was doing one thing right. His left hand was massaging Zoom's long right ear as she leaned into his legs and closed her eyes in bliss. Zoom he had figured out.

It was his right arm that was giving him trouble. He had his right arm stretched out along the top of the sofa, reaching behind Elspeth's head but not touching her shoulders. He wanted to drop his arm down and give Elspeth a cuddle but he wasn't quite sure he should. He was beginning to feel a significant strain in his shoulder.

Elspeth was sitting on the middle cushion of the sofa. Surely she could have chosen the far cushion if she didn't want to be close to him. Then again, her leg wasn't touching his. She had sat leaning forward with her forearms on her thighs for the last fifteen minutes. She looked tired.

Nico wasn't ready to give up. He said, "Tell me about Carmen."

"Her limp, you mean?"

"Yeah. Is that the Huntington's?"

"God, no. It's too soon for that. Last summer she was out biking and got clipped by a car. It threw her into a concrete barricade. She smashed her knee, her hip and her ankle."

"Ouch."

"Yeah. The last year or so has been awful. Carmen was supposed to go to the University of Washington last fall on a volleyball scholarship. That went down the tubes."

"She's an athlete?"

"A good one. She was put on some powerful medication to help soothe the nerve damage and it had some side effects. Personality changes, big weight gain. She's constantly moody. It's been rough on her and on Uncle Duane."

"And her mom is declining?"

"Yeah. Horrible all around. Last summer was the worst."

"You were selling mushrooms and got busted?" Nico flexed the fingers on his left hand. Zoom shuffled her feet and leaned in, begging for the ear massage to resume.

"Busted in May. Out in October." Elspeth sat up and her thigh bumped into Nico's. She seemed not to notice. She said, "Turns out Liberty is much smarter than I am." She rolled her eyes. "What a gig he's got going!"

"Growing liberty cap mushrooms?"

"No! That's just it. *Psilocybe semilanceata* isn't grown domestically. It is a very finicky mushroom with potent levels of psilocybin. People would love to be able to grow it, but no one can. People hunt them in the fall. Liberty caps can be dried, but a good salesman can make an argument that fresh is better. Liberty figured out how to deliver fresh liberty caps out of season. He uses New Zealand truffles."

"Truffles?"

"Yep. The liberty caps like to grow in wet cow pastures. They really grow well where there are sedges and cow dung. It took me a bit to figure it all out, but it is genius in its simplicity." Elspeth grinned at Nico. "Believe it or not, that guy is truly brilliant."

"Go ahead, convince me," Nico said. "Brilliant is not a word I'd put with the guy I met tonight."

"Trust me. He's clever. He uses those big eyes and his dimples to make sales." Elspeth smiled wearily and said,

"You know that I went out to a spring bonfire at his place last year. I wanted to look around and see if I could see any of Liberty's growing techniques."

"You were a magic mushroom industrial spy?"

Elspeth's eyes lit with humor. She said. "I suppose. I knew he sold lots of species of mushrooms. Edibles to restaurants, psychoactive species to users. I wandered around with a beer in my hand and I didn't see any plastic totes or outdoor mushroom beds or any sign of work at all. I was mystified for sure. Then I got moo-ed at."

"By a cow?"

"Yeah. Liberty lives in this old mobile home next to a cow pasture. I bet that pasture is crawling with liberty cap mushrooms every fall. It's a big rolling pasture with some shade trees on one side. The pasture is wet with lots of sedges and grass that insulate and protect the ground all through the fall. That would give an extended season for growth because it provides some different microclimates. I'll bet he can pick mushrooms from mid-September until we get a hard freeze."

"So that's lucky, not brilliant. What's with the New Zealand truffles?"

"I'm getting there. I'm walking around his property, chatting with people, being nice and I see there's a shed. I poke my head inside and I see big, insulated coolers. They're massive – and each has a shipping label. "Truffles from New Zealand. Gourmet product. Refrigerate. Priority shipping.""

"I don't get it."

Elspeth yawned and stretched, brushing Nico's arm. "He has partners who are legitimately shipping truffles from New Zealand. He must also have a friend on some New Zealand dairy farm that is covered with liberty caps in their fall. The various truffle partners air freight mushrooms to Liberty and the psychoactive little liberty caps come along for the ride."

"So they are shipping truffles and liberty caps?"

"Right-o. I peeked in the cooler and saw rows and rows of perforated plastic bins with liberty caps."

"Wouldn't Customs check? I mean a truffle — any truffle — looks like a lump. It doesn't look like a liberty cap."

"How many Customs agents know their mushrooms?"

Nico smiled. "I can see your point. But if you can pick oodles of liberty caps out of a cow pasture, how does our Liberty profit?"

"Unlike customs agents, he knows his mushrooms. He meets the plane at SeaTac, spends a day delivering fresh truffles to upscale eateries in Seattle. He'd get top dollar for fresh, quality truffles and then he'd take a vanload of Liberty Caps to concert sites in the Southwest and Midwest. Even our Northwest mushroom sounds like an exotic product two states away — a New Zealand mushroom even more so. There might be some small differences in the physical product so he would hone in on those differences when selling."

Elspeth shook her head and yawned again. "Even if the mushrooms were absolutely identical to what we have in our backyards, a good salesman can make an overseas version sound fabulous. He sells magic mushies like mad for a couple of days in the Southwest, then back to SeaTac airport to pick up the next load of truffles. I think he works May to June with New Zealand truffles and 'shrooms and September to mid-November with his back yard collection. I'll bet he ships coolers back in our fall to the New Zealand end. He might even ship them some northwest chanterelles."

"Wouldn't the shipping costs eat up the profit?" Nico asked.

"Not if he has some connections to bring coolers in on someone's private jet. It might be free or nearly free. There's lots of trading of favors and goods in the alternative economies. A big cooler holds lots of 'shrooms."

"And his customers think he's a grower."

"Yep. It'd be interesting to know about his truffle connections. How legitimate are they? A chef may not ask too many questions if a nice product is being delivered. The deliveries do need to be quality stuff however. I think that's Liberty's gig. High quality mushrooms, big-eyed sweetness, get cash in hand, boom, out the door — and he's working, oh, six months of the year."

"You're right. He's brilliant."

Elspeth nodded and blinked, owl-eyed with exhaustion. "I guess we should plan on an early start tomorrow. We should call it a night."

"Alright. Nico pulled his arm in and his shoulder sent messages of relief. "Do you want to call and check on Carmen first?"

Elspeth shook her head. "That would just make her mad. She'd think I thought she couldn't make a bus stop drop off." She pulled out her phone and smiled. "There's a text. She says she's home."

"Alright then. Zoom and I get the guest room, right?"

Deep rose patches appeared on Elspeth's cheeks. "Thanks for staying," she said.

"Not a problem," Nico said. "Glad to."

* * *

Lexi stopped at the traffic light at Harrison Avenue and Cooper Point Road. It was always a long light. She reached over to her bag and pulled out the chocolate box.

Lexi lifted the lid. "Milk chocolate or dark chocolate?" she murmured. "Ooh, maybe one of each."

Do not anticipate trouble, or worry about what may never happen.
Keep in the sunlight. Ben Franklin (1706-1790)

Chapter Fifteen

Sunday morning, April 22, 6 a.m.
The Lowenstein Home

Elspeth rolled over in the large bed. The 1200 thread count sheets slid over her body like silk. She snuggled into her luxurious nest, ready to slip back to sleep when a cold nose banged her cheek.

Elspeth's eyes flew open.

Zoom licked her face.

Elspeth sat up and scrubbed her eyes. Right. She was in Mrs. Lowenstein's deluxe bedroom and that meant . . .

That Nico was down the hall in the equally posh guest bedroom.

"Woof."

"I think that means you need to go out," Elspeth said. She checked the bedside clock. 6 a.m. "And it's time for us all to get on the road."

Zoom wiggled a full body dance as Elspeth swung her legs over the edge of the bed.

"WOOF!"

Nico came charging down the hall. "You alright?"

"Fine! Zoom just wants out." Elspeth looked at Nico and grinned. "Great boxers. I didn't know they came with fairies and mushrooms."

Nico shrugged. "My mom."

Zoom whined.

"Okay, Okay," Nico said. "I'll take you out."

Elspeth sat on the bed, enjoying the sight of the dog and manly rear end leaving the room. She was . . . happy. Wow.

Elspeth wrapped her arms around her middle, savoring the moment.

She thought about the day ahead. Breakfast first and then out to fetch Liberty's camera. She should type up Nico's historical section.

Elspeth stopped with a wave of panic. Was she still supposed to meet Nico's parents for lunch? Did Nico really think that was a good idea?

Elspeth scrambled out of the bed. She needed a shower. She needed something to wear.

Sunday morning, 8 a.m.
The Oh Residence
1202 Tamoshan Drive, Olympia

"Hi Mom! How's Vienna?" Jasmine cocooned her cell phone onto her shoulder as she shook cereal into a bowl.

"It's breathtaking. Absolutely charming. Words fail me."

"How's the concert hall?"

"Splendid! Your father sounds amazing. The acoustics are incredible." Madeline Oh bubbled on, "We're going out tonight for 'Tafelspitz' and tomorrow we're going to make the rounds of the sheet music shops."

Jasmine laughed. "Oh boy! Sounds really parental."

"It's fun!" Madeline Oh refused to be baited. "How's Grandpa?"

Jasmine was ready with her lie of omission. "Fine! We went up in the mountains yesterday and found a humongous fungus that is really rare. It was very exciting."

There was no way she would mention finding a body. Her parents, both violinists, had worked hard to land the Vienna gig. Jasmine reasoned that the dead body was now in the hands of the authorities and there was no need to have her parents winging home to fuss and worry.

Her mother had the ears of a bat however. "Did Grandpa get tired?"

"A little. I made him a cup of tea on the backpacking stove and that helped. He's fine, Mom."

"Any memory lapses?"

"A little one. He didn't remember water bears but after some tea he was back to normal."

"A water bear?"

"Small arthropod that lives in moss. It came to him after a bit."

"Do you need us?"

"No!" Jasmine shifted to hold the phone in her hand. "We're fine. Today he goes to play poker with some pontificating geezers and he's looking forward it."

Her mother sighed. "Please don't let him hear you call the retired professors 'pontificating geezers'."

"I'll refrain."

"Who's hosting?"

Jasmine looked up at the wall calendar by the kitchen clock. "Looks like a Dr. Sutherland."

"Drop Grandpa off at the curb and don't go in."

"Is there a problem?"

"Dr. Sutherland is an ass grabber from way back," Madeline Oh said. "He likes young women. The younger the better, says the campus rumor mill."

"Yuck. Grabby Geezer. Barf."

"Just stay in the car. And you have class this week?"

"Biology in the morning. As usual it's a team project and the day before concept presentation we've barely started. I imagine we'll be working like crazy later today. Totally normal. No worries, Mom. Everything is peachy."

Sunday morning, 9 a.m.
The Dwerry Dell

Carmen stood in the kitchen. She picked up her cell phone. She set it back down on the table. She looked at the wall clock in the kitchen. 9:00 a.m. It was early to call. For a Sunday, it was early.

She tried to think about eating breakfast. Toast. That sounded dry. Cereal. That sounded soggy. An omelet. That sounded like too much work.

She'd have to tell Lexi that she finally was having a meal where she didn't want to eat everything in the pantry and the tablecloth too.

Carmen looked up at the clock. 9:03.

She picked up the cell phone and tapped her way to the recent calls box. She tapped the phone to return the call to Jed.

She got his voice mail. His baritone voice barked, "Not here. Leave a message."

"Hi! This is Carmen! From the 3D show? I'm sorry I missed your call. I was taking a friend of my cousin's to the bus station. It'd be great to talk to you. I'm sorry I missed your call. Bye!"

Carmen tapped off the phone and groaned. "Stupid! God, I sounded so stupid!"

Duane Dwerryhouse came into the kitchen and made for the coffeepot. "What's up, sunshine?"

"I'm returning a call. To a guy. I sounded like an imbecile."

Duane filled his coffee mug and sat down at the table. "You sounded fine to me. Cheerful. You sounded cheerful."

"I said, 'I'm sorry I missed your call' *twice*."

"Trust me. He'll like that." Duane smiled at her. "He'll like that a lot."

"I hope I get to find out," Carmen muttered. Then she smiled back at her father. "It's been a while since a guy called me. This one seems pretty nice."

"Do I know him?"

"He was at the Saturday show. I sold him some freeze-dried food."

"Dark hair. 5'10. Muscles. Harley Davidson T-shirt?"

"Yes!"

"Damn. He saw me flatten that lowlife. Sorry about that, Carmen."

"Hey, he called anyway. That means he's brave, right?"

Duane swallowed a sip of coffee and said, "Could be. What's his name?"

"Jed."

"Does he have a motorcycle to go with the T-shirt?"

"I don't know." Carmen rolled her eyes. "No, I will not ride the motorcycle without a helmet."

Duane smiled and took another sip of coffee. "Damn straight. Did you decide on a project?"

Carmen pulled out a kitchen chair and plopped down with a scowl. "I'm supposed to meet with the other students later today. My brain is churning with possibilities and the interesting ones all sound impossible." She sighed. "Jasmine Oh's grandfather is a botanist. She says he has about two thousand slides of local mosses and lichens. Part of me just wants to go hide at her house and watch pictures go by."

Duane laughed. "You never know. Something in the pictures might trigger some thinking."

"I already know the lichen that I think is cool." Carmen sat up straight and beamed a smile that pierced Duane's heart with its unexpected radiance. He swallowed and held back a sniff.

Unconscious of Duane's silent rejoicing, Carmen said, "There's this tree fungus named *Letharia vulpina* or wolf lichen."

"Wait. Is it a fungus or a lichen?" Duane asked. "I'm thinking Elspeth said they were two different things."

"A lichen usually is an algae and at least one fungus growing together symbiotically," Carmen said patiently. "The algae takes in sunlight and makes sugars that it shares while the fungus excretes digestive enzymes and takes up nutrients from rocks and soil that it feeds to the algae. You've seen the wolf lichen — it's that shaggy chartreuse stuff we see in the woods."

"Bright lime green?"

"Yeah. It can be used to dye fabric yellow. Like the tardigrades, it can survive very cold temperatures. It's also poisonous to foxes and wolves because it contains vulpinic acid, which is not toxic to mice or rabbits." Carmen shifted her weight on the hard kitchen chair. "So I'm wondering 'why'? Why would a tree lichen need to be poisonous to foxes and wolves? I mean, it grows up a tree!"

"Huh." Duane finished his coffee. "I'm glad it's up in the trees. Sounds like it'd be bad for dogs."

The whole life of a man is but a point in time; let us enjoy it.
Plutarch (circa 46-120 AD)

Chapter Sixteen

Sunday morning, April 22, 9:10 a.m.
Rural Mason County

Nico pulled the Jeep to the side of the forest road. "There's the mile marker." Large Douglas firs and cedars towered on both sides of the road. The air smelled of evergreens and damp earth. A sprinkling of trilliums sat in a south facing dip, their triangular white petals flashing in the dappled shade.

Nico parked and stepped out onto the dirt and Zoom scrambled out of the vehicle and galloped down the road. Nico waited until she was not much more than a red dot streaking along the brown roadway and then he trilled a piercing whistle. Zoom reversed and came running back, arriving with her tongue lolling out and her tail wafting side to side like a dark flame.

"She's beautiful when she runs. Her red against the green of the woods is so pretty," Elspeth said.

"Yeah. She's great," Nico agreed. "We need to keep an eye on her. I don't want her to wander off up here."

Elspeth kicked a soda can to the side of the road. "We don't want her to be eating this garbage either. If we come back we should bring some trash bags."

"It's disgusting alright." Nico frowned. The small ditch next to the road was strewn with energy drink cans, plastic juice jugs and food wrappers.

"Tweakers on meth?"

Nico agreed. "Liberty said this is a common meet up spot. I'll lock the Jeep. We should pay attention to any motor noises we hear."

"There's the stand of Devil's Club. I've heard you can make a tea from it for treating arthritis."

"And nailing a branch over the door is supposed to keep evil away," Nico said. "Of course, filling the doorway with those kinds of thorns would keep everybody away."

Elspeth studied the wall of prickly shrubs across from the smear of litter. "Look. You can see the deer trail at this angle."

"Good. Devil's Club likes water. There's probably nettles here in the summer. Watch for stone flies."

"Stone flies? They bite?"

"Nope." Nico said. "They don't tolerate pollution. The nymphs have special gills around their anus that they use to take up oxygen from the water. That doesn't work when the oxygen levels are off. If there are stone flies upstream from the trash heaps, it'll suggest that people haven't peed upstream."

He added, "That's a hell of a steep rise there." Water streamed down from the gully, dribbled down a rock face and coalesced into a riverlet that disappeared into a culvert that ran under the road. Bright yellow skunk cabbage speared up through the water, adding an off-putting scent. Nico walked up the road and looked back at the mountainside above the road. "Bit of an optical illusion too. More of a gully up there than you might think."

Zoom ran down the road and again returned at Nico's whistle. He snapped a leash onto her collar and tugged her back to the Jeep. "Any sign of the camera?" he asked.

Elspeth rotated slowly and studied the massive Douglas firs that continued down the slope to her right. "How would he get a camera up far enough on these trees?"

"He didn't. He said it was on a sideways log. Let's walk up the road and see what we find."

Zoom lunged forward and hit the end of the leash. Nico stopped and knelt down to look at the dog at her eye level. "We're not doing that. Walk nicely. Remember?"

Zoom licked his face. Nico made her sit and then stepped off with a tug and the word, "Walk!" Zoom fell in beside Nico. "Good girl!" he praised.

"How do you do that?" Elspeth marveled. She sped walked to catch up with the pair.

"A long run yesterday followed by some intense training. She can't keep a slack lead very long. Her ability to focus has to build." Nico moved forward at a brisk pace. "We'll help her out by walking fast."

The moist smell of evergreens and moss filled the air as they walked. Indian plum hoisted early blossoms and tiny leaves sprouted from the limbs of a red huckleberry bush.

"Any chance of finding some morels?" Elspeth asked. She tried to sound casual, as if she always chatted while speed walking.

"I don't think so. It's about two weeks too early. Do you like morels?"

"I like anything where I can make a legitimate profit."

"Do you know how to tell the *Morchella* species from the *Verpa* and *Gyromitra*?

"Nope. But morels are easy, right? They have the wrinkly cone top."

"I think we better have some training sessions before you kill someone. Several species in the *Gyromitra* genus have a crinkly top that looks like a morel. Some species also contains mono-methyl-hydrazine, which is basically rocket fuel."

"Ugh. That doesn't sound savory." Elspeth found she could manage short sentences without gasping. Nico's lung capacity had to be phenomenal. He was showing no respiratory distress as he lectured and kept Zoom content with rapid forward motion.

He said, "There are people who love to eat *Gyromitra* anyway. The collectors will boil off the toxins and I hear that can reduce the rocket fuel load. But there's no way of knowing how concentrated the mono-methyl-hydrazine is in a particular specimen — and that sort of toxin is cumulative."

He said, "You want the mushrooms that are hollow stemmed, and have a fully attached cap. That should be a true morel. We could spend some time this spring on collecting and identifying."

"I'd like that." Elspeth said no more as she reached a near sprint to stay in pace with Nico.

He smiled at her. Despite all she'd been through she was no complainer. "We'll see if we can find you a morel patch and a buyer," Nico promised. "There was a fire south of here last summer. That'd be a good place to look in early May."

"Look!" Elspeth pointed at jumble of gravel and tree stumps bulging out of the woods just as the road curved. A cluster of cedars loomed behind an enormous cairn of road building detritus. There were logs and stumps mashed into a pile that bristled with branches at odd angles.

"Good eyes." Nico came to a stop. He said, "That's an excellent place. Straight shot back to the Jeep."

Nico unclipped Zoom and the dog celebrated by whirling in a circle. She staggered slightly as the dizzy circling ended then righted quickly to scramble up the cairn of rubble after Nico.

"I see it!" Elspeth pointed to a dark rectangle on a log cantilevered out at an angle over open air.

"Wow. That's out there."

"Let me. I'm lighter. I'll scoot out there and you can sit on this end to make sure it doesn't tip."

"Be careful." Nico gave her a hand up the slope. Her hand was small and smooth. It fit nicely into his.

He smiled at her and she looked up into his eyes and blushed.

Zoom came scrambling up the embankment, shoving into the back of Elspeth's knees.

"Hey, " Nico scolded. "Watch where you're going."

Zoom's feathery tail waved enthusiastically as she surged to the top of the rubble pile.

Elspeth laughed and began her traverse of the log. As she inched out moisture from moss mats soaked through her jeans.

Nico sat on the log, hoping his weight was enough to keep things anchored. He thought that Liberty deserved some credit. It was a challenging place to navigate. A hard dark semicircle of a *Ganoderma* shelf fungus protruded on one side. Elspeth gave the *Ganoderma* a wide berth.

Nico found he was holding his breath when Elspeth reached the small camouflaged box. She had to lie down on the narrow log to carefully unstick the hook and loop strips before pulling the camera up. She briefly straddled the log and then swung a leg over to reverse her crawl back to Nico.

Her jeans were wet and smeared with moss. Strands of her dark hair were free from her braid and were sticking to the sides of her face. No matter. She had the camera. She jumped off the log and Nico stood up, smiling.

She handed the box to Nico with a grin. "Success!"

Nico opened his arms and Elspeth stepped into his hug which quickly melted into a snuggle and a kiss. They stood, heart to heart, under the sweeping boughs of an ancient cedar and kissed again. Nico ran his hands up and down her arms. Elspeth looked up into his face, her own rosy with joy.

There was a metallic clunk.

Nico and Elspeth jumped apart. "That was a car door," Elspeth whispered.

Zoom was already racing down the rubble slope. She reached the road just as Nico began a whistle. It was too late. Zoom dashed down the road to greet the new arrival.

She picked up speed and became a red blur racing for the deputy sheriff's sedan that sat parked behind Nico's red jeep.

Elspeth looked down the road and saw the sedan and the lean deputy sauntering down the road. She cried, "McRae! God, No!" She sat down behind a log and covered her face with her hands. "I am not believing this."

"You know him?"

"Sheriff's Deputy McRae. Yeah. I know him. He's one of the ones who arrested me." Her face was pale with devastation. "Nico, I'll never outrun my past. It will always be something."

Nico put out his hand, palm up. "Come on. We'll face this together."

Elspeth took his hand and stood up slowly. Her wet jeans suddenly felt shoddy and she could feel the wisps of her hair that had stuck to the side of her face. She must look like a tramp.

Nico guided Elspeth down the slope of the rubble pile. They reached the road and Elspeth whispered, "Should I ditch the camera?"

"No." Nico shook his head. "He'll see that. Just act normal."

"Easy for you to say." Elspeth said.

"We haven't done anything wrong."

"He'll find something. I promise you. I'm a felon."

"And you are with me."

Zoom came bounding back, did a loop around Nico and Elspeth and ran back to loop around Deputy McRae.

"Good morning, folks," McRae called as he walked. "This your dog?"

Nico called back, "Yes. She's with us."

McRae took his time sauntering down the dirt road. Elspeth watched him and swallowed hard. It was so unfair. She only wanted to make her way in the world and now her beautiful moment with Nico was ruined by this lanky deputy and her own sordid past.

"I hope she didn't bump you," Nico said.

"No, she's fine. Beautiful dog."

"Thanks."

McRae spoke again. "And how are you, Ms. Meso-Landing?"

"It's Dwerryhouse now. Elspeth Dwerryhouse."

"Got married? Congratulations to both of you!"

Elspeth felt the blood rushing to her face. How embarrassing. She stuttered out, "No. I took my uncle's name. This is Nico Pavlopoulos."

"Nice to meet you. I'm Deputy Don McRae."

Nico took McRae's offered hand. "Nice to meet you too, sir."

"What brings you two out here today?"

"Just walking the dog," Nico said.

McRae put his thumbs into his Sam Browne belt and said, "Let's start this conversation again. You two are in the vicinity of a major crime scene. Ms. Dwerryhouse is a previously convicted felon who looks to be holding a trail camera. Do we want to have a lengthy discussion at my office or can we cut to the chase right now? Think carefully, because I am making a one time offer to hear your side of the story without prejudice."

Nico looked at Elspeth. She swallowed hard, her throat suddenly dry. She felt cold, and clammy and sick to her stomach. Her brain furnished her a mental movie of a college diploma that sprouted wings and began flying away.

She inhaled and said in a rush, "Deputy McRae, I promise you that I am doing everything in my power to do right. I am working about five jobs to earn money for college this fall. I am here to do a paid job for a friend. I am not doing anything illegal, I swear."

"Tell me about the trail camera."

"It belongs to Liberty Hartmann. I think his real name is Peter Hartmann."

McRae nodded. "I know Liberty."

"I'm not working mushrooms. I swear," Elspeth said. "He stopped by and said he'd pay some cash if I would come out and pick up this camera."

"That didn't seem a bit odd to you?"

"Absolutely. He had a story — a weird story."

"I'll bet. What was it?"

Elspeth licked her impossibly dry lips, feeling like the world's biggest idiot. She confessed, "He said he had made arrangements to meet a representative of a pharmaceutical company. He was trying to sell the guy a mushroom strain for the treatment of Alzheimer's disease."

"You are kidding me."

"No. I'm not. I swear I'm not."

Nico interrupted. "Liberty is a slime bucket who gave a psychoactive mushroom to his grandmother. According to Liberty, his grandmother's dementia improved, so he got this goofy idea about selling his mushrooms as a medical cure."

"Are you in the mushroom business, sir?"

"I'm a researcher. I'm a graduate student working to modify a rapid DNA sequencing machine to work in the field to differentiate and identify mycological specimens. Dr. Berbera at Summit College is my advisor." Nico's cool confidence made Deputy McRae's eyes narrow.

"And you believed Liberty's idea?" McRae's eyebrows now arced up in feigned surprise.

"I actually have some very strong doubts about it. I do believe that Liberty thinks his mushrooms have an economic value as a medicine. I also think he's amoral as hell."

"I can see where a person might think that," McRae conceded. His eyebrows snapped down into a straight, no-nonsense line. "So Ms. Dwerryhouse came to get the camera. Why is the camera here?"

"Liberty told us that he arranged to meet this pharmaceutical man out here. He was trying to make his mushrooms sound rare and exotic." Elspeth said. "He was afraid that his idea would be stolen, so he set up a trail camera to document the meeting — only he went to take a bathroom break — a long bathroom break — and that's when the representative showed up with another man in the car."

McRae snorted with the start of a smile creeping onto his face. "Somehow, I am believing this."

"It's the truth," Elspeth said. "The two men went up the ravine back there. One man came out and drove off in a nice car. Liberty went up the ravine and found that the other man was dead and that's when Liberty ran off. He ran that way." Elspeth pointed. "And he thumbed a ride on a logging truck."

"How did Liberty get out here in the first place?" McRae asked.

"A buddy of his dropped him off. Apparently Liberty has lost his license."

McRae pulled out a pocket notebook and a pen. He made some notes and then asked, "How did you two get into this?"

"Liberty realized the camera was still out here. He didn't have a vehicle so he stopped by to talk to me." Elspeth hesitated. She didn't want to get Carmen in trouble. "Look," she said, "it's a little complicated."

McRae said, "I do complicated." He added, "Don't think you do anyone any favors by not mentioning names. The way forward here is to put it all out on the table." His face softened. "Elspeth, more than anything, I want you to be in class this fall and not back in jail."

Nico reached out and took the trail camera from Elspeth and handed it to McRae. "Here. Take it. The idea was for us to delete any pictures of Liberty and then to mail the camera into the authorities. Let's just skip a step."

McRae took the camera. "Good move. Tell me the rest."

"Liberty spoke first to my cousin, Carmen. She had been chatting online with a classmate who said she'd found a body up here."

McRae's eyes hardened. "The classmate's name?"

"Jasmine. I don't remember her last name."

"Anything else?" McRae's casual face had now transformed to hard angles.

"Liberty wanted to leave town. Carmen gave him a ride to the bus station last night. Liberty said he recognized the man who came out of the woods alone."

"Name?"

"Henry Fickham."

McRae's jaw tightened. His eyebrows were now a straight line over a pair of eyes that looked like gray ice. "Henry Fickham."

Elspeth nodded. "There's one more ugly part. I've been working as a sales person at my Uncle Duane's survival gear shows. There are these four guys that have been showing up. They were . . . staring at me. This last show one of them was really rude. My uncle Duane ran them off but one of them, a young guy, showed up last night at the house where I'm cat-sitting. I think he's a nephew of Henry Fickham."

"Troy or Tate Fickham?"

"Troy. He wears a red ball cap. That's it. That's all I know." Elspeth paused and then said, "I could ask Carmen for Jasmine's last name. We should warn her about this Henry."

"I'll take care of that," McRae said.

"You know how to find this Jasmine?"

"Yes," McRae grumbled, "I do.

The Derry Dell
Westside of Olympia

Carmen sat at the kitchen table with her laptop open. "No! No! Damn it!" Her eyes welled with tears. A moment later she was sobbing.

Her father appeared and pulled out a kitchen chair. Duane sat next to his daughter and pulled her into a hug.

She rained tears down on his shoulder. Finally she sniffed and said, "Thanks, Dad."

"Welcome. What's up?"

"Science is supposed to be reproducible. My project idea isn't."

"I'm sure there's a copy machine somewhere that can do it. We can drive to Seattle."

Carmen managed a watery laugh. "No. Not that kind of reproducible." She waved at the laptop. "I gave up the idea of presenting mushroom DNA methylation as a potential cure for Huntington's disease. It just seems too far out there. So I switched over to the tardigarde DNA idea."

"Where the little beasties were borrowing DNA?"

"Horizontal gene transfer from other species," Carmen agreed. "Jasmine and Taz are both psyched on the idea." Carmen pointed to the story on her screen. "Originally some scientists found some 6,000 genes in tardigrades that seemed to be borrowed — but now another team has done the same work and they're saying that the tardigrades don't have much borrowed DNA. They couldn't reproduce the original work. The original work team may have picked up contaminants."

"Ouch. Embarrassing?"

"Probably. It also means my report idea just got flushed. And my professor is a jerk. I don't want to ask her for an extension."

"And you miss Mom."

"Oh, God. Yeah."

"You are eighteen years old. I think you got a lot on your plate. So, I've got a plan for you." Duane patted Carmen's shoulder. "Want to hear it?"

Carmen sniffed again and dragged a knuckle under her nose. "Sure."

"You're part of a team for a reason. Message your team with what you found. Let them have a few hours to freak out and think on it. We'll go see Mom later today and then you meet with your team. You'll pick another path or you will figure out how to overcome the obstacle."

Duane smiled at his daughter. "And you'll have the additional adrenaline boost of being at deadline. Works a treat."

"Love you Dad."

"Love you back."

Near Grass Lake Park
Olympia

A stout man moved down the grassy shoulder of Kaiser Road. He carried a bucket and a long-handled grabbing stick. Sunday morning was his favorite time of the week. He would walk three solitary miles collecting trash while his wife attended Sunday school at the mega-church on the corner. He could not abide preaching or litter and his Sunday morning ambulation and trash collection served as a bridge between his furies and his wife's faith. They both reached Sunday lunch having had a morning that served the soul.

The church services were underway. The roadway would be quiet for the next hour or more. He shuffled past a car parked awkwardly on the roadside. He stopped. He could see a blond young woman slumped at the wheel of the car.

Fingers trembling, the man pulled out his cell phone and called for an ambulance

When a person is down in the world, an ounce of help is better than a
pound of preaching.
Edward G. Bulwer-Lytton (1803-1873)

Chapter Seventeen

Sunday morning, April 22, 10 a.m.
Mason County

"**N**ico, I am so sorry." Elspeth said as they loaded Zoom into the jeep.

"About what?"

"About bringing you to the attention of law enforcement."

Nico looked at her. He could see taut lines of strain in her face. "Don't worry," he told her. "We have done nothing illegal. We told the truth. We assisted law enforcement when we could. That guy should have no beef with us."

"Should and does are two different things," Elspeth said.

"Are you on parole or anything?"

"No. But," she swallowed. "Those guys. They will hound a person. Once you are a bad guy, they just never let up. I've heard some horrible stories."

"Hey." Nico put his arm around her shoulders. "You are not alone with this."

"I should be." Elspeth looked up at him. "This sort of thing could completely derail your project. Your reputation could be ruined."

"This sort of thing," Nico said firmly, "is no big deal. But if it will help you feel better, we'll talk it over with my parents. They've worked in the Mason County Emergency Room a long time and they know a lot of the officers. Let's get an outside opinion before we freak out."

"I can't meet your parents!" Elspeth wailed.

Zoom leaned out of the back of the Jeep to give Elspeth a face wash. Elspeth hiccupped and pushed Zoom away.

Nico stepped closer and pulled Elspeth into his shoulder where she leaned in and wept. Nico kissed her hair and then her forehead. "Listen," he said. "My parents see people in rough circumstances every day. Nothing makes them happier than to see a person come back from a bad place."

Elspeth sniffed and hiccuped.

Nico kissed her forehead again. "What's most important to you right now?" he asked.

"College. Hopefully without too much debt," she answered. "If I can get a college degree, then that says something." She swallowed and continued with a steadier voice. "I want to earn my degree."

"Right. So I'm bringing a young woman to lunch who values education."

Elspeth managed a watery laugh. "That sounds . . . pretty good."

Zoom woofed.

Nico smiled. "I think she's saying I'm bringing two beauties with me to lunch."

"Oh boy. And I thought I was good at sales."

"Come on. Let's get out of here."

Elspeth looked down at her streaked jeans. "I need to stop at my place for a change of clothes and my charging cord." Elspeth said. "I don't want to meet your folks slimed like this."

"We can stop. Don't worry. My folks are going to love you no matter what."

Elspeth rubbed her face. "Thanks. Thanks for backing me up. If you hadn't been there I think I'd be in jail now."

"Was that the officer who arrested you before?"

"No. He was part of the team who served the search warrant and he was there when I was questioned. It was a federal officer from DEA who was a total jerk."

"If you get called in again, we'll go with a lawyer."

Elspeth didn't know whether to laugh or cry. She went with a strangulated sniff. "I can't imagine your folks loving that."

"Are you kidding? They have been hounding me to get out of the basement and have some adventures. You're smart, hard working and totally beautiful. How can they complain?"

This time Elspeth did laugh. "You're very kind."

He shifted gears on the Jeep and asked, "So when you start college this fall, what will be your major?"

"I always thought I'd study biology but after busing tables I'm starting to think I should be a nutritionist. People eat the mushrooms *in the salad*."

"Ah, yeah?"

"Come on, Nico! Mushroom walls are built with chitin — the same stuff that makes up insect shells, fish scales and lobster claws. You have to cook mushrooms to release any nutrients. Uncooked chitin can trigger an immune response too." Elspeth took a breath and raced on with, "Now, with cooked mushrooms you get all the B vitamins, potassium, Vitamin D and, the new hot foodie thing is choline — That's a macronutrient that helps keep energy levels up and brain cells functioning. Choline helps with DNA methylation and we all know that's important! But you have to know what you need. A person with Parkinson's disease might not want increased choline."

Nico grinned. He said, "Feeling strongly about this, I see."

"Absolutely. You should see what people are eating! They pick out the mushrooms, maybe because those are perceived as expensive, and then they leave the rest of the salad. But melted cheese? We practically never have any melted cheese left on the plate."

"Guilty," Nico admitted. "I'm way more a nacho guy than a salad guy."

"Melted cheese hits the taste buds with loads of salt and fat. It tastes great! But we should be eating half a plate full of roughage and not nearly so much of the other stuff. Don't even get me started on the sodas."

"Yeah. My mom is going to love you."

"Sorry. I get a little intense. My customers keep saying stuff like, "Gee, I wish I was skinny like you," but they don't see that they're eating a gazillion calories after sitting through a movie while I'm spending the evening hauling dishes and going home with a bowl of shredded chicken that I share with a cat. It makes me a little crazy."

"Ah, you might want to dial back the outrage a bit. I don't think we change things with the big finger wag."

Elspeth sighed. "I know. So many of us are struggling. We have to buy what we can." She leaned back in the seat. "I was lucky in prison. I was able to work on my feet in the laundry. A lot of the jobs were on a computer or sitting at a sewing machine. So many of the women had depression and anxiety. Totally reasonable. Add in crappy institutional food and there was diabetes and high blood pressure everywhere."

She looked out the window at the vast expanse of forest. "I am so very lucky. I'm out here now. It is just so beautiful.

"How about Outdoor Ed?" Nico asked. "You could teach."

"Not with my conviction," Elspeth said. "And now I've had further brushes with the law, like, this morning?"

Nico said, "Stop worrying about it. We turned over the camera to law enforcement within five minutes of finding it. The deputy's body camera was on, so that is documented."

"He had a body camera on?"

"Yeah. Black unit on his vest with a little green light."

"I thought that was a radio."

"He had one of those too."

"Great. Now I'm documented."

Zoom leaned forward from the back seat and gave Elspeth a lick, then washed the side of Elspeth's face until Elspeth gave in to a smile. "You're alright, Zoom. And I'm going to keep going until I'm alright too."

Harrison Avenue, Olympia 10:40 a.m.

Ricky Lee Fickham parked his rusting Suburban outside the office of Westside Storage Solutions. His father sat in the front passenger seat. Russell looked down the row of shuttered doors on storage units and said, "Looks locked up as tight as a Virginia virgin."

A laugh came from the second row of seats where Tate Miller sat. He said, "I gotta nice long key."

Ricky Lee frowned. "There's no telling which units belong to Dwerryhouse."

"Office girl might tell you," Russell said. "If you can find some charm. Hah! Mebbe I should go."

Ricky Lee's frown deepened. The last thing he wanted was to watch his father succeed at sweet-talking some female. It was mystifying how mesmerizing Russell could be when he put his mind to it.

"I'll check it out," Ricky Lee said. "You just wait." His large belly jiggled slightly as he stepped down from the vehicle and stalked with a wide gait to the glass door of the office. He heaved the door open and scowled as he waddled in. He focused a hard stare at the pierced kid standing behind the service counter.

The young man made a point of smiling.

Ricky Lee felt a wave of hate well up from his gut. He knew it came from hating his father and hating his life but he couldn't do anything about either and he hated that too. He narrowed his eyes and focused his hate on this young male at the counter who had the audacity to be handsome while sporting an ear full of hoops and a short barbell through his right eyebrow. The kid wore a black T- shirt that asked, "What the Frack?"

"You one of them anti-Fa?" Ricky Lee growled, jerking his chin toward the kid's shirt.

"No sir. I support clean energy paths. We're working here to have a neutral carbon footprint. You may have noticed we have solar panels on our units to run our security lighting. Would you like a tour?"

Ricky Lee shook his head. The last thing on this goddamned earth that he wanted to do is hear his father's opinion on a tour of solar panels.

"I'm looking for 3D Survival. This address was on their website."

The pierced kid nodded. "We work with 3D to have parking lot sales in the summer and fall. That won't begin until late May."

"I need to talk to Dwerryhouse," Ricky Lee said. "Now. Not in May."

The young man eyed Ricky Lee with a dawning wariness. "Their website has a contact form. That would be your best bet."

"You got a home address for him?"

"I'm sorry, sir," the counter clerk said. "We don't share personal information on any of our customers. You can use that website contact form to request a meeting. That's all I can recommend."

"Never mind." Ricky Lee turned, shoved open the glass door, and stomped back to the battered Suburban. He hoisted himself into the big vehicle, slammed the door shut and cranked the ignition hard.

The pierced young man watched as the Suburban pulled forward. There was a giant bearded man in the passenger side seat and a thin faced young man in the back. He watched until the dirty clunker roared onto Harrison Avenue before bringing out his cell phone to make a call.

"Duane? It's Danny over at Westside Storage Solutions."

The Derry Dell
Westside of Olympia

Duane was still on the phone with Danny when Elspeth walked in with Nico and Zoom. Duane waved a hello and directed them with his thumb toward the kitchen.

Elspeth pulled Nico along by the hand. They found Carmen at the kitchen table, sitting quietly. She held up her index finger to her lips.

Elspeth and Nico silently joined Carmen at the table. Zoom sat down and plunked her head in Nico's lap for an ear rub.

Moments later Duane turned around, storm clouds of concern on his face.

Elspeth rushed to say, "Uncle Duane, this is Nico Pavlopoulos."

Nico stood up and held out a hand.

Duane took it. "Duane Dwerryhouse." He studied Nico. "You the graduate student?"

"Yes sir. This is Zoom."

"Sweet." Duane motioned to Nico to sit as he pulled out a chair for himself. "Ladies, we have problems."

Carmen said, "I heard. The Fickhams?"

"Yes. Danny at Westside Storage said a carload of three dirty guys showed up looking for 3D Survival. Big bearded guy, young guy and the one that came into the office was fat, surly and wore a red checkered wool jacket. Danny says he stank of cigarettes. That says the Fickhams to me."

"Are they after you or Elspeth?" Carmen asked.

"Maybe both. Shit." Duane's eyes flashed. "I made that idiot lose face and now he's gonna want to kill someone. Like me. God, I hate it when I make a dumb move."

Elspeth swallowed hard. "Uncle Duane. There's more. I tried to do a favor for a friend and that was a bad idea. Nico and I ended up talking to a law enforcement officer this morning. There was a murder out in the woods and it may be connected to a Henry Fickham."

Duane sighed. "That's the really dangerous one, right?"

"I'm afraid so. And now I went and put myself in front of the eyeballs of the law." Elspeth tried to sound flippant but her eyes welled with tears.

Duane reached out and took her by the hand. "Elspeth, I'm glad you're being honest. We're going to need our lines of communication to be crystal clear. Let me get another cup of coffee," Duane said. "And let's hear it all."

Love me, love my dog.
St. Bernard of Clairvaux

Chapter Eighteen

Sunday, Lunch with Dr. and Dr. Pavlopoulos
1555 Country Club Road NW, Olympia

"Could a psychoactive mushroom treat Alzheimer's disease? Oh, I think that's an interesting question," said Kristyna Pavlopoulos. The wiry middle-aged woman passed a bowl of pasta salad to Elspeth and added, "We know penicillin came from a bread mold and the cancer drug taxol is made by a fungus on the yew plant, so there is some precedent."

"Vinblastine is from the rosy periwinkle," said her husband. Theo Pavlopoulos was a lean and graying version of his son with the same charming smile. The Pavlopoulos home was an elegant long rambler with wide French doors that opened onto a huge swath of grass. Today the doors were closed as a spring rain descended.

Kristyna took a sip of red wine. "Right! Vinblastine is responsible for a huge reversal in death rates in childhood leukemia. Prior to vinblastine most children with leukemia died. Now most survive."

"Let's stick with fungi," said Nico.

"Hmm," his mother said. "We've got another antibiotic, cyclosporine, and the anti-cholesterol drug lovastatin."

"And many, many fungi are used medicinally in Asia," his father added. "But here we're talking about psychoactive responses. What works in the brain?"

"Lion's mane. And definitely psilocybin mushrooms!" Kristyna said. "Elspeth, have you tried any?"

The question was casual but this was Nico's mother. Elspeth swallowed hard as she decided that her Uncle Duane was right. Honesty and clarity were her best cards. Nico's parents deserved to know who she was. So be it. Nico's parents were going to give her points for honesty even if it came with a pleasant but firm goodbye.

Elspeth said, "I tried magic mushies twice. Both were failures. The first time I was nervous and threw up. The second time I was even more nervous and I had an anxiety attack and couldn't even swallow. I'm a bit of a control freak and that means I really don't have the right mindset to enjoy that sort of relaxing. I'm better off with a board game."

Kristyna beamed. "Oh, I'm right with you."

"We're lucky that Liberty's Grandma didn't have her brain turned off permanently," Nico said. "I can't believe he gave her, well, drugs."

"We see some ugly things in the ER," his father said.

"Is there any chance his stupidity helped her?" Elspeth asked.

"Who knows?" Kristyna replied. "Psilocybin in mushrooms changes to psilocin, which binds to serotonin receptors. Psilocin can also increase levels of dopamine in some parts of the brain."

She continued, "But we don't even know that the grandmother was suffering from Alzheimer's. She might be a stroke victim, severely depressed, which is called 'pseudo-dementia,' or simply be an elderly person with a vitamin B12 deficiency. There are many ways to end up with the same symptoms."

"My father suffered from Huntington's disease," Elspeth said. "He definitely had dementia at the end."

There was a silence.

Kristyna reached across the table and gently put her fingers on Elspeth's wrist. "Not everyone inherits the Huntington genes," she said.

"I know. I got tested. I'm in the clear."

Kristyna and Theo exchanged a relieved look. Theo asked, "Do you have siblings?"

"No. I do have a cousin, Carmen. Her mother — my Aunt Yera — is in hospice right now with Huntington's. She has moments of clarity but not many. We all know there won't be a real relapse. Not at this point. Carmen hasn't been tested. She's only eighteen. She says she just can't get her head around the consequences of being tested. Not right now."

"How very frightening."

"It is, but Carmen is a fighter. Her college biology project might be looking for a wild mushroom to methylate the CAG repeat of Huntington's."

"Wow! That's impressive!"

"I'm really proud of her." Elspeth paused, and added, "I'm hoping to join her at college this fall. Nico may have told you — I got in trouble last year but now I'm working to save money to start school this fall."

"She's working four jobs," Nico said. "Sometimes five."

"Good for you," Kristyna said. "What kind of trouble?" She looked from Elspeth to Nico.

Elspeth sat up straight. The small amount of pasta salad she'd eaten sat like a giant lump in her stomach. She set her fork down, cleared her throat and said, "I grew and sold psychoactive mushrooms for the better part of a year. I went to prison for five months and now I am out of the growing business. I would like to be a nutritionist."

Kristyna Pavlopoulos didn't miss a beat. She said, "Ah, so that's how you came to have the mycological background for Nico's transcription work. That makes sense."

Her husband said, "Elspeth, does the prison time mean you are ineligible for a Pell grant?"

Elspeth nodded. "I have a drug conviction. To qualify for a Pell grant I have to have two clean urine tests and I have to complete a drug rehab program. The first part is easy because I never was a user but it's impossible for me to get into rehab right now. I am a low death risk so I can't bump a heroin user off a publicly funded spot. I wouldn't want to anyway — and I can't afford a private rehab stay. I'm stuck."

"Well, that's idiotic," Kristyna said. She reached out and patted Elspeth's arm. "I'm delighted to hear that you value good nutrition. Perhaps you can talk Nico into giving up his cheese puffs."

At least she's not kicking me out the door, Elspeth thought. *Yet.*

"And how's your proposal going?" Theo asked his son.

"Not as well as I would like." Nico ran a hand over his face. "Fungal species identification is complex and I'm not sure if this is where I want to spend my life." He turned to Elspeth and said, "Whatever expertise I develop will be where I can expect to spend the next several decades."

Nico looked at his parents. "If I back out of this idea, then I'm not sure what I'll do."

"Are you still thinking a Ph.D?" his mother asked.

"Yes. I want to do research and I want the research to help people. It makes sense to stick with some form of mycology too."

"It's alright to take some time," his mother said. "Get it right."

"Within reason," his father amended.

"What? You don't want to support me in my old age?" Nico teased.

Before his parents could respond there was a high-pitched bark from down the hall.

"I think Zoom has had enough of the chew bone in the laundry room," Kristyna said. "Let's finish lunch and get her outside. I'd love to see you put her through her paces."

"We should meet the puppies too," Nico said.

Minutes later Zoom was romping with Nico on the big lawn. Nico ran squishing through the wet grass as Zoom raced ahead. She arced to run in happy circles.

"Zoom is well named!" Kristyna laughed.

"It's nice to see Nico with a dog again," his father said. He turned to Elspeth and said, "Nico had a Great Dane for several years. Great dog. We lost him overnight to a gastric torsion. It was heartbreaking."

"Nico was shattered," Kristyna agreed. "He couldn't stand the idea of getting another Great Dane and I couldn't live without having a dog. We compromised on Springer spaniels."

"Which turned into your passion more than his," Theo observed.

"I know." She called to Nico. "Shall we teach Zoom to Find?"

"Sure!" Nico called back. "Will you video record us on my phone?"

Kristyna disappeared into the house and came back with a handful of aromatic cheese chunks and Nico's cell phone. "Ready!"

Nico and Zoom came trotting over.

"Here," Kristyna handed the cheese to Elspeth. "Show those to Zoom but don't let her have one."

Zoom became keenly interested in Elspeth's closed fist.

"Now if you will go out behind that grape arbor and squat down," Kristyna instructed. "Don't call. Wait for Zoom to find you and give her a treat."

Elspeth did as she was told. She heard Nico say, "Zoom! Find Elspeth!"

Zoom dashed to the arbor and gobbled a cheese bite from Elspeth.

They practiced with Elspeth hiding behind a compost bin, behind a patio chair and back behind the grape arbor before Kristyna said, "Enough! She's got it!"

Zoom came wiggling over to Kristyna who pronounced her a most beautiful dog despite the mud now dripping from the long hair on Zoom's legs and belly. "Let's put you back in the laundry room," Kristyna cooed, "So we can show Elspeth the new puppies."

"Actually I'd like to run her through the dog wash," Nico said. He took his cell phone from his mother and handed it to Elspeth. "Will you send the video to Mrs. Lowenstein?"

"Good idea! She'll be pleased to see Zoom is learning some manners." Elspeth replied. She sent the file and then followed Nico's mother into see the new arrivals.

The puppies were squirming brown and white blobs. Elspeth was handed one to hold and stroke as Kristyna whispered, "They'll be a lot cuter in a month. Do come back and see them."

"I'd love too," Elspeth whispered back.

"Super. Sounds like you and Nico are enjoying your time together."

Elspeth felt her face flood with warmth. She had to be a bright pink. Thinking about it made her even warmer. She managed to say, "He is such a nice guy. I feel really lucky to know him."

"He clearly thinks a lot of you," his mother said. "This is the first time he's ever asked us to have a young lady over for lunch."

Elspeth stroked the puppy in her lap. "I would never do anything to cause him trouble," she said. Then she groaned. "Except I already did. We went this morning out to the woods to pick up a trail camera for a friend named Liberty. I should have known better. It turned out to be a mess. There's a chance that the camera recorded a crime. We gave the camera to a deputy. I'm so, so sorry. I am not going to do anything with Liberty ever again!"

Kristyna laughed. "I appreciate your honesty. Take your time, Elspeth. Many people hit a few bumps in their life path and end up stronger and finer for it."

"That's kind of you to say." Elspeth handed her the puppy and watched as the puppy was gently returned to its mother.

Kristyna said, "Be smart as you go. If you need a prescription there is a walk in clinic on First Street in Shelton."

Elspeth stood up, mystified at the offer. She met the family's other two charming and silky clean spaniels before Kristyna ushered her out of the kennel area and led her to the dog wash.

The Pavlopoulos dog wash was a former bedroom turned tiled dog spa. Zoom stood dripping in a giant elevated tub as Nico and Theo rubbed her down with towels. Nico coaxed the dog out of the tub and down a ramp to an overhead blower.

By the time Elspeth finished talking about the puppy viewing, Zoom was combed out and radiant.

"Wow. I didn't know she could look so good," Elspeth said. She looked around the room. Triple rows of blue ribbons hung from a corkboard. A sizeable trophy case sat wedged in one corner. On one shelf there was a large trophy and a photograph of a young Nico with his Great Dane. Junior Champion. Elspeth blinked in amazement at the shelves of grooming tools. Even the towels were deluxe.

"We went overboard," Kristyna laughed. "Our jobs are stressful so it's fun to come in here and make our dogs look beautiful."

Nico gave Zoom a head rub. "We should go."

Elspeth turned to Nico's parents. "Thanks for lunch. I had a great time."

"Come back soon!" Theo turned to his son. "Don't forget that Vannak and Bopha bought a farm. I'm sure they'd let you take Zoom out for a run there."

"Good idea. I'll check in with them."

In the Jeep with Zoom looming into the gap between the front seats, Elspeth exhaled. "Your folks are terrific," she said. She laughed. "And the dog spa is impressive."

Nico smiled. "Yeah. They put that in when I was in seventh grade. I wasn't doing well in school and the opioid epidemic was hitting Mason County. One weekend three teenagers died and my dad came home and drank two bottles of wine. Mom said we all needed dog therapy. She didn't waste any time. A week later I had a Great Dane pup and Dad had a remodeling project. We've been dog mad ever since."

"Your mom talked about getting a prescription." Elspeth said. "What was that about?"

Nico went red as he hunched over the steering wheel. He turned onto Cooper Point Road in silence.

"Nico?"

"My parents! My dad said the same thing to me!"

"What?"

"Birth control," Nico muttered. His ears turned a deep crimson that came close to Zoom's shade of red.

Elspeth slapped her hands over her mouth, feeling the blood rush to her face. "Oh. My God! Oh. Wow."

"Sorry, Elspeth. They're doctors. They think differently." His hands gripped the steering wheel of the jeep with knuckles that were turning white. "We can be just friends."

"Friends with benefits?" Elspeth asked carefully.

Nico scowled. "That seems to be a recipe for one person or the other to be used and discarded." He slowed the Jeep to steer around a branch in the road. "I like you. A lot. I'd like to date." He moved the Jeep back into the right lane and added, "Exclusively."

Elspeth's heart stuttered. "Nico, it's such a bad idea."

"Why? You like me. I like you."

Zoom leaned in between the seats and tried to lick Nico's face. He pushed her back with a sharp, "No!"

Elspeth blinked back tears. "I don't think you understand how much of a gap there is between my world and yours. I'm a convicted felon. It's like resting on a rock shelf on a mountain. I am a long hard climb from seeing the view from the top and it is really easy to tumble back down the mountain."

"I think you're overstating things." Nico shoved the shifter up a gear. "You're employed. You have a plan."

Elspeth's laugh verged on the hysterical. "Every ex-con has a plan. We're famous for them."

"What's the most important thing right now then?"

"Getting my act together to take classes this fall. I've got to come up with about two thousand dollars to take a part time class load at the community college."

"If you get a semester of college under your belt, then what?"

"Then I'm in a better place. But the grind keeps coming. While I'm in school I have to keep earning for the next term. There just aren't enough hours in the week. I need some sort of specialty where I can earn more per hour but most of those kinds of job require a professional license which an ex-felon can't get."

Nico scowled. "My parents like you," he said.

"I like them." Elspeth sighed. "I like them a lot, and I think you are so awesome."

Zoom leaned in again and this time licked Elspeth, who patted the red setter and said, "And you are the world's most beautiful dog."

Nico hunched over the wheel of the Jeep and muttered, "Great. I finally find a girl who likes me, mushrooms and my dog but she won't have me."

"Zoom isn't your dog."

"She will be." Nico looked over at Elspeth. "When I want something I can be very persistent."

Elspeth swallowed, a lump in her throat nearly gagging her. She sniffed and said, "It's not about persistence. It's about reality."

"Reality stinks."

"Yeah. Sometimes it does."

"Make the best use of what's in your power and take the rest as it happens." Epictetus (circa 55 -135 AD)

Chapter Nineteen

Sunday, 1 p.m.
The Fickham Family Homestead, Kamilche Peninsula

The narrow dirt road twisted through a clear cut ragged with stumps and blackberry vines. Henry Fickham steered the cream-colored Lexus through the ruts with some care. The car still had its original plates. He should put a screwdriver in the glove box and look for another light Lexus in town. If he could do a little midnight exchanging of plates then he could keep the car for a few more days. He liked the seat warmer and the deep tones of the wood trim.

As the car bumped into a rut, Henry scowled. He didn't like bringing this beautiful car out on this poorly maintained road. There was nothing clean, repaired or sleek in anything that had to do with his family. His half-brother, Ricky Lee and his nephews, Troy and Tate, were wimpy, dirty, whining losers. His father, Russell, however, was efficiently brutal and still terrifying enough that he responded to his father's call.

The road curved and ended in a sprawling rural slum of shabby buildings and discarded vehicles set against a forest of large Douglas firs and cedars. A mildewed boat on a trailer with two flat tires jutted out from behind a listing wooden shed. Two yellowing camping trailers and a mold-streaked RV paralleled one edge of the clearing. A gray barn with closed large doors sat to the left of a dirty shipping container.

Waist high salal with its leather-like leaves rimmed the compound. Bright yellow shafts of miniscule flowers speared up from rugged specimens of Oregon grape while the next layer of understory showed the dark leaves of evergreen huckleberry and the lighter leaves of red huckleberry bushes.

A mound of Himalayan blackberry vines came close to covering an old boat motor and orange trumpet honeysuckle vines with twinned leaves snaked over the remains of a fence. A flicker demonstrated its undulating flight and white rump patch as it flew away from Henry's arrival.

Henry parked the Lexus near the boat trailer and picked his way over the rutted parking area before jogging up the steps of a battered mobile home. He opened the door without knocking and noted that Troy jumped in alarm at seeing him.

Troy would bear some watching.

Russell and Ricky Lee looked up from their recliners near the television. "About time," Russell grunted.

Henry stopped at the kitchen and picked up a beer before joining them. "Move," he said.

Troy got up from a dandruff-coated brown couch without complaint.

"Get Tate," Russell ordered. Troy slouched off down the hall to rap on a bedroom door. Moments later Tate and Troy took up positions behind the sofa, leaning on the faux wood paneling that bent under the weight of their slight frames.

"Troy has a girl in mind," Russell said. "There's one for Tate too. The father is a problem."

Ricky Lee slurped his beer and said nothing.

"Go on, Ricky Lee. Tell Henry what happened," his father ordered.

"Guy named Dwerryhouse hit me. He's related to the girls. He got a drop on me," Ricky Lee muttered. "Didn't see it coming."

Henry sipped his beer. "Not surprised," he said.

Ricky Lee shot him a murderous look.

"How do you know this girl?" Henry asked Troy.

Troy startled again. "Saw her last year at a bonfire. Then we saw her at a survival gear show. Sales girl. She has a cousin that's a sales girl too."

Henry took another sip. "Why bother me? Aren't the four of you enough to handle two girls?"

Russell laughed. "I can manage two girls on my own. The thing is that these girls have somebody dying in the Evergreen Path hospice. Isn't that where your girlfriend works?"

Henry froze. He made himself take another casual sip of beer. "How do you know there's a family member in hospice?"

Russell laughed. "Two girls. Pretty. I figured maybe somebody had sent them flowers, so I called around to a few florist shops. Said I wanted to send some flowers to 'Ms. Dwerryhouse,' but I didn't know the address. The third shop I called said they knew which hospice she was in. So I tugged on that line." Russell tipped back in the recliner and finished his beer. He threw the empty can at a heap of cans in the corner and belched. "Only three hospices in town. Wasn't hard to call around and find her. Duane Dwerryhouse's wife."

Henry sipped his beer. His father could be charming and chillingly persuasive on the phone. He didn't know how his father knew about Lucinda — but somehow Russell knew.

He took another sip of beer. "I've got a lot of girlfriends. Which one works at the hospice?"

Russell laughed a chilling, derisive snort. "The only one you care about, buddy. Lucinda Sutherland who lives over on Deer Fern lane with her crippled old man. You were there last night until about ten."

Tracking device, Henry decided. Somehow his father had gotten a tracking device on his regular vehicle. He had taken his truck to Lucinda's. Russell did have a knack. For an old man, he certainly embraced technology. The Lexus he was driving today might acquire a tracker while he was here. Maybe that was why Troy was so jumpy.

Henry stared at the oblong stain that colored the pale wall behind the dandruff-flecked couch. He had worked so hard to be shed of this place. There were few things he hadn't bought, sold or ferried and he finally had some joy with a little money put by and Lucinda in his life.

Lucinda knew what it was to come from nothing. She liked nice things. So did he. No one had ever given him Jack-Shit until Lucinda. It was amazing what a man could do with some brains and tools on his side.

He would do what it took to keep his old man away from Lucinda.

Did his old man know about the fentanyl business?

Henry looked around the room, taking in the tattered drapes, the stained furniture and the carpet filthy with fir needles and clumps of moist soil. The sooner he was out of here the better. He asked, "What's your plan?"

Sunday, 1 p.m.
West Olympia

Jasmine heeded her mother's advice and declined her grandfather's invitation to meet the members of the poker group. She dropped him off at the curb of the Sutherland's home and said, "I'm supposed to meet up with my biology project team this afternoon."

"I think Chen can give me a lift home."

"Okay. Love you, Grandpa. Win all their money!"

She watched as Dr. Oh made his way up the walk. His pace was measured and careful. The day in the woods had been too long.

Jasmine thought of the giant shelf fungus they'd found. It was unlikely that such an uncommon species had ever been evaluated for medicinal properties. Jasmine slowed for an intersection. She might be wrong on that. Perhaps a Northwest tribe used it.

She turned onto Cooper Point Road. Reishi, Jasmine thought, is definitely a shelf fungus that could be helpful. The polysaccharides in reishi boosted the immune system, which, in turn, could limit the growth of some cancers. Her brain retrieved the genus. *Ganoderma*. That was it. There was an Asian reishi, *Ganoderma lucidum* and an American species, *Ganoderma oregonense*. With a species name like "lucidum," did the Asian species help with memory loss? Could she get Grandfather to take some reishi capsules? She should learn some more about the fungus.

Her thoughts made the drive home pass quickly.

Jasmine smiled when she saw the Mason County sheriff's sedan sitting in her driveway. McRae!

McRae was not smiling. He leaned against his unit with his long arms folded across his chest.

Jasmine parked and slid out of the car, calling, "Fancy meeting you here!"

Her charm had no effect. "Is everything Okay?" she asked.

Don McRae unfolded his arms and walked over to her. "No."

"Want to come in and tell me about it?"

"No. Here is fine."

Jasmine glared up at him. "What is wrong with you? Eat a toad for breakfast?"

"There's a trail camera with your picture on it."

"What?"

"A seller of psychoactive mushrooms installed a trail camera at the roadside where you and your grandfather were yesterday. The camera took your picture."

"Who has the camera now?"

"We do." McRae sighed. "I'm worried about you, Jasmine. There's also a picture of a really dangerous man who went up that trail with our victim. He's a local named Henry Fickham and he is seriously bad news."

"Why isn't he in jail then?"

"We're working on it. He's associated with the disappearance of half a dozen people. We're thinking now that he leaves bodies out in the undergrowth where most of the time no one ever goes — except for you and your grandfather."

"Does this Henry know about Granddad and me?"

"Unknown."

"How about the mushroom seller?"

"He's left town."

A scattering of raindrops fell, darkening the concrete parking pad.

"Are you sure you don't want to come in? I can make some tea. We could talk."

"Jasmine." McRae sighed. "Where are you going?"

"In the house!"

"No. I mean in life. Are you staying in Olympia?"

"This spring I am. I'm taking an honors biology class at the community college. I deferred full time classes to take sort of a gap year."

"Why?"

Jasmine shrugged. "I got really exhausted my senior year. I applied to twenty colleges and then I tried for scholarships. My parents convinced me to rest up last summer and I went overseas last fall. I'm healthy now."

McRae studied her. He said, gently, "Anorexia?"

"No. I'm genuinely scrawny, not sick. No worries there! My self-esteem is rock solid. My problem was that I got too intense." Jasmine said. "My parents intervened. I'm a ton better now. I meditate every day. It was the right thing to put off going away to college. It's also given me some special time with my grandfather. I'll be ready when I go east."

"The college is ?"

"Columbia University."

McRae snorted. "Yeah. That fits. You're going to Columbia."

"What's wrong with Columbia?

"It fits you. It doesn't fit me. I'm a twenty-five-year old deputy in a rural county in western Washington. I did four years in the Coast Guard and have, so far, about fifteen college credits. I'll finish my degree in about a decade and it won't be from Columbia. Not even close." McRae's gray eyes looked hard as flint.

Another shower of raindrops sprinkled the cars and pavement.

Jasmine said, "I think you should come in for a cup of tea."

"I don't think that's a great idea." McRae's jaw barely moved as he ground out the words. "You've got ideas that aren't going to pan out."

"My grandfather tells me often," Jasmine said, "that we can never count on meeting the next sunrise." She reached out and put her hand on McRae's arm. "That has to be particularly true for a deputy."

Jasmine looked up into his eyes and asked, "Isn't life for living?"

"The future emerges from the past."
Proverb from Senegal

Chapter Twenty

Sunday, 1:30 p.m.
The Sutherland home

"There's more beer in the fridge in the garage," Dr. Sutherland rolled his wheelchair up to the table of elderly card players. "But it's down two steps."

"I can get it." Dr. Oh said. He stood up carefully. "Any special requests?"

"Extra hop IPA for me," said Dr. Whitener. "A sharp bite for a sharp mind."

This generated a bark of laughter from Dr. Chen. "Modest as always, are we? Although I approve of your choice."

"I venture forth, then, on safari!" Dr. Oh said. "Send a search crew if I fail to return!"

"It's not that big a house," Dr. Sutherland laughed.

"It's a very big house," said Dr. Chen. "You have done amazingly well on a professor's salary."

"Lucinda's work has made a big difference," Richard Sutherland said. "We've loved living here." He looked around the bamboo-paneled room with satisfaction. "Although when the day comes to move, we'll need a special buyer who likes a lavender kitchen and a black carpeted game room."

"I'll say," muttered Whitener.

"It is unusual," Dr. Sutherland agreed. "Our own special interests represented by color. We've had three decades of fun."

"Better than my marriage," Chen conceded. "Three days of fun and fifty years of me escaping to the office."

"So that's why you dedicate each research paper to your wife!" Whitener crowed.

Dr. Oh smiled as he shuffled down the hall. He enjoyed the jousting of Chen and Whitener. He'd been pleased when they'd invited him to join the poker gathering. He had known Sutherland only slightly from the college. Botany was on the opposite side of the campus from the English Department.

He passed an open door to an office and paused for a look. It was time to replace his computer. He could see what Richard used.

He wouldn't step into the office. That would be rude. Dr. Oh stood in the doorway and saw a computer tower and a very large screen. The screen saver was on. Pictures of girls went scrolling by. Blondes, brunettes, and redheaded girls braided with photos of young blacks and Asians.

That was odd. Sutherland must have many grandchildren. Or perhaps he supported a charity that helped schoolgirls.

Dr. Oh returned to the beer quest. He shuffled to the kitchen and through the laundry room to the door to the garage.

He turned on the light and saw that the garage was pristine. There was a tarp-covered roadster parked to the right. That must be Richard's old car. How sad he could no longer drive.

The refrigerator sat at the end of a long workbench. As he made his way slowly to the cooler he marveled at the neat organization of the garage.

Dr. Oh stopped and stared at the large pegboard filled with tools. Every tool was outlined in black marker to show its place. Every tool in residence had its base encircled with a band of black electrician's tape.

The hammer outline was missing its hammer.

Dr. Oh took his time. He studied the wall of tools. He looked at the workbench and shuffled down to its end to survey the floor. No hammer. He went to the refrigerator, looked over the beer collection and loaded an assortment of bottles into a six-pack carrier.

He shut the refrigerator door and made his way back to the laundry room, turning at the door to complete another survey of the quiet garage. He carefully opened the laundry room door and set down the six-pack before moving up the steps with deliberate care.

Dr. Oh navigated back down the hall, stopping in at a powder room with a lavender sink and toilet. After urinating, he washed his hands, studying his reflection in the mirror framed with painted lavender pansies. He was uncertain. That was not a normal sensation for him to have on a Sunday afternoon. He picked up the six-pack and made his way to the game room at a slow pace, thinking deeply. Finally he set the six-pack carrier of beer bottles down on the table and carefully took his seat.

"We were about to send out a search party," Whitener said.

"I'm an old man. I had to take whizz." Dr. Oh looked across the table to Richard Sutherland and said, "I had an adventure yesterday. My granddaughter and I found a man in the woods who had been hit in the head by a hammer."

"Really? Was he alright?" Richard's face wore a look of mild surprise.

"No. He was dead. We called the sheriff's office and they came and took the body away. The hammer too."

"Jesus, Oh! Did they take you in for questioning?" Chen asked.

"The sheriff had lots of questions. We told them all we knew and then we went home. It was in Mason County off a forest road." Dr. Oh passed around beer bottles and added, "The thing is, the hammer had a band of black tape on the end of the handle. I heard there were initials on it too."

Richard Sutherland sat very still.

"That's a dumb crook," Whitener observed.

"Or maybe someone stole some tools," Dr. Oh said. "Richard, I noticed your tool set has that sort of banding – and you are missing a hammer from the pegboard."

Chen cackled. "You think Richard was up in the woods murdering people?"

"Like I said, maybe someone stole some tools. Is there any chance someone took things from your garage?"

"I haven't been out there in months," Richard said calmly. "I'll check with my wife when she comes home. We shouldn't be bothering the police if Lucinda knows where our hammer is." Richard picked the cards. "I believe it's my turn to deal."

Sunday, 1:30 p.m.
The Dwerry Dell

It took a nanosecond to recognize the number. Jed! Carmen gripped the phone and swiped it open rapidly before bubbling out a "Hi!"

Duane smiled and did his best to amble rapidly out of the kitchen as his own cell phone jingled.

"Hi yourself," Jed said. "How are you?"

"Great!" Carmen sank into a kitchen chair, joy coursing through her body. She took a breath. It was time for Dwerryhouse courage. She said, "Actually, not so great. My class biology project is in disarray, my mother is in hospice and my dad and my cousin are being stalked by some really creepy guys, but other than that, I'm good."

There was a pause. "Is now not a good time then?"

"I'm being honest. My life is complicated. Is . . . complicated Okay?" Carmen held her breath.

"Yeah. Complicated is Okay."

Carmen exhaled.

"Tell me," Jed said, "Are the creepy guys the same ones that were at the survival show?"

"Yes. We think so. They've been asking around town about us."

"You need some help?" Jed's voice was low and strong.

Carmen's heart soared. She tried to sound casual "I wouldn't mind some company," she said.

"I could do that," Jed said. "Are you playing volleyball any these days?"

"No. I had a bike crash that was ugly. I'm still trying to get healthy from that. How did you know I played volleyball?"

"I saw you play last year at the regionals."

Carmen felt a huge lump swell in her throat. She said, "I'm not that person any more. I'm fat and lame and completely different."

"Nah. You are still you. Your heart is the same," Jed replied.

"My heart?"

"Yeah. That's what is so beautiful about watching you. You don't hold back. Everything you have, you deliver."

Tears streamed down her cheeks and, damn it, her nose was clogged. Carmen snatched a napkin off the kitchen table and blew her nose. "Thanks," she managed.

"Welcome. Getting back to volleyball soon?"

"Probably not this year. I have two more corrective surgeries to go. Right now the worst is getting off my medication. It makes me fat and really mean."

Jed chuckled. "Is that what's wrong with the world? Wrong medicine?"

Carmen felt a smile creep on her face. "Fixable?"

"Yeah. Sounds fixable."

Carmen wiped her eyes and said, "It's really nice to think that."

Duane appeared in the doorway, worry on his face. "Gotta interrupt," he said.

"I'll call you back," Carmen promised Jed.

"I'll be here."

Carmen tapped off her phone and turned to her father.

"Baby," he said, "I just got a call from Ramon at the hospice."

"Mom?"

"Yeah, but it's also Lexi."

"Lexi?"

"She was found dead in her car." Duane's eyes were direct and worried as he added, "Ramon didn't know the cause of death, but with a young person we think about a drug overdose pretty quickly."

"Dad, that's not possible. It's just not." Carmen stared at her father and shook her head. "Lexi doesn't do drugs. We made a pact. We're going to clean up our bodies. No more cigarettes after this week. We were even talking about eating all organic."

"I'm sorry. She was found at the wheel of her car this morning and it looks like it she drifted off the road. Not a big crash. Just coasted over."

"There's no way she was taking recreational drugs." Carmen looked out the window and jutted out her lower jaw. "We need to talk to Officer Martinez. Somebody needs to be looking into this."

"We've got more problems, baby. Ramon says your mom is struggling today. I think we should be there. We may be getting close to the end."

Carmen's hands flew to cover her mouth. "Oh, my God." She exhaled. "I know. I'm supposed to be ready." She shook her head. "I'm not." She swallowed and said, "I was going to meet with Jasmine and Taz. I'll call them and cancel."

Duane shook his head. "Why don't we head over to the hospice and see how Mom is? Maybe we can get some more details about Lexi from Ramon or someone else. If Mom is resting, maybe you and your friends can find a space to work."

"Okay."

"I am so, so sorry, baby."

Carmen wiped her hand under her nose, mopping up the leakage triggered by her father's gentle tone. She sniffed, then swallowed and said, "I should call Jed back too."

"If you want him there, it's fine." Duane reached out and hugged his daughter. "Be a hell of a first date, but if you want him there, it's fine with me."

"Love you, Dad."

"Love you too. We're gonna get through this."

"I know." Carmen wiped her nose again. "I just wish it wasn't all so complicated."

Sunday, 1:40 p.m.
Evergreen Home Hospice, Olympia

Lucinda checked her watch and then checked the roster. Ramon was on with Mrs. Dwerryhouse until the shift changed at three but he had refused the opportunity to work a double shift. It was expensive to bring in a temp from the staffing agency. With Lexi gone, there had been no other option.

She hoped the temp arriving would be one of the usual clueless youngsters. The temps were convenient scapegoats in so many ways. Missing medicines, bolloxed records, even unusually speedy deaths could be shoved under the umbrella of 'incompetent temp'.

Her thinking broadened as she contemplated the opportunity the presence of a young temp might present. She should check in on Mrs. Dwerryhouse later this afternoon. It might be that Nature was already lending a helping hand and Lexi's friend would be too consumed with grief to be asking any difficult questions.

Lucinda checked her watch for a second time. Henry's plan was diabolical and potentially so very lucrative. They were so close to implementation that it was silly to be nervous now. She was not a nervous person. Still, she did have half a kilogram of highly toxic fentanyl powder sitting in her garage.

There was a tap on her office door. "Enter," she called.

The door opened and Billy, the maintenance man came in, rear first, as he balanced boxes on a handcart. "Three boxes marked personal for Jeffrey Zhang," he said. "Ramon said you might know who that is."

"Thank you, Billy. Jeffrey is our pharmaceutical rep. It's test products that I'll take home to evaluate." Lucinda said smoothly.

"Want them loaded in your car then?"

"Not yet, but thank you. Could you just put them in the corner for now?"

"Yes ma'm."

Lucinda waited until Billy departed to allow a smile of satisfaction. The large box should be the expensive tablet press. The medium box should contain the excipient powder that would form the bulk of the tablets she would press. The smallest box should contain a set of assorted pill dies and several coloring agents. She would be able to swap out the diameter of the press nozzle to make pills from as small as two millimeters to as large as twenty millimeters.

Lucinda studied the boxes to see if there were any oddities that Billy might have noticed. The return addresses on the boxes were discrete. There was only a post office box and a zip code. She knew that the sender preferred anonymity.

Henry had thought of everything. As a pharmaceutical salesman, Jeffrey Zhang's name calmed the waters should anyone notice the boxes contained prescription production machinery. Lucinda's precise signature on the receiving form could be easily explained away.

She smiled. Dear Jeffrey would not be complaining. Henry had managed that detail splendidly.

Their new machine could produce up to five thousand pills an hour. Henry's truly brilliant idea was the purchase of the assortment of pill molds. Once set up, they should be able to manufacture fentanyl pills in a wide range of appearances.

Theirs would be a customized online business on the dark web. A customer wanting to hasten the end of an ill parent or partner would need only to send along a cell phone photo of one of the patient's current prescription tablets and a hefty payment. Lucinda and Henry would create and mail replicas of the pill made of fentanyl. For an additional fee they could provide a labeled prescription bottle with multiple tablets.

Lucinda felt her lips curve into a smile. Yes. She was excited. Their services would be popular. Who wouldn't want a speedy end for a difficult family member? She had compiled a list of the un-squeamish attorneys she had met in her years as a hospice administrator. It would be easy to quietly advertise her bespoke services.

Perhaps they should have names for different packages. 'Happy Trails' for a single pill and 'Angel Paths' for a larger amount. She smiled. She loved to make Henry laugh. They could have an entire evening of fun developing names for their services.

They would begin with pressed pills and would expand into capsules, perhaps by the fall.

Lucinda refused to check her watch again. Henry would call soon. In the meanwhile she should clean up the facility records. She would be retiring from this job by summer's end. The Medicare ghosts needed to vanish with her.

"Closeness without conflict only exists in a cemetery."
Proverb from Finland

Chapter Twenty-One

Sunday, 3:30 p.m.
Sheriff's Office, Mason County

Detective Raposo hunched over a computer keyboard and pecked in his notes. Deputy McRae walked by and reversed with a back track.

"Hi, Boss," McRae said. "I didn't know you were on today."

"I am now," Raposo muttered. He looked up and said, "I sat through a three-hour lunch where Brooke, her mother and my mother debated whether alabaster was darker or lighter than ivory. Finally, praise God, they moved onto flower girl dresses. When they started in on the merits of apricot versus peach, I bailed."

"I think, for you, apricot. Definitely the apricot."

Raposo snorted. "Noted. What have you been up to?"

"I looked at the pictures from the trail camera. We have multiple frames showing our victim and Henry Fickham exiting the cream-colored Lexus, but only partials of the plate. I've gone through the possibles and our most likely is a vehicle registered in Vancouver to a pharmaceutical company. I tried their toll free number and left a message."

"Good!"

"And I just met with Jasmine Oh. I warned her about Henry Fickham. She said she'd call in if she sees anybody strange in her neighborhood." McRae chose to omit the details of having had a cup of tea. Raposo didn't need to know everything.

"Let's hope Henry never finds out that she and her grandfather found a body. Hey, I went over your interview footage with Elspeth . . . Dwerryhouse. Good stuff. I remember her."

"Me too. Scared stiff but wouldn't cave. One of those times when you wish your suspect had a lawyer."

"Yeah. She took it in the shorts." Raposo leaned back in his chair. "I went to school with Henry Fickham."

"No kidding. What was he like?"

"Impoverished. Never had a pencil. Back in those days they made the free lunch kids get tickets to turn in for a lunch tray. Everybody knew Henry was free lunch. In middle school Henry quit showing up at the cafeteria. He'd hang outside. Said he wasn't hungry."

"Bullied?"

"Not too much. He was scary tough even then — but he got the ten thousand social slices. His clothes were always dirty.   Once his stepmother showed up to pick him from school. Big sunglasses on that didn't cover a black eye."

"Violent dad."

"Big time. Old Russell Fickham is a very bad man." Raposo flexed his fingers over the keyboard. "I was about to bring up the records on Henry and his old man. We suspect Russell has dumped more than one body in the woods."

"Where we'll never find them."

"Not often. After six months, they're lost to the mushrooms of the undergrowth."

Sunday, 2:30 p.m.
Evergreen Path Hospice, Olympia

"This morning was rough. She's resting well now." Ramon, the nurse, stood at the counter of the nursing station as he spoke with Carmen and Duane.

"Are we near the end?" Duane asked.

Ramon hesitated. "In this case it is hard to say. She seems to rally when she has a chance at quality sleep — Dr. Park may have some better insight."

"He said any day now," Carmen said grimly.

"I'm so very sorry."

"Thanks, Ramon." Carmen felt tears prickle and she blinked rapidly to beat the tears back. She swallowed and said, "I heard about Lexi. I just can't believe it."

"We're all stunned." Ramon looked up and saw Lucinda Sutherland striding down the corridor toward the nursing station. "I should get moving," he said.

He vanished into a patient's room before Lucinda reached the counter.

"Good afternoon," she said. "Is Ramon able to meet your needs this afternoon?"

"Yes. He's been great," Duane said. "We were surprised to hear about Lexi."

"What a tragedy," Lucinda said smoothly. "I understand it was an accident on the way home."

"She called me when she got off shift," Carmen said, miserably. "She was so excited that she was going to be helping my mother again. And she said you were so nice with your gift of chocolates."

Lucinda carefully rotated her head and looked directly at Carmen. "She mentioned the chocolates?"

"Yes. She said they might not make it all the way home."

"How very sad."

"I told my father that Lexi would never do drugs. We had a pact."

"I've got a call into my friend at the police department," Duane added. "We want to make sure they really check out this accident."

"How caring you are," Lucinda said. She picked up a clipboard from the nurse's station. "Do please excuse me. I have some calls to make."

"Um, Mrs. Sutherland?"

"Yes?" Lucinda turned her full focus back to Carmen.

"Would it be alright if two other college students and I worked in the front lounge this afternoon? We have a biology project proposal due tomorrow."

Lucinda studied Carmen for a long moment and said, "Of course! In fact, there is a better space you can use. There is an executive boardroom at the back of the building. It has comfortable chairs and a large table. I'll open it for you."

"Thank you."

"I'm glad to help."

West of Olympia

Henry Fickham drove the cream Lexus down Highway 101 and pulled off at the Steamboat Island exit. He needed gas. He needed gum. He needed to get the rank taste of his family out of his mouth.

He wasn't interested in helping Troy and Tate to lay hands on two young women. The women sounded like people who would be missed. Troy had set his sights too high. He should have picked out one of the salal pickers or mushroom hunters who migrated through the Cascades and Olympics every spring, summer and fall. One of those sad foreign women would be missed by family and friends but not reported to the law. Not ever.

His father was on his usual power trip thinking he was somebody if he could intimidate or destroy. No question, his old man was a sick fuck.

And Ricky Lee had his goddamn ego in the mix. If he wanted to get even with Duane Dwerryhouse, he could do it himself. Henry had bigger fish to fry.

The Lexus handled beautifully. He should check underneath the car and in the wheel wells to see if Russell had stuck on a magnetic tracking device. He had already checked under the dash and the OBDII port was clear. He might be alright. The magnetic trackers didn't work as well. His father may have given up using them.

Henry shook his head. Damn. He should put a mesh or lead sheet over the car's dash GPS unit. That would make the unit inoperable and, hopefully, impossible to locate by law enforcement.

Henry parked at a service station as his cell phone chimed. He looked to see the caller. Lucinda.

"Hey," he answered.

"My heart, I have problems," she said.

Henry parked and leaned back into the cushioned leather seat. Lucinda sounded tense.

"I'm listening," he said.

"My husband just called. One of his elderly poker-playing friends is a retired botanist. A man named Dr. Oh." Lucinda spoke crisply, but Henry could tell she was rattled.

She said, "Dr. Oh told Richard a story about going into the woods yesterday with his granddaughter and finding a body. They reported the body to the authorities who collected the body and a hammer with a black band on the handle."

"Shit."

"Precisely. I'm assuming you wore gloves."

"Of course. But I didn't think anyone would ever wander up that gully. Certainly not this soon."

"Richard says he acted unconcerned and that he would check with me. He implied I can say that a landscaper or maid must have stolen from us." Lucinda inhaled and added, "But we don't need anyone poking around the garage. Not with the powder in the cabinets — and I don't think we want the pill press stored out there. Not now."

"This poker player — he only was out in the garage just this afternoon?"

"Right. He's new to the group. That may be why the nosy old fart was looking around when he went into the garage for beer. Richard assures me he said he would discuss the missing hammer with me and we would call the police if need be. Dr. Oh is not supposed to call the authorities — but what if he does?"

"Or the law calls him to talk over something and he mentions your tools." Henry thought furiously. "Not good."

"There's more."

"What?"

"The nursing aide, Lexi, called her little friend, Carmen Dwerryhouse, and she said . . ."

"Wait! Who?"

"Carmen Dwerryhouse. About eighteen or nineteen. Dark hair."

"And she has a relative with you in hospice, right?"

"Her mother."

"And is there another Dwerryhouse girl? Black hair, pretty?"

"A cousin named Elspeth."

Henry shifted in the car seat, thinking hard. Perhaps things were coming together instead of falling apart. He might be able to erase a challenge for Lucinda while appearing to help his father. "Go on."

"Apparently Lexi called her little friend after she left here and told her that I had handed over a box of chocolates. Now Carmen is saying questions should be asked because she doesn't think Lexi would have taken a recreational drug." Lucinda added, "If this girl talks to the police, they may examine any leftover chocolates. I don't know what was left in her car." Lucinda groaned. "You said the carfentanil worked quickly. Maybe it worked too fast."

"That's why we're changing to the fentanyl. Don't worry. We may be in luck, sweetie." Henry tapped the steering wheel. "This could work out."

"Oh, Henry, please think of something, fast."

"How about diabolical?"

Lucinda managed a weak chuckle. "I'd love it."

"My nephews have an interest in the Dwerryhouse girls. My idiot brother wants to even a score with a . . . Duane Dwerryhouse."

"That's the husband of Yera, our patient. Father to Carmen."

"Right. Any other family members?"

"Just Elspeth. There's no one else listed on Yera's visitor list."

"It's Sunday afternoon. Are any of the Dwerryhouses visiting?"

"Duane and Carmen. He's in sitting with his wife. Carmen just asked to use a staff room for a meeting with a couple of other college students. I said they could use the executive boardroom."

"Excellent. You said the botanist is an old guy?"

"I think so."

"Can you find out where he lives?"

"Richard should know. Or I can look in the old faculty directory."

"Why don't you run over to this guy's house with some brownies. Special brownies. Thank you brownies." Henry's voice lilted with pleasure.

"Why am I thanking Dr. Oh?"

"For being a friend to your disabled husband who is feeling alone and neglected by former colleagues after a long and distinguished career."

Lucinda laughed. "Play the violin a bit, shall I?"

"Right. Who wouldn't take the brownies? You said he's an old guy. If he keels over, no one will be surprised. So use the fentanyl in the brownies."

"Ah. I could do that. That would take care of one loose end."

"Be careful with it. Ideally it should be mixed in with something so it doesn't float off."

"Icing then. Or a pudding layer."

"Yeah. Something like that. Listen, I'm going to turn around now and go back out to my father's place. I'll let my family know where the Dwerryhouses are this afternoon. This could work well. Leave the back door to the building unlocked when you leave today and don't go back. You don't want to be there when this goes down."

"Okay. Your father and brother will take care of the Dwerryhouses?"

"That's my plan. They can at least collect the daughter and that can be the lure for the father."

"What about the cousin, Elspeth? I don't think she's a student."

Henry thought a moment. "Can you find a way to suggest that she come visit her aunt today? If that doesn't work, then maybe Troy and Tate could pick her up later. Troy seems to know where she's staying. The important thing is that you and I are nowhere in sight when the Dwerryhouse family disappears. My old man and my shitty little brother can be on the hospice security tapes. Not you and not me."

"I like it," Lucinda said. "Oh, Henry. I like it a lot."

"Opportunities come but do not linger."
Proverb of Nepal

Chapter Twenty-Two

Sunday, 4:30 p.m.
Sheriff's Office, Mason County

"Thank you, sir, for calling." McRae hung up the phone and stood up and stretched. This detail would interest Raposo.

McRae ambled down to Raposo's office and poked his head in. "I think we've got a name for our dead body."

Detective Raposo leaned back from his keyboard and said, "Do tell!"

"There is a cream-colored Lexus assigned to one Jeffrey Zhang, a pharmaceutical representative. I got a call directly from a regional manager who tells me that Jeffrey had meetings in Olympia yesterday, including a meeting with a Peter Hartmann who was to share information on a 'mycological species'."

"That'd be Liberty and his magic mushrooms."

"Right. Apparently Mr. Jeffrey Zhang was supposed to call in to the answering service at the end of the day and he failed to do so. The manager tried Zhang's cell phone multiple times this morning with no pickup."

"Did we find a phone yesterday?"

"Nope. Just the camera on the ground with no chip."

"Maybe the phone is with the car?" Raposo leaned back in his office chair. "A car like that should have LoJack."

"Yes, indeedy. The manager gave me the details. I was just about to see what we could find."

"I'll help," Raposo offered. "Give me Jeffrey's cell phone number."

"Thanks, boss. I appreciate it."

"Anything that's not identifying apricot."

McRae laughed and sketched a salute.

The Lowenstein Home

The word processing was not going well. Elspeth sat at Mrs. Lowenstein's dining room table with a headset on and her laptop computer open. She had a cup of tea to her right and Mr. Midnight sat on the table to her left, paws tucked under his chest as he watched her fingers move with his unblinking yellow eyes.

Elspeth typed. Stopped. She highlighted and deleted a section and began again.

It was no use. Nico was too much of a distraction. The worst of it was she couldn't tell him that he was making her bonkers because he was quietly sitting at the other end of the table with his face in his own computer screen.

He was breathing too loud.

Elspeth sighed. No. He wasn't breathing too loud. He was just being . . . Nico. Handsome, smart, likeable Nico who wanted to date her.

And she wanted to date him.

She exhaled and started to type again. Her fingers hit the keyboard like ten bloated torpedoes.

"Crap!" Elspeth swore.

Nico looked up. "Troubles?"

"I can't do this."

"The transcription?"

"Yeah. Your voice is in my ears."

"Ah, isn't that how transcription works?"

"Normally, yes." Elspeth scowled. "But now it is your voice. Your voice. I can't concentrate."

Nico smiled. "I'll take that as a good sign."

"You won't when you get a bill for ten thousand hours of incompetent transcription."

"You wouldn't."

"Probably not." Elspeth sighed and took off her headset. "I should make some coffee. Maybe some caffeine would help." Before she could stand up, her cell phone chimed. She tapped the phone and said, "Hello?"

"Ms. Dwerryhouse," The caller began, apology in her tone, "I am so sorry to bother you."

"It's fine." Elspeth said, "What's up?"

"This is Mrs. Sutherland. The administrator at the hospice. Your aunt is . . . well, I am so sorry." Lucinda continued with a submissive tone. "I'm really not supposed to be making a call like this and I hope you won't mention that I did, but I thought you might want to be here with your uncle this afternoon."

Elspeth looked at her watch and blinked. 4:30! Most of the afternoon had evaporated. She still needed to collect her check from the restaurant and she hadn't come close to finishing the transcription for Nico. She said, "I need to run one very fast errand. I should be there by five or five-thirty. Please tell my uncle I'm coming!"

"Oh, no need to rush like that," Lucinda replied smoothly. "There is really no need to be racing. It's just that we suspect the final decline is beginning."

"Right. I'll come as quick as I can."

"Wonderful."

Elspeth tapped her phone off and turned to Nico. "My aunt. She is near the end. I need to pick up my check at The Azul Kitchen and zoom over to be with Uncle Duane."

Zoom launched herself up into Elspeth's face with an enthusiastic lick.

"Down!" Elspeth ordered. "I didn't mean to say your name."

"Zoom and I can go for a run," Nico said. "Should I come to the hospice later? I don't want to bother Duane but I'd like to be there for you."

"I think it'd be alright. I'll text when I know." Elspeth bent down and began lacing on a shoe. Glancing up she said, "I need to be there for my uncle and Carmen. I may not get this transcription done soon."

"I will wait for you," Nico said. "You're worth the wait." His face was stern with the afternoon shadows touching one side with gray.

"Are we still talking about transcription?" Elspeth asked softly.

Nico stood up and came around the table. He knelt down next to her chair and put his hand out.

Elspeth sat up, one shoe on, one shoe off. She stared at him. Nico gazed back, keeping his eyes steady on hers.

She swallowed and reached out to put her hand in his.

He brought her hand to his lips and kissed her knuckles. "I know things are so very hard right now. I want to be your friend and help you through this. And then, when you are ready, I want to find out if we suit each other. I don't want you to worry about how long that might take. I'll wait for you."

Elspeth's eyes filled with tears and she launched herself into his arms.

They went sprawling onto the floor as Nico kissed her face and stroked her hair. "I'll wait for you. Until you are ready. If that's okay by you."

"Big time 'yes' on that." Elspeth reached up and cradled his face. "I have to go."

"I know. I'll take care of Zoom and Mr. Midnight."

Elspeth sat up. She finished the one shoe and started lacing the second. "Are your parents going to be okay with me? I mean, really okay?"

Nico smiled. "I didn't date much in college. I mean, I tried, but the girls I knew were aggressive and I was taking entomology. We did an entire week on the many species with predacious females."

"Like the praying mantis that eats her partner after mating?"

"Oh, that's a quick death. A female midge jams her proboscis into the male's head once they are joined. Then her saliva melts his innards into slurpee and she sucks him dry."

"I meet your paranoia and raise." Elspeth said. "I have moments when I can't stop thinking about the two-ton elephant seals that are so enthusiastic that they gang up and drown females in the surf."

"Hey, not two tons here."

"Yeah, but then there's also the cowpea seed beetle that has a spiked penis. And the blue whale that has a ten foot penis and the spiny anteater with a four-headed penis, . . . "

Zoom barked.

"Right. We both need to get going." Nico reached out and stroked Elspeth's arm. "No weird parts. No savagery."

"Deal."

The Fickham Compound

"Troy, get the handcuffs," Russell said. He brought the foot of the recliner down and heaved himself to standing. "Don't forget. We slap 'em hard and get their hands secured."

Ricky Lee said, "I'll get the socks."

"What's the sock for?" Tate asked.

Russell grinned and said, "Stuff a sock in her mouth and tie it in with a rope and she can't scream. We do that quick after the hands are done."

"Why don't we use some of that roofie drug?" Tate asked, turning to Henry Fickham.

Henry stood in the doorway, arms crossed. He studied the warping faux pine paneling a moment before saying, "I don't deal in it. I don't need my women unconscious."

Tate nodded. "Yeah. I guess. It's just. . . seems kinda hard on them with handcuffs."

Russell snorted. "You won't get far with seduction, Tate. You ain't got the charm or the moola. Better off just showin' 'em who's the boss."

Tate swallowed and nodded.

Troy came out of the bedroom, clicking the ratcheted curve of the handcuffs through the anchor piece. "Don't worry, Tate. When you put your hands on some boobies, you'll be ready to party, real quick."

"How about a little pick-me-up?" Henry murmured.

"Yeah," Tate said. "That'd be good."

Russell's eyes gleamed. "When we get them here, they go in the shed overnight. We'll get them feeling a bit shaky. I got some special tenderizin' in mind. In the morning, you boys take a strap to them. By afternoon they should be ready to take to the mattress."

Tate wrinkled his nose. "That old thing has mushrooms growing out of it. It stinks."

Russell guffawed. "Damn straight. Got forty years of them 'biologicals' in it. Don't worry, boy. You'll be on top."

You do not teach forest trails to an old gorilla.
Congolese proverb

Chapter Twenty-Three

The Sutherland home
4:45 p.m.

Richard heard the garage door opener grinding. Lucinda. His long fingers stacked poker chips into their elegant case as he thought through his approaches. He would, he decided, be angry.

Lucinda came in through the kitchen, setting her lavender purse and a grocery bag on the gray granite countertop. She paused to hang her coat on the hook by the garage access door before calling out, "Richard?"

"In here." Richard began jamming poker chips in with vigor. He finished and slammed the case shut.

"Your poker group finished?"

"Obviously." Richard yanked the case into his lap and rolled the wheelchair over to a cabinet. He reached down and yanked the cabinet door open and flung the case in. He slammed the cabinet door shut with a bang.

"What's wrong?" Lucinda asked calmly.

"What's wrong? Your lover boy uses my tools to commit a murder and you want to know what's wrong?"

"Richard, I do not need this right now. I do a lot to make you comfortable and happy." Lucinda paused. She said, "The new photos are outstanding. We could make a quarter million dollars. Maybe more."

Richard stopped his wheelchair and smiled. "That good?"

"A whole new fantasy format."

"Does Henry know?"

"Yes. He advises me to quit selling the tween porn videos. And soon. It is lucrative, I'll admit and I know you have . . . an obsession. Our challenge is that it is increasingly easy to be caught and the penalties are more than we want to bear."

"Where are the pictures?" Richard asked.

"Typical. I take the risks, you enjoy the benefits." Lucinda leveled a steady look at her husband. "I have many irons in the fire and I am a bit exhausted. I do plan to retire this summer. You know what that means."

"That we divorce and I'll need to find live-in help."

"Yes."

Richard rubbed his palms together. "I understand, my darling. You deserve a rest. May I have the pictures?"

"I need to know how much of a problem this Dr. Oh is."

"I convinced him that we would notify the authorities about our hammer."

Lucinda noted the "we." Richard was back on her side. His addiction called for the photos she had. Nothing else mattered to him now.

"Henry suggests that I take care of Dr. Oh," she said. "I was going to go do that now."

"Henry's instincts are good," her husband admitted. "Oh left with Chen about ten minutes ago. He should be home by now. Alone. His son and daughter-in-law are in Europe and his granddaughter has a study group."

"Excellent. Do you have an address for him?"

"Yes. It's in my contacts folder on the computer. May I have the pictures?"

"Of course, dear." She opened her lavender purse and took out a flash drive. "Here."

"You are so good to me." Richard accepted the small red rectangle and began rolling his wheelchair down the hall.

Lucinda unpacked the grocery bag, setting out a chocolate pudding mix, a quart of milk, a tub of frosting and a plastic bin holding a chocolate muffin on the kitchen countertop. The Sunday afternoon bakery selection had been minimal with no brownies, no fudge and only a few offerings of muffins. She had finally decided that her best approach was a chocolate muffin that she could top with a pink frosting to turn it into a giant cupcake. The sickly pink ooze pictured on the frosting tub was flecked with red 'cherry flavored' gummy chunks. She had to have the frosting. It would mask her additions.

It was the work of just a minute to pour the pudding mix into a ceramic bowl and to mix in two cups of milk. Lucinda slid the bowl into the refrigerator to set and chill.

She walked out to the garage and stopped at the workbench to don vinyl medical gloves and a facemask before unlocking a storage locker. A small cardboard box sat, double-bagged in plastic, on a high shelf.

Lucinda took the box down and set it on the workbench. She carefully slit the plastic wrap and then the box top. She was relieved to see that the fentanyl inside was already bagged into many tiny servings. She took out one small baggie and resealed the box and taped shut the slit plastic. She restored the box to the storage unit shelf and stripped off the gloves and disposed of them before stepping over to the workbench to pluck out a fresh pair of gloves. With pristine gloves on she shut the locker doors and reset the padlock. Picking up the one tiny baggie in a gloved hand, Lucinda left the garage and returned to the kitchen. She set the baggie down on a disposable napkin on the counter.

She retrieved the pudding and gently sprinkled in the contents of the fentanyl packet, using a spatula to fold in the powder. She used a clean teaspoon to dig a small crater in a muffin top and filled the crater with a spoonful of pudding. She opened the frosting container and used a butter knife to cover the muffin top with a thick spread of the frosting. She placed the frosted muffin into a plastic gift box and snapped on the lid.

Lucinda finally removed the facemask and breathed deeply. It was exhausting to keep such careful focus on hand control. Henry had told her that it was dangerous to use loose powder so mixing the fentanyl into the pudding base made the product safer for her but even that small extra step had been unexpectedly draining.

She studied the bowl of leftover pudding. She did not want to go through the process of divorcing Richard. There would surely be constant negotiations over one little thing or another — and he had that horrible, superior way about him. Somehow Richard never let her forget that he had chosen her out of the college typing pool.

He'd needed a presentable handmaiden.

And she had been one. She had stepped and fetched and cleaned and cooked and earned her degree while doing it. She had been to hundreds of faculty teas, student events and college fundraisers as a dutiful and well-groomed wife. She had finally escaped those soul-killing exercises to build her own career, but even then she had remained Richard's little dogsbody at home.

She'd been the mastermind of the side businesses. Not Richard. He didn't deserve half the profit. Or half the value of the house.

She picked up the bowl of poisoned pudding and put it in the refrigerator.

Lucinda carefully washed the spatula, spoon and butter knife and disposed of the baggie, gloves and mask.

As she picked up her car keys she listened. She could hear Richard down the hall in his office, humming with delight.

He would be hungry later. Perhaps he would find the pudding. It was something he could swallow.

She could hope.

Meanwhile, she should visit with Dr. Oh and then take herself to a place with a security camera to record her presence. There was a nice coffee shop in downtown Olympia across from the city hall. That would do. Lucinda picked up the bakery bin and her lavender bag. She would go for coffee after visiting Oh. Her laptop was in the car. She could sort out some of the Medicare files. She might even eat dinner downtown. Perhaps Henry could join her.

The driveway at the Lowenstein Home
4:45 p.m.

"I must have left the lights on," Elspeth said. She cranked the key in the ignition of her Civic and got only a click.

Nico stood on the driveway, reining in Zoom as she danced at the end of a leash. "I've got jumper cables. I can give you a jump."

Elspeth checked her watch. "That'll take time. I've got to get to The Azul Kitchen by five to get my check. Crap!"

"Better idea, then," Nico said, pulling his out his keys. "You take my Jeep. I'll call my dad. He can bring his truck over and we'll get the car going. Zoom and I can bring the Civic over to you at the hospice."

Elspeth scrambled out of the Civic and planted a kiss on Nico's cheek. "Thank you, thank you!"

"Go already!" Nico said.

The Evergreen Path Hospice
4:45 p.m.

"Jed,I'm so sorry it took so long to call you back."
Carmen leaned against the wall of the hospice boardroom.
"I'm at the hospice now."

"How's your mother?" Jed asked.

"She seems the same to me. She spasms with chorea and
struggles to breathe so she's on some major medication.
Some moments she knows I'm here but most of the time
not."

"I'm so sorry," Jed said. "Can I come sit with you?"

Carmen blinked back tears. "That would be super," she
sniffed. "I've got a project that I need to organize with two
other students. That should take an hour or so. Dad and I are
going to be here for a while."

"I'll show up in about an hour."

"Thanks. See you then."

Jasmine Oh stuck her head in the doorway. "Hey, boss!
This our workspace?"

Carmen smiled. "We're women on the way up. The
boardroom is where we live!"

Jasmine smiled and pulled back from the doorway to
chirp, "Yo! Taz! We're in here!" Jasmine returned and took a
seat at the long table.

A heavy figure in a long white T-shirt, relaxed jeans and
skateboarding shoes slouched in, dropping a book bag on the
table. Short dark hair spilled forward over a pale face. "Hey."

"Hey, yourself."

"We got problems," Taz said. "Your Huntington's
project concept is too well developed conceptually and
impossible for us to pursue physically. It's a cool concept but
there's nothing further for me and Jasmine to do. The
tardigrade concept is worse because we don't have the chops
to design a distinguishing set of tests. And I'm not sure we

176

want to put ourselves into the whole reproducible results mess."

Carmen nodded. "Back to the drawing board, and fast. Any ideas?"

Jasmine said, "I've got one. My grandfather and I found a big shelf fungus on a stump in the woods yesterday. It's really enormous. I couldn't remember if it was a brown rot fungus or a white rot fungus, so I looked it up. I found one reference that said it might be both."

"Not up to speed here," Taz said. "Give me the basics."

"Brown rot fungi secrete enzymes that break down the hemicellulose of plant walls to hydrogen peroxide," Jasmine said. "The hydrogen peroxide seeps through wood and causes the wood to shrink and break into chunks."

She wiggled her fingers and said, "White rot fungi spread their little rootlets, called hyphae, through the wood, secreting enzymes as they grow that digest cellulose and lignin. That makes wood soft and spongy."

"Shitake and honey mushrooms are white rot fungi," Carmen added. "White rot fungi are the only things on the planet that can break down plant lignin. If we didn't have brown rot and white rot fungi, we'd be standing on miles-deep piles of dead tree trunks."

Taz laughed. "And you're telling me that this fungus you and Grandpa found is a switch hitter? Count me in!"

Jasmine laughed. "I hadn't thought of it that way. I was just interested when I found literature that said different things and one biologist who thinks it might be both."

"Fungal sex is bizarre," Carmen added. "There isn't male or female."

"Maybe a place to start," Taz mused, "would be to see if there are other fungal species that have both brown and white rot phases."

"You start there," Carmen agreed. "This wood rot must have commercial applications."

"Like old home restoration," Jasmine agreed. "I'll poke around on the economics of rot."

"And I'll look at the biochemistry," Carmen said, opening her laptop.

Taz asked, "Do we have a time limit on the room?"

"I don't think so. We have the place to ourselves."

Mason County Sheriff's Office
4:45 p.m. Sunday

"Ready?" Raposo asked.

"Yep. Let's go see what the Fickham family is doing this fine afternoon," Deputy McRae replied.

From outside Raposo's office window there was the sound of squealing tires followed by a bang. High-pitched screams cut through the afternoon.

Both men looked through the window and saw that a church bus had rammed into the back of a camper trailer being pulled by a pickup. Girl's faces were pushed against the windows of the bus and their screams began to crescendo.

The deputy and the detective sprinted for the door.

"Realize that everything connects to everything else."
Leonardo DaVinci (1452-1519)

Chapter Twenty-Four

The Fickham Compound
4:45 p.m.

"Everybody ready?" Russell Fickham asked.

Troy grinned. He was flying high and ready thanks to a quick snort from his Uncle Henry's cocaine supplies. "Damn straight!" he said. "Let's go, Grandpa!"

Russell laughed. "Glad to see you got your courage up." He said, "I'll take the Suburban and Tate is with me. Ricky Lee and Troy, you're in the sedan. When we get there, we park in back and go in the back door and down the hall to this board room."

Tate nodded. He, too, was flying high and happy after a visit to Henry's stash.

Troy asked, "What about you, Uncle Henry?"

"I've got deliveries," Henry said smoothly. "You don't need me for this."

Troy eyed his uncle, blinking rapidly and thinking about what he had heard through the window from Liberty about Henry and the dead pharmaceutical representative. The deliveries might be worth serious money.

Henry stared at Troy, daring him to speak.

Troy looked down and busied himself with the handcuffs, pushing the curved metal piece into the locking mechanism and out again. It was beautiful to watch the ratchets work.

"Any security cameras on the back of the building?" Ricky Lee asked.

"My friend turned them off," Henry lied.

"Alright then," Russell continued. "We lightfoot it down the hall. I'll go in first and grab the closest girl. Knife to the throat and we should have no screaming." He looked at Ricky Lee. "Remember what comes next?"

Ricky Lee nodded. "Handcuffs on, gags in. Out to the car, fast."

"Handcuff 'em in back. A girl with her hands in front can cause trouble."

"What if the dad Dwerryhouse is there?" Tate asked.

"He belongs to Ricky Lee," Russell replied.

"He won't get a drop on me this time," Ricky Lee said.

"Good." Russell opened the door of the mobile home. "Let's get your girls. It's about time somebody made me a great granddaddy."

Near the Mason County Sheriff's Office

Deputy McRae directed traffic around the crashed church bus as Detective Raposo executed a quick triage. A hefty man was climbing out of the truck, carrying a rapidly barking dog while the church bus rocked with screams.

Raposo put his head in the church bus and yelled, "Quiet!" Fifteen middle school girls and a frightened young woman driver instantly fell silent.

"If you are bleeding, will you please raise your hand?"

No hands waved.

"Anyone have a bumped head?"

A chorus of voices began.

"Quiet!" McRae roared. "Raise your hand if you have bumped head!"

No hands went up.

"Raise your hand if you think you need an ambulance."

No hands went up.

"Thank you. I am now going to check on the people in the other vehicle. You may whisper among yourselves. I do not want to hear any more screaming."

Raposo stepped off the bus and nearly collided with the pickup driver who yelled, "She back ended me!" as the small dog yammered like a pile driver.

"Quiet!" Raposo roared.

The dog blinked then erupted into a staccato round of barking. His owner reached up and put gentle banana-sized fingers around the dog's muzzle.

"Let's see some ID," Raposo growled.

Fifteen minutes later two more officers had arrived and Raposo signaled to McRae. "Let's let Gomez and Johnson take it from here."

McRae was glad to step away from the traffic directing. "What was all the screaming about?"

"That, my friend, was the teen soprano section of the First Baptist Church, which, Thank God, has installed seat belts on their bus. Much drama, no injuries."

"And the dog?"

"A Jack Russell terrier. More drama. Some embarrassment when the driver realized he had not plugged in his trailer brake lights."

"We still headed up to the Fickhams?"

Detective Raposo checked his watch. "It's getting late, but I could go. You got any gas left in your system?"

"It's murder, boss. I can go all night."

"Good man. Give me a few minutes to record some notes on this accident and we'll get on the road."

* * *

The Evergreen Path Hospice

Jasmine, Carmen and Taz hunched over their laptops as the hospice boardroom echoed with the sounds of thirty fingers clicking on keyboards.

"I'm finding oceans of stuff," Taz said. "Ninety-five percent of all plants have a fungal partner that help root systems take up nutrients. You've got your endo-mycorrhizal fungi that do this melding with the plant root and set up, like a farmer's market. The fungus brings in phosphate and other minerals that the plant takes up and the plant delivers sucrose and glucose to the fungus." Taz inhaled and added, "and there's the ecto-mycorrhizal fungi that cover the surface of the root tip like a condom — but either way the fungi expands the root uptake zone by a factor of a thousand. That's mind blowing."

"And the transport is incredible," Taz continued. "Carbon can be moved from a birch tree through the fungal mycorrhizae and into fir trees. It's part of how ecosystem succession unfolds."

"The economics are huge," Carmen said. "When there's functioning mycorrhizae, then chemical fertilizer costs can be cut in half.

"I'm off in bizarro world," Jasmine said. "Did you know there are fungi that trap and digest soil nematodes? Fungi eat anything."

"The fungi are everywhere," Carmen mused. "Building, transporting, deconstructing. It's a whole global economy that I just haven't been seeing."

"More bizarro," chirped Jasmine. "Bushmen of South Africa hunt truffles and may carry truffles to counteract the toxin on poisoned arrows."

"Truffles," Carmen mused. "Lots and lots of money spent on truffles."

"Only found growing in association with certain trees," Taz called. "Oregon white truffles like Douglas fir growing on slopes and French truffles like hazel nut trees." Taz's fingers flew across the laptop keyboard. "Ninety-nine dollars an ounce on Amazon. Free shipping."

"Ninety-nine dollars an ounce? Wow!" Carmen said.

"Focus," Jasmine laughed. "We're all wandering. We're supposed to be focused on fungal rot of wood."

"I've got one here. *Neolentinus lepideus,* called the Train Wrecker mushroom because it digests railroad ties — even the ones treated with creosote." Carmen said. "Smells like anise."

"What's anise smell like?"

"Licorice." Carmen answered. "Says here this species is widespread and is often the fungus that is decaying manmade structures."

"That sounds like it has economic impact," Taz said.

"Ooh! Ooh!" Jasmine cried. "Cool! Listen guys! *Neolentinus lepideus* is a brown rotting fungi. It was originally *Lentinus lepideus.*"

"Be still my heart," Taz deadpanned.

"No, you don't get it. *Lentinus* is a white rotting genus. Remember, brown rotting fungi eat cellulose and white rotting fungi eat lignin. *Lentinula edodes* is shiitake, probably the most important medicinal mushroom out there. Twenty bucks a pound, but you can grow it yourself. Anyway, the Train Wrecker and the Shiitake were thought to be closely related, but then, through the rotting, scientists figured out they were different, which leads back to why are they different, which leads to . . ." Jasmine paused dramatically.

"Insights into diversity and evolution and how we all got to where we are," Carmen said, "All with economic impacts."

* * *

Room 16B The Evergreen Path Hospice

Duane Dwerryhouse held his breath when his wife stirred. He didn't want to wake her. Yera moved and a harsh gargle started in her throat. Her head twitched and her eyes flew open. She looked up at her husband and smiled.

He couldn't help it. Tears flowed down his cheeks. He had doubted he would see the beautiful shine of recognition in Yera's eyes again. He wished Carmen were here, but he was afraid to leave his wife now. She closed her eyes and coughed.

Duane reached out and took her hand in his. He said, "It's alright, baby. If you are tired and need to go, I understand."

Yera coughed again. An ominous wheezing rose from her chest. She looked at Duane with confusion drifting over her face and then she turned her head away.

He held her hand as she drifted back to sleep.

Evil is easy and has infinite forms.
Blaise Pascal (1623-1662)

Chapter Twenty-Five

Sunday, 5:45 p.m.
The Oh Residence

The sound of the doorbell jarred Dr. Oh awake. He roused to find that he had fallen asleep in his favorite armchair. The *Journal of Botany* issue he had been reading had slid off his lap and lay open on the floor. It took several moments to stand, step over the publication and make his way to the front door.

Dr. Oh peered through the door's sidelight window to see a silver-haired woman of middle years wearing a lavender raincoat and holding a plastic food bin. She wore the frozen smile that Dr. Oh associated with spouses of upwardly mobile academics. He opened the door and said, "Hello."

"Hi," Lucinda said, holding out the bin. "I'm Richard Sutherland's wife. I wanted to say 'thank you' for being so kind to Richard this afternoon. His retirement transition has been challenging."

"My pleasure," Dr. Oh said. "He was doing us a kindness by hosting."

"I feel just awful that we hadn't met before," Lucinda said brightly. "I work as a hospice administrator and in recent years I rarely made the college faculty events."

"You are brighter than the professors then," Dr. Oh said dryly.

Lucinda beamed. "How kind — and it was good of you to bring the missing tools to our attention."

"Do you know who took them?"

"No," Lucinda said. "I suspect my gardening help."

"Will you call the police, then?"

"We have." Lucinda lied smoothly. "A Detective will be out tomorrow to talk to us." She extended her hands a fraction further so the gift box almost touched Dr. Oh. "Do take this. We so appreciate your efforts."

Dr. Oh took the bin. "You really didn't need to do this."

Lucinda smiled brightly. "I thought it was the least I could do."

After she left, Dr. Oh pried open the gift bin and studied the offering. It looked like a very large cupcake. He didn't really like sweets. Chips and salty pretzels were more to his liking. He sniffed the cupcake. Store bought. He could smell the preservatives in the pink frosting. It would be good manners to eat it and say something nice about it.

Except, he thought, that only encourages ladies to do things that are irksome. He had never understood the complex inter-weavings of gifts, thanks, and their associated sets of indebtedness. Perhaps it was best to not say anything and so discourage further unwanted acts of appreciation.

Dr. Oh set the gift bin down on the kitchen counter. He wanted a sandwich. He'd think about having the cupcake later.

The Evergreen Path Hospice

The Fickhams parked in the rear parking lot of the hospice. The four men silently closed car doors and assembled at the back door of the building. Ricky Lee tried the doorknob. It turned in his hand and he drew the door open. Russell nodded, stepping through the doorway. Troy followed, feeling strong from his uncle's cocaine. Ricky Lee stepped in, letting go of the door as Tate slid in the narrowing gap, grinning, as the door swung shut.

Russell Fickham took the lead. He moved rapidly down the back hallway to the brown door labeled "Executive Boardroom." He slid a machete out of its scabbard.

Troy's eyes jittered at the size of the unsheathed blade. The thought of blood spatter made his stomach jump.

Russell opened the boardroom door and stepped inside.

A plump girl was closest, with her back to the door as she hunched over a laptop computer. Russell smoothly grabbed her braid and pressed the machete to her throat.

"Anyone of you scream, anyone of you fuss and I will take her head right off."

Jasmine and Taz froze.

"That's right," Russell crooned. "No typing on those keyboards."

Ricky Lee slid through the door, followed by his sons. Ricky Lee circled around the table and put his meaty hand on the back of Jasmine's neck. "You get one chance to live, girlie. We're going to close your mouth and put you in cuffs. You cry, you die."

Tate handed his father the handcuffs and watched as Ricky Lee wrenched Jasmine's arms back to lock in her wrists. Leaning forward, he stuffed a sock in Jasmine's mouth and tied it in place.

Troy bounced in place, trying to watch all three captives at once. He felt like he should be doing something but Russell and Ricky Lee were taking up all the oxygen in the operation. Troy felt his hands float up as if he was going to box with someone. He stared at his hands and dropped them only to have them begin to rise again. He was definitely high. He felt great.

"Well, what the hell do we have here?" Ricky Lee leered at Taz. "You a soft boy or a tough girl?"

Troy's eyes focused on Taz. Here was a place for action. Troy began to move.

Taz's dark eyes flashed with hatred as Troy came around from the other side of the table.

Troy leaned down and stared into Taz's face. "I'd say we have a weirdo, Pa."

Taz erupted out of the chair only to be met by a double-handed shove from Troy. The chair went rolling back as Troy charged forward, riding high on cocaine. Troy yanked Taz up as the chair careened into the wall.

Troy fired his fists into Taz's middle. As Taz collapsed on the ground, Ricky Lee moved in and added three fierce kicks to the stomach.

Taz curled up, moaning. Troy kicked Taz again, aiming for the kidneys. Taz rolled under the table and lay still.

Carmen clenched her teeth as Tate tried to shove a sock in her mouth. Russell's fingers tightened in her hair. Carmen ignored the pain and kept her mouth closed. Tate tossed the sock on the floor and wrapped a long strip from a T-shirt across her mouth. He tied the strip tight and stepped back.

Russell angled the machete against Carmen's neck and leaned down to whisper in Carmen's ear, "We've got your friend. We don't need you. Be smart. Put your hands behind your back. Don't go causing problems."

Tears of rage prickled her eyes as Carmen moved her hands to behind her back. Tate clicked on a pair of handcuffs.

Russell surveyed the room. "Troy, your girl isn't here. Will the Asian do?"

Troy looked down at Jasmine. "I dunno," he said. "I kinda got my mouth set on Elspeth."

Russell's laugh was dark and dirty. "That one's small. Let's call her the appetizer." He added, "Get their phones. We'll see if we can get Dwerryhouse to bring the other one along." He yanked Carmen up by her braid. "Come on, Pocahontas. We're going to move you back to the woods." He barked, "Check the hall, Tate."

His weasel-faced grandson opened the boardroom door and peeked down the corridor. Emboldened, he opened the door wider and put his head out. "All clear."

Ricky Lee leaned down and looked under the table at Taz. He said, "Hey. Wierdo. Tell Dwerryhouse no police. He brings the cops in and the girls are stew meat. Got that? We'll be in touch."

"Come on, then. Let's get them loaded." Russell propelled Carmen toward the hall, as Tate and Ricky Lee lifted Jasmine off her chair and carried her to the door.

"Troy you bring up the rear. You watch out for Dwerryhouse."

Near the hospice

Elspeth drove Nico's Jeep carefully. She slowed as she neared the hospice, thinking it might be wise to park in the rear parking lot. Too many Sunday afternoon hospice visitors were elderly and she didn't want Nico's shiny Jeep collecting a parking lot ding. She slowed further for a speed bump. A flash of pink motion from the right had her braking fast. The Jeep came to a halt alongside an island of rhododendrons.

It was the same shade of rich rose pink as Carmen's favorite sweater. Was Carmen sneaking out for a smoke again?

Elspeth nursed the Jeep over the speed bump as she peered through a break in the rhododendrons. It was Carmen! Elspeth could see her cousin being propelled down the walkway by Russell Fickham. Carmen's hands were behind her back and there was a ratty white ribbon of cloth around Carmen's head and mouth.

Next came Tate and Ricky Lee, carrying a slender, dark-haired girl. Troy Fickham in his greasy red ball cap brought up the rear. The group moved rapidly.

Elspeth scrunched down in the driver's seat as her hands scrambled for her phone. Fingers shaking she dialed Nico and frantically waited as his message inbox came on.

"Nico here. Leave a message."

"Nico! I'm at the hospice. The Fickhams are kidnapping Carmen! I'm near the hospice back parking lot." Elspeth swore. She should have called 911 first. She punched the phone icon to hang up. Her fingers fumbled as she tried to tap in 911 and then the cell phone screen warned her that the battery was low. She tried to steady herself for another try when a car horn honked.

Elspeth looked in the rear view mirror and saw a luxury sedan behind her.

"Damn it!" Elspeth flung her phone down on the passenger seat. She sat up and pulled the Jeep to the curb. A sour faced couple pulled around the Jeep and turned into the hospice lot just as a battered Suburban exited with Russell Fickham at the wheel. He threw a look to his left as he turned the vehicle right but he didn't make eye contact with Elspeth. She made herself sit still as first the Suburban and then a beige Toyota bounced over a pothole then picked up speed and disappeared around a curve.

Elspeth put the Jeep in gear and followed. She hit the pothole and her cell phone slid off the passenger seat and into the foot well. Elspeth held on to the steering wheel and floored the gas.

In the Boardroom

Taz lay under the boardroom table with waves of pain pulsing with every heartbeat. Of all the cruelties that Taz had experienced in a lifetime of being unique, this beating was the worst. Everything hurt.

Was it possible to have an exploded kidney? It felt like it. Taz gingerly uncurled. Help was needed. Fast. Carmen and Jasmine could be found. Taz rolled over and began to crawl, using fingers dug into the carpet to propel forward.

Taz reached a wall and began plotting a path to get upright. First put one hand on the seat of a chair. Push. Swallow a scream of pain. Push again. The left hand on the tabletop. Push with the legs. Almost upright.

Taz saw the small red box on the wall and fell forward, fingers out splayed. Xyr's fingernails caught the small red bar. Taz pulled down and a fire alarm began its ear splitting wail.

A block from the hospice

Nico was close by in the old red Civic. His father's massive Ford truck had a powerful battery that had made short work of bringing Elspeth's battery to life. He'd thanked his father, loaded Zoom into the front passenger seat and was near the hospice when his phone chimed. He ignored it.

He pulled into the front visitor's parking lot and cruised the length of the building seeing no empty slots. Late Sunday afternoon seemed to be visiting time. Zoom hung her head out of the open window and leaned into the wind.

Nico pulled out of the front lot and circled the building. He was just pulling into a parking spot when the fire alarm erupted. Nico scrambled out of the Civic, slamming the door shut. "Stay!" he shouted at Zoom as he ran for the hospice rear door.

Elspeth. Where was she?

The door opened as Nico reached the building. A nurse shoved a doorstop under the door and ran back inside, turning to dart through a set of fire doors swinging shut on a long corridor of patient rooms. Nico stepped inside the building and inhaled. There was no smell of smoke. Before he could take another step, Duane Dwerryhouse burst through the double doors.

"Carmen's in the boardroom," Duane called as he sprinted past. Nico followed. He had to find Elspeth.

The men found Taz leaning against the wall under the fire alarm box, pale and groaning.

Taz looked up and said, "Four men. Nasty. Took Carmen and Jasmine."

Duane's eyes turned to blue chips of ice as the fire alarm continued to wail.

"You pulled the alarm?" Nico asked.

Taz nodded.

"Okay. I'll run tell the staff there's no fire."

"No police," Taz gasped. "The man said he would . . ." Taz winced and said, "be in touch. Took cell phones."

"Where's Elspeth?" Nico demanded.

"Who?" Taz croaked.

"Elspeth! Carmen's cousin. Dark hair. Beautiful."

Taz shook her head. "I haven't seen her. She wasn't here. But maybe she was outside?"

Duane looked up at Nico and said, "I'll try Elspeth on my phone. Go say there is no fire. It was an accidental pull. Then get back here. We'll make a plan."

"On it." Nico ran for the door.

It requires more courage to suffer than to die.
Napoleon Bonaparte (1769-1821)

Chapter Twenty-Six

Sunday, 6 p.m.
In the Suburban

Carmen's shoulder screamed in the sharp pounding way of an abused joint. Her body was resting with her weight pressing down on the outside of her right shoulder. She had been shoved into the back of a stinking Suburban and Jasmine had been tossed in on top of her.

The corrugated metal floor was damp and oily and only an inch from her nose. Carmen wiggled and transferred her weight to her right elbow. She squirmed into a sitting position as Jasmine slid to the left. Carmen's eyes focused on a screw head protruding from the back of the seat bench. She leaned in and hooked the rag of her gag onto the screw head.

She tried leaning back. The rag stretched but the dirty cloth in her mouth stayed in place.

Tate Fickham looked over the back of the seat bench and saw her. Carmen looked up at him, making her eyes steady on his. She pleaded with her eyes.

He reached over the seat back and yanked the gag out of her mouth. "No yelling," he warned.

"Fine," Carmen rasped. "Please help Jasmine. If she throws up in that gag she could choke to death." Carmen tried not to think beyond this first task. When her mind darted to the thought of Russell Finkham putting his hands on her again, she could feel her brain begin to seize up. Better to focus on Jasmine.

Jasmine rolled over and looked up, her own eyes desperate with fear. Tate smiled. "Sure," he said. He twisted on the seat bench to look down on the girls. "My God, you are so fine," he said as he pulled off Jasmine's gag. "You best be quiet," he added.

"Tate," Russell Fickham called from the driver's seat, "Don't go being soft on those girls. They've got plenty of piss and vinegar in themselves at this stage."

Tate looked down at the two young women. They stared up at him with strained faces and terrified eyes. "I think they're smart, Grandpa." Tate said. "They know they're not going anywhere."

When Tate popped in ear buds and turned to face the front again, Carmen shifted to put her mouth next to Jasmine's ear and Carmen began to whisper.

Carmen spoke quietly as the bed of the Suburban jostled and swayed. "Crappy shocks. Wouldn't you know it? We get kidnapped by a gang with crappy shocks." This did what she wanted. She got a quarter smile from Jasmine.

"It really stinks," Jasmine whispered back. "Who are these guys?"

"Creeps," Carmen said, "Family name is 'Fickham.' Four Fickhams. They have been stalking my cousin, Elspeth. My Dad punched one of the guys yesterday. I think they want revenge."

Jasmine whispered, "Will they ask for ransom?"

"I don't know. I know my Dad will be mad as hell and he will come get us."

"If we can figure out how to tell him where we are."

"Yeah." Carmen's heart sank. There were thousands of acres of forest surrounding Olympia. They could disappear forever and never be found. Tears welled in Carmen's eyes as she thought of her father searching for her for years. He would. Carmen gulped. And she never even had a chance to kiss Jed. Hell, she hadn't even had a chance to say much more than 'Hi' to Jed.

That was so unfair.

Jasmine whispered, "I have a friend who is a deputy. He warned me about a man named Henry Fickham."

"He's related to these guys but I haven't seen him yet. Have you?"

"No. None of these guys is Henry?"

"The old man is Russell. The fat one is Ricky Lee. The two young ones are Troy and Tate."

Jasmine swallowed hard. "That's a lot of Fickhams."

Carmen nodded and sniffed. She wasn't even able to wipe her nose. Her shoulder hurt. She twisted to shift her weight and fiercely whispered, "This is stupid. Those Fickhams do not know who they are messing with!"

A curve in the road had Carmen sliding into the wall of the Suburban, slamming her shoulder. She inhaled. She was her father's daughter. She knew that survival started with reconnoitering, asset counting and a plan.

Reconnoitering. She was in the back of an old, large vehicle. There was not an exit available to her.

Assets. She had herself and Jasmine. Lots of brains. No tools.

Plan. Carmen whispered to Jasmine, "When you get the chance, see if you can squeeze your butt back through your arms. If you can get your arms in front, then you'll be able to grab. That will give us more options."

Jasmine nodded and began to wiggle.

"Not now!" Carmen hissed. "Once they leave us alone."

"Alright. I think I can do it. I'm good at yoga."

"Good. I know I can't. My butt's too big."

"Your butt isn't that big!"

Carmen rolled her eyes. "Trust me. Bringing handcuffed hands back to front takes either long arms or a skinny rear and some flexibility. Stay alert. Look stupid and agreeable."

Jasmine nodded as the Suburban bounced and swayed. "What is that smell?" she whispered.

196

"Blood," Carmen whispered back. "Whatever was back here before was bleeding."

On the road

Elspeth found it was easier to keep her eye on the maroon Suburban than on the beige Toyota. She held her breath as the Suburban approached the light at Delphi Road. With luck it would turn red and she could use the stop to scramble for her cell phone.

No such luck. The Suburban gunned through a green light and roared down the hill, past Bay Mercantile at the flats of Mud Bay and then accelerated onto Highway 101.

The beige Toyota followed.

Elspeth trailed several cars back. She swore when a pickup slowed to turn into the tavern at Mud Bay. She was able to keep the Suburban in sight, catching up to it as the highway curved. The important thing now was to see if the Suburban stayed on Highway 101 to Mason County or veered left to take Highway 8 to Elma, Montesano or Aberdeen.

She debated slamming on the brakes and diving for the cell phone but changed her mind when she saw the Suburban picking up speed. She tightened her grip on the steering wheel and vowed, "Carmen, I'm coming. By God, I am not going to lose you."

Elspeth took a breath and followed the Fickhams to Mason County.

At the hospice

The April sunshine was waning as Jed Twanea steered his motorcycle into the parking lot of the hospice. A jangling fire alarm choked off, leaving a profound silence. The front foyer of the building teemed with staff members and seven patients on gurneys.

"False alarm," a nurse called. "A visitor had a fainting spell and hit the alarm box going down."

A groan went up followed by some determinedly cheerful chatter as staff began wheeling patients back into the building. Jed parked the bike and walked up to the entrance.

"Let me help," Jed said to a tall male nurse's aide who was steering a gurney loaded with a very large man.

"Thanks. Can you steady that side and hold up the tubing?"

"Sure."

Jed accompanied the patient and gurney down a long corridor to a room where the aide reconnected an oxygen line and a call button before gently taking the patient's hand. "All set, sir?"

The large man in the bed nodded and closed his eyes.

Ramon, the aide, signaled to Jed that they should exit the room.

"Thanks again," Ramon said.

"No problem. I'm here to see Carmen Dwerryhouse. Her mother is a patient. Can you tell me the room number?"

"You need to sign in at the nurse's station to be directed to a patient's room, but I don't think she's with her mother. I heard Mrs. Sutherland say that Carmen could work on a project back in the boardroom. Down the corridor, take a left, go through the double doors."

A moment later Jed put his head into the boardroom and saw Duane Dwerryhouse holding a water bottle up to a dark-haired person sitting on the floor. "Mr. Dwerryhouse?" Jed called.

Duane's head swept up and his blue eyes glared arrows at Jed before recognition set in. "You're Carmen's friend."

"Yes sir. Jed Twanea."

"I'd shake your hand, but we've got a situation unfolding. Do you remember that toerag I clocked yesterday morning?"

"Chunky smoker?"

"Right. Ricky Lee Fickham. Taz here tells me that the four Fickhams were here with knives and handcuffs. They took Carmen and her friend, Jasmine, and left a message for me not to call the police."

Nico came jogging in from the hallway. He said, "Things are cool up front about the alarm but Elspeth isn't answering her cell phone. She left me a message that she saw the Fickhams leaving the building with Carmen. I think she's following them in my Jeep."

"Damn! I kept thinking we should get that Find-the-Phone app up and going on the girls' phones but I never got around to it."

"I've got a car tracker app on the Jeep," Nico said.

"Let's take a look." Duane stood up. "Nico, this is Jed, a friend of Carmen's."

"I'll do anything you need to help," Jed said.

"Great." Nico tapped his phone and said, "Looks like the Jeep is going out Harrison Road to Mud Bay. I would guess they're going onto Highway 101."

"Let's go." Duane turned to Taz. "Can you manage?"

Taz nodded. "I'll call my brother to come get me."

"Good." Duane reached in his jeans pocket. "Shit! Carmen has the car keys."

"I have Elspeth's Civic. We can take that." Nico paused. "Zoom is in the car."

"The big dog?"

"Right. She, ah, sits in front. She didn't like the back seat."

Duane swiveled to Jed. "Got room for me?"

"On my Harley."

"Oh Hell No. I want to survive this." Duane scrubbed his face with both hands. "Okay. Backseat to a dog. Let me get your numbers into my cell phone and let's get going. Jed, keep behind us. We'll be tracking the Jeep and trying to close the gap. Once we get close, we'll pull over and make a plan."

"No police?" Jed asked.

"Fickhams said not to call, but my real worry is that it will take the authorities too long to do us any good. If the Fickhams are headed up 101 they are headed to Mason County on a Sunday afternoon. We're crossing jurisdictions and response time is long in the woods. We should start now and recon fast."

"Give me a minute to get ready," Jed said. "I've got my bike leathers in my saddlebags. If we're going up the highway, it'll get cold."

"Sure. Go. Meet us around back."

"Mr. Dwerryhouse?" Taz croaked.

"Yeah?"

"I hope you beat the snot out of them."

"That is my intention."

Woe to those who scheme iniquity.
Micah 2:1

Chapter Twenty-Seven

Sunday, 6:15 p.m.
The Suburban, traveling north on Highway 101

"Tate! God damn it! Tate!" Russell Fickham bellowed over the road noise generated by the old Suburban as it rattled and swayed down the highway.

In the next bench of the vehicle, Tate jolted into awareness and removed an ear bud. "Yeah?"

"Answer the god damn phone. It might be Dwerryhouse."

Tate looked down at the two pink cell phones on the bench seat. One was chiming loudly. He picked up the phone and tapped the phone icon. "Hello?"

He smiled as he said, "Ah, hi. Nah. This is . . . a friend. She's, ah, kinda tied up right now." Tate looked over the top of the bench seat and grinned down at Carmen and Jasmine, huddled on the floor of the luggage area.

"Yeah," Tate said. He listened for several moments and said, "I got that. Hey, don't worry if it gets late. We got a big project. Might go all night." Tate listened again and said, "I'll be sure to tell her. Bye now." He tapped the phone off.

"That was Jasmine's grandfather." Tate said.

"The skinny little Asian is Jasmine?"

"Sounds like it."

"What did grandpa want?"

"To tell her that he's not very hungry so he's just going to watch some television. And," Tate grinned, "And to say that Mrs. Sutherland brought by a cupcake to say thank you about a hammer."

"Mrs. Sutherland?" Russell laughed. "Jasmine's grandpappy had better watch out. From what I heard about Henry's squeeze, she's one stone cold bitch."

"Where did you hear about her, Pop?"

"Clemmie over at Mason Savings traded me some news for cedar shingles. She said that they had this woman taking out a thousand in cash every Thursday afternoon, like clockwork. Cold bitch at the drive up window. One day Clemmie saw Henry make the pickup instead, which she thought was interesting so she clued me in. And, you know what?"

"What?"

"Clemmie says the Feds are interested in people making lots of deposits of cash but there isn't such a tracking of people who are taking money out."

"So the lady has a big trust fund or something?"

"That's the interesting part. The lady has online accounts that collect money from a video distributor. Lots and lots of three-dollar deposits. "

"She's an actress?"

"No, you dumb shit. She's selling some sort of video. What kind of video makes money?"

"Porn?

"Finally, you're showing some brains, boy."

"Why would she be bringing over cupcakes to somebody's Grandpa?"

Russell steered the Suburban into the passing lane to roar around a logging truck. "Gather information?" he shouted as the Suburban shook. "Or poisoning the old fart."

"Henry's fentanyl would do it," Tate agreed.

"Henry's got fentanyl?"

"That's what Troy told me."

"You watch your Uncle Henry, boy. He's always got something up his sleeve. He's never been the one-note asshole like your father."

Ricky Lee scowled from the passenger seat but said nothing.

Russell let the Suburban drift back into the right lane before saying, "Check the other phone. Can you get to the contacts list?"

Tate picked up Carmen's phone and tapped the screen. "We need the password."

"Use your god-damned brains, son. Tell the girl you need it."

Carmen heard Russell and thought furiously. It would be a good thing if her father got a call. He would begin to know where to find her. She could always change her password later.

When Tate's face appeared over the seatback, she was ready. "It's 8912" she said.

Tate crowed, "Got it!"

Russell said. "Go to contacts. Find Dwerryhouse. It might be under ICE"

"He sells ice?"

"No, idiot. That's 'In Case of Emergency'."

"Got it."

"Gimme the phone." Russell reached back and took the phone as the Suburban picked up speed. He tapped the call icon and held Carmen's phone to his ear as he steered left-handed down the freeway. "Dwerryhouse!" he barked. "I got your girl. Don't do anything stupid like call the police. I'll be in touch." Russell thumbed off the call and tossed the phone back to Tate.

In the back of the vehicle, Carmen and Jasmine bounced on the corrugated metal floor and breathed in the air laden with the smells of death.

* * *

At the hospice

Duane's hands shook as he heard Russell's message. He tapped the phone off and felt his stomach flip. Should he call the cops? He made himself inhale and exhale. Too risky. He needed more intel.

It didn't help that he was folded up in the back seat of Elspeth's Civic as Nico floored the gas to get the little car up to speed on Highway 101. Duane had never liked small spaces. Zoom pranced around in the front passenger seat until she was facing Duane. She stretched back and gave Duane's face a lick.

Duane pushed Zoom's nose away and looked down at the second phone in his lap. Nico had given him his phone with the Jeep tracker app activated.

"Can you tell where they are?" Nico asked.

Duane looked at Nico's phone. "Your Jeep is near the Holiday Valley exit. I'm assuming Elspeth is keeping behind the Fickhams."

"Duane, are you sure we shouldn't be calling law enforcement?"

Duane let out a breath. "I was just asking myself that, but, yeah. I am sure. Not yet. It takes longer than you might think to get a SWAT team in place. If we can catch up with Elspeth, we might get an idea of where these losers live. I'm not thinking we'll be taking these guys on in a hand-to-hand fight. We want to see if we can infiltrate and liberate. In that case we might be faster and more effective than the cops." Duane closed his eyes and let a wave of dismay roil past. He knew his tone of voice sounded like he was describing a wall spackling project instead of rescuing his daughter. He took a deep breath and opened his eyes. His voice was staying calm, so he just had to keep the rest of himself in line. He had to do what needed to be done.

He caught Nico eyeing Jed in the rearview mirror. The Harley was having no trouble keeping up with the Civic. Nico said, "Jed seems competent."

Duane stared down at the tiny icon on Nico's cell phone. "We're about to find out."

* * *

Java, Java, Joe on Harrison

Lucinda Sutherland sipped a latte and stared at the spreadsheet on her laptop. It was astonishing to see the total cash outlay for the pill machine, the fentanyl and the processing supplies. She'd purchased gloves and masks from an assortment of outlets, not realizing her total expense. Unfortunately bulk buying might have triggered questions. She should have collected supplies slowly from the hospice storeroom. If she had liberated boxes of gloves carefully, no one would have noticed.

It was too late now. She would remember to keep an eye on this expense line in the future.

She toggled a key and brought up the draft of the new Lu-Hen Services web page. She loved the name of her company, although the dark web page development genius had been dreadfully expensive. Lucinda smiled. The pimply teen had chosen a gym locker at a 24-hour gym as his payment path. Henry had simply made a small contribution to one of the gym trainers and soon they had the name of their website developer. No matter. The kid had created an excellent website that was close to complete. This path would be much more secure than the video sales site. Lucinda sipped her coffee. One should pay readily for quality work. The teen was safe from her. His death would raise too many questions from his doting mother.

Lucinda brought up her work calendar. It was time to close the account at Mason Savings. Six months was long enough. She would open an account next in Lewis County. That would be lovely. She could shop the outlet stores in Centralia. She had the cash.

She made a schedule and reviewed the worksheet on her Medicare patients. Money management was so exhausting. It took care to keep deposits from triggering questions.

Lucinda checked her watch and decided to call Henry.

He answered on the first ring.

"Where are you?" she asked.

"Near my father's place," Henry replied. "I'm up in the woods. I want to make sure they get here with the girls."

"What is your thinking?"

"That some photos of the girls being unloaded might be some good insurance to have."

"Always thinking ahead. That's one of the many reasons I love you."

"How are you?" Henry asked.

"Exhausted. I'm reviewing the accounts and everything looks fine. I'm finding a few areas for improvement, as always." She sighed. "It's just we have so many irons in the fire."

"Just a little longer, love. Remember, we are professionals."

"I am so glad you see me that way."

"Lucinda, we are not our past. We are not where we came from. We are what we have made ourselves to be."

Lucinda blinked back sudden tears. "Thank you," she murmured. "Thank you for seeing me that way."

"You are so smart and so hard working. You are also so beautiful."

Lucinda laughed. "Oh, thank you, sweetheart. In a minute I am going to spill the last of my coffee in my lap and I was regretting the mess I am about to be."

"I assume you need to be a mess for a moment then."

"Yes." Lucinda smiled. "I need to have some drama with a cleanup so the barista will remember me. I did as you suggested and took the old man a filled cupcake. There was leftover pudding and I set that in the fridge. I am so hoping that Richard is hungry."

"Ah. That could snip one loose end."

"Yes. I've decided it is silly to go through a divorce. Why have half when we could have all?"

"You'll be so upset at his sudden death that you'll have to leave town?" Henry chuckled.

"Of course," Lucinda said.

"Day by day, what you choose, what you think and what you do, is who you become." Heralitus (circa 535-475 BCE)

Chapter Twenty-Eight

Sunday, 6:40 p.m.
The Oh Residence

Dr. Oh frowned as his fingers tapped the kitchen counter. He did not care for the tone or accent of the young man who had answered Jasmine's phone. It wasn't something concrete that disturbed him. It was more the overall flavor of the exchange.

His knees hurt. Perhaps that was the real problem. He had experienced too much exertion in the woods. How irritating. There had been a time when such an excursion had been typical outing before breakfast. There had been many, many days when fieldwork had him scrambling up and down rugged terrain from dawn to dark.

There were no more daylong excursions in his future. He was too old.

Dr. Oh scowled at the frosted cupcake sitting on the kitchen counter. It smelled of commercial preservatives. No wonder so many of the young people had their faces in their phones with food like that being offered. Didn't they know that artificial dyes could trigger an allergic reaction?

He laughed. "Oh, you fool" he said out loud, "You're becoming such a grumpy old man. Natural Red Number Four is carmine. We get carmine from boiling dead bugs in ammonia."

With a smile on his face, he picked up the cupcake and studied it. "Do you happen to contain *Dactylopius coccus?*"

With his mood improving, Dr. Oh thought about eating the cupcake. He had been resting for some hours. Surely the glucose gates on his thirty-seven trillion cells were at the closed or nearly closed position. Adding glucose to his system now would result in blood carrying glucose that could not be delivered. The glucose would be filtered out in the kidneys or stored in the abdomen as fat. Oddly, glucose would also be stored at the back of the throat where it would narrow the airway.

He already had an old man's potbelly. His granddaughter had informed him that he was snoring more. The only way to open the cellular glucose gates to accept more glucose delivery was through movement. Despite his aching knees, he needed to walk before consuming this cupcake.

Dr. Oh looked out the window. The late spring sun sparkled around lengthening shadows, promising another hour of good light. He could shuffle down to the end of the block. There was a big-leaf maple there, leaning out of the woods. Its massive moss-covered arms supported an array of licorice ferns. *Polypodium glycyrrhiza* was such an elegant and appropriate name. "Poly" for "many", "pod" for "foot" represented the forked rooting system that helped the fern cling to the tree branches. The "gycyrrhiza" meant "sweet root." Originally the licorice smell and sweet taste of the roots had botanists thinking the chemical made by the fern was glycyrrhizin, which could be found in the licorice plant, *Glycyrrhiza glabra*, and which was fifty times sweeter than sugar. The fern's sweet roots, however, were due to the presence of polypodoside, which was typically six hundred times sweeter than sugar.

Dr. Oh looked back at the frosted cupcake. He should admit to his ulterior motive. There was a recently retired pharmacist who had moved into the home next to the licorice ferns. She was a handsome woman of just sixty-eight. His last conversation with her had been delightfully intellectual and far ranging. He could knock on her door and request permission to collect the licorice ferns, explaining a scientific curiosity and a desire to compare sweetness patterns between fern and cupcake.

If the conversation went particularly well, then perhaps dinner out might follow the sweetness testing.

After all, he wasn't dead yet.

In the Jeep

Elspeth hung onto the steering wheel of the Jeep as she stabbed on the brakes and moved behind a bus-sized RV. The beige Toyota ahead of her was rocketing down Highway 101 and it wasn't keeping up with the Suburban. Her eyes ached and her fingers were cramping. Tailing vehicles was hard work. She didn't want to be so close that she drew attention. She also didn't want to lose sight of the Fickhams.

"It'd help if there weren't so many damn people out here." A pickup swung out behind her and roared past the Jeep and the motor home. Elspeth knew she had to do the same. She put on the turn signal, moved into the left lane and pushed down the accelerator, hands white-knuckling on the steering wheel as the Jeep hurtled down the highway. Ahead of her, the beige Toyota exited the freeway, so she swerved back in front of the RV and signaled to exit.

The motorhome driver blasted his horn in irritation.

"Sorry, sorry, sorry." She rode the Jeep's brakes down the exit ramp as she left the highway behind. She switched to ramming her foot down on the gas pedal as the Toyota disappeared around a right-hand curve. It would be so very easy to lose the Fickhams now.

She sped around the curve and then braked hard again when she saw the Suburban and the Toyota turning right onto Bloomfield Road. Her cell phone slid on the floor well, inching closer to the passenger door. Elspeth concentrated on shifting gears. Phone calls for help would have to wait.

In the Lexus

Henry Fickham pulled the cream-colored Lexus off the road so that the car rolled behind a large swath of tall evergreen huckleberry bushes. He was at the edge of his father's property. He used a screwdriver to remove the back license plate and replaced the plate with one that he had liberated from one of his father's collection of wrecks. He opened a Buck knife and carefully peeled the expiration sticker off the Lexus plate and reapplied it to the corner of the borrowed plate with a dribble of adhesive.

He smeared the plate with some mud and stepped back to review his work. The exchange looked good enough to escape notice. He tossed the original license plate into the brush and slid the screwdriver into his back pocket. The pharmaceutical company might already have notified law enforcement that Jeffrey was missing. A cream-colored Lexus was findable and he didn't want himself found with it.

The next tasks were to hike through the woods to his father's place, take some pictures of the girls being unloaded by Ricky Lee and his worthless nephews and then he'd drive the Lexus up to a Tacoma chop shop. If all went well, he'd be back in Olympia by midnight.

Lucinda was right. They had too many operations going. Henry scowled. Her instincts said it was time to pull out of the video operations. She was right. More than six months was tempting disaster. Richard might complain. Then again, Lucinda was clearly ready to shed Richard.

He didn't like the videos and he wanted Lucinda out of the video business. Henry rubbed his face and blinked to bring some moisture to his tired eyes. The money would do them no good in jail. He needed to be nimble. They should ramp up the customized fentanyl business and live a quiet little life. It was time for Lucinda to get out of the videos and the Medicare billing. She needed to be out well before the next audit. He should ask her the accountant's schedule. She would know.

An April evening breeze was rising. Henry zipped up his jacket and strode down a deer trail to his father's place.

At the Sutherland Home

Richard Sutherland had his wheelchair pulled up to the computer, his adrenaline rising. Lucinda had said this round of photos and videos had merit. He agreed. He was, he thought, a most excellent judge.

A photo expanded on the screen showing a naked little girl of about eleven. She was partially wrapped in a feather boa and wore a rhinestone tiara. Delightful. Richard craned his neck to study the image closely. The velvet curtains behind the girl added richness to the photo. Yes. This was a keeper. He would name this girl . . . Lucy.

Richard smiled. Lucy. An old fashioned name that charmed. Yes. This was a Lucy.

He tapped a tab to bring up the Journal of Psychological and Physiological Exploration and logged in the members section. Richard hovered the selecting arrow over the "Sensitive Topics" button and clicked. He filled in a second password and his entire collection of young girl pornography listed on the screen.

Richard grinned. Piggybacking on a scientific journal's website was a stroke of brilliance. Like a remora suckerfish attaching itself to a shark, Richard could coast along in the slipstream of the journal. All it had taken was the knowledge that the journal editor and website administrator were one and the same as a beleaguered dean at a large university. Who had time to monitor a closed discussion group that generated no complaints?

It was the work of a moment to add the new photo to the line up. He knew Lucinda was tired of her job as a middleman and merchant. Too bad. The photographer was gifted but computer deficient. The market was steady and the income significant. Lucinda was necessary to keep the customers supplied. He could ignore this new boyfriend of hers. Lucinda should quit whining. Everything was fine.

Richard unzipped his pants. He hoped Lucy had more poses.

In the Civic

Zoom leaned her head out the window of the Civic, her tongue lolling. Her long ears streamed back like ribbons in the wind. Her rear end wiggled and erupted in a gaseous gust.

"God! Open the window some more!" Duane grumbled.

"Sorry. She seems to have something going on digestively," Nico apologized as Zoom's fecal-smelling fart spread through the car.

Jed was keeping up on his Harley, staying a steady hundred yards back as the Civic sped down the exit from Highway 101. Moss-covered limbs of leaning alder arced over the road, doing little to disrupt the light rain.

The road dipped and turned. The trees changed to enormous Douglas firs that hemmed in the view. Occasionally Nico caught a flash of a roof of a house, tucked into the woods. Most of the area was forest in a thousand shades of spring green.

Duane studied the Jeep's icon on Nico's cell phone. "We're catching up to her. It looks like you want to go right on the next road."

"Right we go, then." Nico barely touched the brakes as he made the turn.

* * *

Deputy McRae and Detective Raposo were headed south on Highway 101 as a light rain began to fall.

"Ever been to the Fickham's place?" Raposo asked.

"No, Sir. I've not had the pleasure."

"It's quite the place. Old Man Fickham — that's Russell — has a little of everything. There's a backhoe, part of a dump truck, boats, RV's, sheds, at least two mobile homes in rough condition and about twenty acres of woods, — mostly a mix of Douglas fir and cedar. The undergrowth is remarkable. I've never seen a thicker mess of sword ferns, blackberry vines and salal. It all stretches back to one hell of a bog."

"Not an easy place to search, then."

"The worst. I helped search that site about a decade ago when we had a missing salal picker named Jesus. His brother kept insisting that Russell owed them money but when Jesus went to collect, Jesus went missing. We poked our noses all over that property while Russell stood around wearing a shit-eating grin."

"No Jesus?"

"Not even an eyelash." Raposo shifted his long legs and leaned back in the passenger seat. "We didn't have cadaver dogs in those days. I always wondered what we might have found in we'd searched that bog with a hound."

"Does Henry Fickham live out there?"

"I don't know. He's about forty-five now so he may live elsewhere. I figured we'd look for the cream Lexus and see what we see."

"Sounds good. I want the casino exit?" McRae asked.

"Yeah. Turn under the freeway and we'll head past the Squaxin Island Reservation and then to Bloomfield Road. When we get close, we should pull off and walk in. The driveway is tricky. It looks like it stretches back through the trees forever, but there's an odd bend around a hill and you're at their place."

214

Raposo and McRae passed the turn off to the Squaxin Island Museum and were almost to the turnoff to Bloomfield Road when a red Civic came hurtling along from the opposite direction. The Civic roared right onto Bloomfield Road.

"Man, they're going fast," Detective Raposo said just as Deputy McRae said, "I know that dog!"

McRae turned onto Bloomfield Road and put on the sedan's whirling lights. He gave a blast of the siren. As he tailed the Civic, he said, "That red dog was with Elspeth Dwerryhouse and her boyfriend up at the murder site this morning. Nico something. He was driving a red Jeep."

"Yeah. I saw your video," Raposo agreed.

With the patrol car on his back bumper, Nico had no choice. He had to pull over.

"God damn it to hell," Duane cursed from the back seat.

Jed, on the Harley, came up behind the sheriff's sedan. As Nico brought the Civic to a halt, Jed gently swung his motorcycle around the cars and drove down the road at a sedate speed.

"Shit, shit," Duane swore. The Jeep icon on Nico's phone had just come to a stop.

"Here I stand. I can do no other. God help me."
Martin Luther (1483-1546)

Chapter Twenty-Nine

Sunday, 7:20 p.m.
The Fickham Family compound

Elspeth saw the beige Toyota turn left onto a dirt road. It seemed to pause near a bank of evergreen huckleberry bushes before resuming its way down the road. She assumed the Suburban was still ahead of the Toyota, so she slowed at the juncture and carefully turned onto the rutted drive. She saw the Toyota vanish at a bend in the road.

She rolled the Jeep forward a dozen yards before bringing the vehicle to a stop. It was time to let someone know where she was. Elspeth put the Jeep into neutral and pulled on the parking brake before unhooking her seatbelt and reaching down to search for her cell phone. She knew it was on the passenger side floor but it took several moments to retrieve it. The slender phone had slid under the passenger seat and rested against an empty water bottle.

After an undignified, rear-end-up retrieval, Elspeth had her cell phone. She would call the police. She should also call Nico and Uncle Duane. The cell phone showed a single dot of signal strength and the red line of low battery was glowing as well. No matter. She would walk back to the road and see if she could get a better signal. She only needed a few minutes of power to make her calls.

Elspeth was still looking down at the cell phone screen as her left hand reached for the door handle. She pulled the door open and had her left leg descending to the ground when the door was yanked from her hand.

She looked up to see the grinning face of Troy Fickham. He held a knife in his right hand.

"Good to see you, gorgeous," he said. "Let's have the phone."

Elspeth made herself hand over her precious cell phone. It was like parting with beloved pet. She felt her heart rate soar as Troy took the phone and stepped back from the Jeep. Elspeth watched, aghast, as he turned off the phone and flung it into the undergrowth. Waves of nausea threatened to erupt in a spew of vomit. She swallowed hard and tried to memorize the spot where the phone had landed.

"I saw you trailing us. Next time you gotta follow someone, try something not as conspicuous as a red Jeep." Troy grinned. "Of course there's not gonna be a 'next time' if you don't do exactly as I say." He motioned with the knife. "You're gonna move over to the passenger side and put both hands on the dashboard. I'm going to get in and we're going to go down to my family's place. Any shit from you and I'll slice your guts out and keep the Jeep."

Troy leaned forward and added, "Nobody finds a body in these woods. You'd be bones in a week and forest slime the week after that."

Elspeth swallowed hard. She had to play for time. Her hands were shaking so hard that she pressed them on the Jeep's door. It took another hard swallow before she managed to say, "I understand."

Troy nodded as he waved the knife. "Of course, if you are going to be nice, then we can get along." He looked down at her and smiled. "You could be my woman. You are a fine thing, Elspeth. I could keep you a long time."

Elspeth knew she should say something agreeable but no words came. Finally she just swallowed hard and moved to the passenger side.

In the Suburban

Jasmine slid and bounced on the stinking metal floor of the Suburban as it bumped down the dirt lane. Every now and then her body bounced off of Carmen's and that was preferable because Carmen was at least soft in a few places. Jasmine saw that the scenery out the window was changing. Earlier there had been distance between the vehicle and trees. Now Douglas firs, cedars and big-leaf maple loomed over the vehicle. They were off the asphalt and moving a long way from other traffic.

She had been seeing flashes of gray clouds and an occasional burst of sunshine. Now the sky was hidden behind the trees. The day was rapidly receding into evening light.

Jasmine could not stop thinking about the conversation between Russell and Tate. Tate Fickham had said something about her grandfather getting a cupcake that might be laced with fentanyl. Whoever 'Mrs. Sutherland' was, she was not to be trusted. Henry seemed to be Tate's uncle. A drug dealer.

She had to find a way to a cell phone. She would call home and tell her grandfather not to eat the cupcake. Jasmine found tears leaking out as she tried to think of her neighbor's phone number. It was in her contacts list. If she could reach the Bayatis, maybe Mrs. Bayati could check on her grandfather.

The intense stench of the Suburban floor made it hard to think. Her shoulders ached and her left knee throbbed. She made sure to flex her fingers every few minutes.

A pair of dips jostled Jasmine close to Carmen again. Carmen whispered, "My father will be coming after us. We have to hang on. We don't fight until we have a real chance and then we fight like hell."

Jasmine nodded and sniffed.

"I need to pee," she said.

Carmen said, "I know. Fear piss. If you gotta go, then go."

The Suburban took another turn to the left and came to a halt.

Tate Fickham looked over the back of the Suburban seat and addressed the young women. "We're home," he said.

At the Civic

Duane opened the rear door of the Civic and levered his body out, knowing the officers exiting their patrol car would not like this. As he expected, Deputy McRae and Detective Raposo reacted instantly.

"Hands on the car!" Raposo shouted as he opened the patrol car door. He stood behind the open car door as McRae finished calling in the Civic's license plate number and made sure the dash cam and his shoulder cam were recording.

Duane obeyed, splaying his fingers on the roof of the Civic and making his body relaxed. He called to Nico, saying "Keep your hands on the wheel. Be very polite."

Nico needed no encouragement. He sat rigidly still even as Zoom moved in to lick his face with excitement. He could hear the sound of Jed's Harley receding until the sound of motorcycle suddenly disappeared.

McRae stepped out of the patrol car and unsnapped the strap on his pistol. "Sir," he called. "Are you armed?"

"No!" Duane replied. "We have no weapons and intend to comply. We are in pursuit of four men, who have abducted my daughter and her friend. We would appreciate your assistance."

Raposo and McRae exchanged a glance. Raposo said, "Sir, we are going to handcuff you for everyone's safety, but we will also listen to what you have to tell us."

"Let's get it done," Duane said.

Raposo took only moments to handcuff Duane and pat him down.

McRae signaled Nico to exit. McRae made short work of handcuffing Nico who did his best to copy Duane's controlled features.

"Talk to us," directed Detective Raposo.

"I had a confrontation with a Mr. Ricky Lee Fickham yesterday at a show at the fairgrounds," Duane said evenly. "He made a disparaging remark to my niece, Elspeth and I clocked the guy. Officer Martinez of the Olympia PD was there and defused the situation. He had the Fickhams leave."

"We know Martinez," Raposo said. "Then what?"

"The Fickhams left. Four of them. Russell, old man with a long beard, Ricky Lee about age forty, and two more, Troy and Tate, who are in their early twenties. Last night Troy Fickham showed up at the house where my niece is housesitting but Nico here was there and ran Troy off."

Nico felt that was a bit of an overstatement, although now was not the time to explain more fully about the loudly crackling madrone leaves or Zoom's hearty barks. He said, "Troy was driving a beige Toyota sedan."

"Did you call this in?" McRae asked Nico.

"No, sir. We didn't. We went out this morning to retrieve that trail camera. Elspeth is wary of law enforcement. Remember?"

"Don't get smart," McRae growled.

Nico fell silent.

Duane picked up the story, speaking rapidly, "My wife is in hospice. She may not survive the week. We were at the hospice this afternoon and my daughter, Carmen, was using the hospice's boardroom to do some school work. She was working with two other college students. The Fickhams showed up. I don't know how they knew we were there. The Fickhams took Carmen and her friend, Jasmine."

"What's Jasmine's last name?" McRae's gray eyes were suddenly hard as granite.

"I'm not sure. I just know she's a student. She's very petite with black hair and dark eyes. The other student with them is named Taz, who got punched but managed to pull a fire alarm. We were able to get on the road behind the Fickhams by following Elspeth," Duane spoke rapidly, "We think my niece, Elspeth, saw the girls being taken from the back of the hospice. Elspeth is in Nico's Jeep and we've been following it on Nico's cell phone. The Jeep stopped just a few minutes ago."

Doubts are more cruel than the worst of truths.
Jean-Baptiste Moliere (1622-1673)

Chapter Thirty

Sunday, 7:35 p.m.
The Fickham Family compound

"**W**ell lookie who Troy found!" Russell had just opened the rear doors to the Suburban. He smiled as the red Jeep with Elspeth and Troy bounced across deep ruts and came to a halt nearby. "We got us a collection."

Carmen had a fierce desire to lash out with her feet in the hopes of connecting with Russell's crotch. She resisted the temptation and lay still. She was too stiff to get on her feet and run and she didn't have any idea of a good path to safety. She satisfied herself with a stare of unrelenting hatred that seemed to amuse Russell even more.

"Ooh, we got a fiery one here," he said. He turned to Ricky Lee and said, "Get some cuffs on the new one. Tate, go get me a couple buckets of water."

Elspeth left her hands on the dashboard, desperately trying to come up with options as Troy kept the knife near her face. She noted it was a full tanged knife as was typical of an expensive blade. That fleeting thought was soon cursed as a complete waste of time because Ricky Lee opened the door to the Jeep. He pulled Elspeth off the seat and yanked her wrists behind her back to snap on handcuffs.

Russell pulled Jasmine out of the Suburban. She swayed a moment before rallying to make a visual sweep from left to right. Towering Douglas firs and moss-covered big-leaf maples rimmed the rutted oval of dirt where the vehicles sat. On the left, a stained yellow mobile home with sagging steps sat surrounded by mounds of wood chips and slash. There was an RV to the right with a thick roof rug of green moss and brown leaves. The drizzle of the day was easing off to some occasional spits of rain.

Russell had her arm in a tight grip. She felt his fingers digging into her upper arm as he yanked her across the parking lot to a tall, bent pipe with a faucet top connected to a black spotted green hose. Jasmine tried to follow Carmen's advice and put her best stupid face on as she gently flexed her fingers. The handcuffs were snug. Her hands became less stiff as she put her fingers through a set of micro-stretches.

Tate Fickham came out of a shed with two five-gallon buckets that he filled at the hose stand. It was an oddly silent tableau as all eyes watched the water pour out of the hose end.

"Not too full!" Russell barked. "About half will do. Leave the buckets there." He rotated back toward the Jeep and said, "Troy, you get a grip on your girl. Ricky Lee, you come get this little one. Me and Tate will take the big girl."

Troy took Elspeth's arm and pulled her forward. "Are we waterboarding 'em, Grandpa?" he asked.

"Nah. That's CIA stuff. We'll just get them a little seasoned," Russell laughed. "Never had three before. It'll be kinda special. Come on." He handed Jasmine over to Ricky Lee. Jasmine stood still and watched as Russell reached in to pull Carmen out of the Suburban.

Jasmine's heart soared as she watched Carmen kick out with one foot. It was her left foot. Her strong foot. Jasmine felt her stomach swoop down in dismay as Russell sidestepped the kick and reached in to slap Carmen. Jasmine heard him say, "I like a challenge, missy. You remember that. I can take you right here and now, so you'd best mind your manners."

Carmen lay still. Tate walked over, gingerly assessing her. Russell scowled and waved his hand forward. Tate put a hand on Carmen's arm and she didn't resist. Russell grabbed her other arm and the two men hoisted Carmen out of the vehicle. She emerged, sandwiched between Russell and Tate, who propelled her forward.

"Mattress shed," Russell barked. "Let's go."

Troy sheathed his knife and tightened his fingers on Elspeth's arms. "Over there."

The young women were marched over the ruts to a dirt trail that ran behind a hillock of Himalayan blackberry vines. A gray shed with two high dirty windows leaned away from what had once been a greenhouse. Carmen eyed the shards of broken glass that shimmered in the dirt. A glass shard might be useful.

Troy and Elspeth reached the shed first. He held on to Elspeth's arm with one hand as he used the other to pull a rusty spike out of a hasp to unlock the shed door. He let go of Elspeth long enough to pull the door open, the door groaning as it moved.

A cold moist cloud of air seeped out of the shed. Troy grinned at Elspeth before pulling her inside. She gasped at the drop in temperature. As her eyes adjusted to the gloom, she saw a large mattress on the plywood floor of the shed. The cover was ripped and stained. Her skin prickled as she registered the jumbled swath of oozing glowing mushrooms that crowded and sprouted from the interior of the mattress. The luminescent mushroom caps had chestnut brown caps that melted to eerie yellow rims. The mushrooms shimmered with shiny goo.

Carmen and Jasmine were shoved inside.

"Against the wall there," Russell said. He turned to Tate and said, "Get the water."

Ricky Lee and Troy stood in the door to the shed, smirking.

"Okay, Ladies," Russell said, "You are going to lose your shoes and your pants. You give us any trouble whatsoever and you will lose a lot more."

Russell stepped back to the sliding door and motioned Ricky Lee and Troy forward. "Get 'em undone."

Carmen and Elspeth exchanged glances. Now was not yet the time to fight. "Comply," murmured Carmen. Jasmine looked up at her with a frightened face that floated like a mask in the darkness.

"Comply," Carmen repeated.

The women stood still as Ricky Lee and Troy pulled off shoes and jerked jeans down and off. Troy gathered the three pairs of pants and slung them over his shoulder. Tate tossed their shoes into a corner of the shed.

Russell picked up a bucket and flung cold water on the women. Jasmine gasped and Elspeth rocked in shock. Carmen tossed her head to scatter the water off of her face. Russell threw a second slosh of water and said, "Alrighty, then. We're gonna go get us some dinner and a few brews. We'll be back later to warm you up."

He threw the buckets down on the ground outside the shed and motioned to Troy to shoulder the door shut. The women heard the rusty spike being slotted into the hasp.

Jasmine was shaking violently. Teeth chattering, she said, "My God, we're going to die of hypothermia."

"The hell we are," Carmen replied.

Outside the shed

Henry Fickham emerged from a thicket of salal and scrolled through his cell phone. The phone video feature had captured the three women being pushed into the shed. Troy's face was clear but he really only had Russell's back. Henry scowled. He wanted footage of Russell most of all.

The setting sun sent slanted rays of light through the woods. The large fir trees were already shadowing the shed. Henry debated whether to go or stay and try for more footage. In the distance he heard the sound of a motorcycle. A bat swooped and flitted over the open area.

The presence of the bat decided Henry. Bats avoided rain. If this bat was out feeding, then it was likely that the lifting clouds would continue to clear. Henry turned up his collar to the evening breeze and sank back into the undergrowth. He would wait and see what happened next.

"It does not matter how slowly you go as long as you do not stop."
Confucius

Chapter Thirty-one

Sunday, 7:50 p.m.
Bloomfield Road

"It's almost eight on a Sunday evening," Duane said, speaking rapidly. "It's getting dark but we'll be able to see well enough for reconnoitering for approximately another forty-five minutes. Normally for an abduction you'd want to bring in a SWAT team but that can take two to three hours to assemble. Maybe more because we're in rural Mason County."

McRae looked over at Detective Raposo. Duane was right.

"Let's go take a look together," Duane said. "Let's see where the Jeep stopped. Nico and I will take direction from you. We don't want anyone hurt. We're unarmed. We don't have short tempers or stupid illusions of grandeur."

"We should leave you here," Raposo said, "and take a look ourselves."

"Zoom can find Elspeth for me," Nico countered. "We've been playing a game called 'find Elspeth' and Zoom is great at it."

"The Fickhams might easily shoot a dog that shows up on their property," Raposo countered.

Nico nodded. "I know — but Zoom is really fast and it might be the quickest way to figure out where Elspeth is."

"We can't wait much longer," Duane said. "That young man on the motorcycle is with us. He's Carmen's new beau. I imagine he's about to circle back and take a look here. If he sees we're being taken in or held up, then he'll likely continue on his own."

"Ah, hell," Raposo grumbled. "I'd rather have you with me than go in without. Don, set these guys loose."

McRae took Duane's handcuffs off first. Duane raised his hands above his head and waved.

A motorcycle revved up in the distance and soon Jed was coasting up to stop by the Civic and the patrol car.

"I know you," McRae said. "Oil spill response team?"

"Yessir. Jed Twanea." He turned to Duane. "There's a dirt drive about half a mile up the road. I got there in time to see a red Jeep disappear around a curve. I figured I'd better hang back until I knew how you wanted to handle this."

Raposo arched an eyebrow and said, "I'm Detective Raposo. Why don't we let me take the lead on organizing this?

Jed looked from Duane to Raposo and back again. Duane gave a quick nod. "Yessir," Jed replied.

"The bike is too loud," Raposo said. "Find a hidey spot for it and you can ride with Deputy McRae and me. We'll all drive up to this turnoff and park the patrol car and the little Civic to block the road. Then we'll walk in. It's about a quarter mile drive with a bend. Right after the bend, it opens up to a compound of junker cars and buildings. We'll go quietly and in a group."

Sunday, 8 p.m.
The Shed

"First, we're all going to pee." Carmen said.

"How do I get my underwear down?" Jasmine asked through her chattering teeth.

"We'll help each other. Once your bottoms are off, just lean back against the wall, spread your legs, and pee. It will reduce the water in your body core. You need to do this to keep your body warm. We should be glad they took our pants because wet cotton jeans contribute to hypothermia."

Jasmine looked at her friend. "We should be *glad* they took our pants?"

"For the moment. Yeah. Trust me."

Jasmine couldn't summon the muscle control to roll her eyes. She shook with shivers as she watched Carmen back up to Elspeth.

It took some considerable contortions for Carmen to drag down Elspeth's panties but then Elspeth leaned against a wall of the shed and ooched down into a squat. She then demonstrated public peeing.

"My mother would just about die if she was here," Jasmine said through chattering teeth.

"Not dying is the whole point," Elspeth replied as she stood up. Carmen backed up to her cousin and the two wrestled Elspeth's underwear back into coverage mode.

"Jasmine, come on. You're freezing. Let's do you," Carmen said. Jasmine's teeth continued to chatter as she followed directions.

"Lean your back against the wall," Carmen said.

"I know. I know."

"Squat," Elspeth said. "Think of a waterfall."

Jasmine felt her urine begin to descend, with some hot splashes hitting her ankles. She did her best to widen her stance and to not splash onto her underwear that sat stretched at half-mast at her knees.

"Wow. I do feel better. Disgusting, but better."

"Me now," Carmen bossed. Her tight underwear and poor balance made the process challenging despite both Elspeth and Jasmine helping.

"I hate having my hands behind my back." Jasmine said. "Is this where I move them to the front?"

"Not yet. We need to make sure they don't check on us. Elspeth, we need to bookend Jasmine. Lean in close." Carmen instructed.

"Right. Friction?"

"Yep." Carmen shoved her bosom against Jasmine's front. "We're going to all be jumping up and down. A lot. You're in the middle and you jump too. Just pretend you're a kid at a favorite band concert in a mosh pit."

"Okay," Jasmine's teeth still chattered a bit. "You really think this will work?"

"Trust us, we're in the survival business." Elspeth replied. "Movement and friction produce warmth." She looked at her cousin. "Is your ankle going to hold up to jumping?"

"One way to find out," Carmen replied.

"Don't break anything," Elspeth warned.

Carmen's sudden grin flashed white in the gloom. "Worries are for wusses."

"Uncle Duane never says that."

"He does say you have do what you have to do. Come on. Two, four, six, eight," chanted Carmen as she began jumping.

"Who do we appreciate?" Elspeth chanted back.

"3D! 3D! 3D! Survival!" Carmen and Elspeth whispers were fierce as they jumped.

Jasmine began jumping up and down, thinking the cold shed was hosting the weirdest cheerleading squad ever.

Sunday, 8 p.m.
The Sutherland home

Richard Sutherland slammed a fist on the desk. "No! God damn it! No!" as his computer screen went dark. He knew exactly what had happened. He had heard a small boom moments before. Yet another squirrel had investigated the corner transformer box and had met an electrical demise.

It was infuriating. The electrical grid was supposed to be able to handle short interruptions. A squirrel could complete an electrical circuit when it touched the energized transformer near the top of the utility pole while still standing on a grounded element, like an incoming wire. What was supposed to happen was an instantly fried squirrel dropping to the ground followed by a resumption of energy flow. But three times in the last year there had been a 'continuous fault' as the electrified squirrel remained aloft, continuing to arc electricity until the system shut down.

Richard furiously rolled his wheelchair down the hall toward the kitchen. With the power out, he had to use the wall phone in the kitchen to call the utility company. His cordless phone from the office was useless. This time he would insist that the company place a barrier around the transformer. This interruption of his work was unbearable.

He checked his watch. Lucinda was still gone. She had better had left some dinner. He was hungry and in no mood to heat some soup.

The Shed

Carmen and Elspeth were breathless by the time Jasmine quit shivering.

"We're not done," Carmen said. "Let's march." Her handcuffed arms ached ferociously as she began stepping in place.

"Right," Elspeth said. "Lift those knees. We march and reconnoiter."

"Reconnoiter? Do you always talk like Marines?" Jasmine asked.

"Rangers!" Carmen and Elspeth said in unison.

"What did you mean when you said you were in the survival business?" Jasmine asked.

"My Dad runs a survivalist gear business. We're his sales help," Carmen explained. "He gives lots of seminars and demonstrations."

"We may not be Rangers ourselves," Elspeth said, "But you can't listen to hours of demos without learning something."

"So, now we march around our space and reconnoiter," Carmen said.

The shed was only the length of small garage and the slanting light of the cloud-covered and setting sun coming through the two high windows barely illuminated the space. The women marched in place for a moment before shifting apart. Carmen marched over to the mushroom-filled mattress with Jasmine following. The floor of the shed sagged from rim to center.

"I know these mushrooms," Jasmine huffed. Her pale face continued to look pinched although she no longer shivered. "Waxy caps. They are a complex group that is currently under revision."

"Keep marching," Carmen ordered.

"Keep talking," Elspeth said. "It will calm our brains and then we can make a plan."

"Okay. Some waxy caps make slime. You can see all the ooze on the mushroom caps and stems. Everyone thought," Jasmine paused and inhaled. She lifted her knees high as she marched in place. She continued, "That there were dull-colored waxy caps in the genus *Hygrophorus* and colorful waxy caps in the genus *Hygrocybe*." She inhaled again and said, "Then someone started looking at the DNA and it was clear that there were all sorts of things that looked alike on the outside but were worlds different inside."

"A big deal?" Elspeth asked.

"Huge. Mycologically speaking. The colors of the mushroom tell us something about what the DNA is doing. Red means there might be betalain, which is the same compound that gives beets a red color. My grandfather is really interested in red colorings." Jasmine's heart pinched as she thought of her grandfather. She shook her head and refocused on the mushrooms in front of her. "I don't think these have betalain."

"They are really chrome yellow and brown. Wouldn't that be red mixed with yellow and then add some blue?"

"I don't think plant colors work exactly like paint mixing. I think these might be a type of parrot mushroom, which is a break out from the colorful *Hygrocybe*. The *Gliophorus psittacinus* is the classic parrot mushroom, but those are usually green — you'll know them when you see them because they are an eerie mushroom —- a glowing, glistening fungi that is really cool to see in the woods."

"Can we eat these?" Carmen asked.

"Oh, we can eat them. The question is can we survive them." Jamine stopped marching and smiled. "Old mycology joke. I think these might be edible — if I have the genus right. I think we're better off going hungry. "

"I'm not risking it," Elspeth said firmly. "Let's do an asset list so we don't have to think about foraging."

"Right," agreed Carmen. "We have . . . three women in handcuffs without pants."

"They left our shoes." Elspeth countered. "We have a disgusting mattress with slimy mushrooms."

"No cell phones," Jasmine said. "Do you think our phones are still out in that Suburban?"

"Hard to say," Carmen replied.

"Troy took my cell phone and threw it in the bushes near the turn off to the drive," Elspeth said. She couldn't keep a quiver out of her voice.

Carmen looked at her cousin, concern on her face. She said, firmly, "We'll get it back eventually. Right now a cell phone is not a great tool. We shouldn't depend on them. They might not have battery power, they might not have a signal and help will take too long to get here." She turned toward Elspeth. "You drove in, right?"

"Yes. We're on the Kamilche peninsula. The road in from the asphalt is dirt and gravel with some bends in it. It's about a quarter mile to the asphalt. I didn't see any houses close by."

"If one of us gets to the asphalt, there's a chance of getting picked up?"

"I think so. Eventually. We might also be able to see a house light off in the distance once it's dark."

"Keys to the Jeep?" Carmen asked.

"Troy took them."

"Okay. We need to think our way out of this."

Jasmine knelt down to peer at the bed of mushrooms. The caps moistly reflected the last of the day's light with a chrome yellow glow. "I have a theory. The floor joists are at least somewhat rotted away. The weight of the mattress must have pushed the plywood flooring down to be in contact with the earth," she said. "The floor rotted through and the mycelium and mushrooms came up through the mattress. It must have taken years."

"Maybe decades," Elspeth said. "So gross." She shook her head. "There is no way I'm having sex on that. Not with Troy or any of those losers. Come on, Jasmine. Think!"

"I am thinking!" she protested. "So this shed has been here a long time. There's fungal growth through the floor. Can we escape through the floor?"

"No," Carmen replied. "We were on the floor next to the wall and it was solid there. What about wood rot in the exterior walls?"

"Brown rot or white rot?"

"I don't think it matters!"

Elspeth backed up to one wall. "We don't want to kick walls with our toes. We should use our heels." She began testing one of the shed's vertical wallboards by swinging her heel back. "How's your ankle?" she asked Carmen.

"Hurts a bit," Carmen admitted.

234

"Then let me and Jasmine do this."

Jasmine backed up to a wall and began tapping the boards with one heel.

"We left off one thing on our asset list," said Carmen over the heel thumping.

"What's that?" Jasmine asked.

"My father. You know he's coming."

Gliophorus
psittacinus

235

"A mouse does not rely on just one hole."
Titus Maccius Plautus (254 -184 BCE)

Chapter Thirty-Two

Sunday, 8:20 p.m.
On the road

McRae parked the patrol car across the turn off to the Fickham compound. Nico slanted the Civic in next to the patrol car to block the road. He clipped a leash onto Zoom's collar before opening the door. She leapt across his lap and out into the cool evening air.

The rain had stopped and the clouds were lifting, leaving the washed air rich with the smells of earth, firs and ferns. Zoom squatted, peed, and then danced at the end of the leash. Her auburn coat flashed with gold streaks in the diminishing light.

Raposo leaned into the trunk of the patrol car and pulled out a black shotgun.

Duane watched, his fingers flexing.

Raposo looked at Duane and reconsidered. He stored the shotgun back in the trunk. "We'll do this without any big guns," said Detective Raposo to McRae. The detective turned to Duane and said, "We're walking in. We're taking a look as we go. If we can, we're having a conversation. You are not a deputy and you are not being deputized. We are conducting a search for three missing women but we do not have a search warrant."

Jed took a step to the right and leaned against a Douglas fir, crossing his arms and pushing out his elbows.

Raposo chose to see Jed and not the small, worn "No Trespassing" sign behind the young man that dangled from one nail driven into the tree.

"Deputy McRae and I will go first," Raposo said. "Duane, you and Nico and the dog follow us. Jed, you are behind them. Any sign of trouble, and you turn around and get the hell out of here. Agreed?"

He took in the quick nods and said, "Let's go."

The Shed

Elspeth's heels were already aching. Jasmine was thumping her heel against the wooden walls with enthusiasm. So far the walls seemed to be solid.

"Think!" Elspeth demanded of her overwrought brain. She stopped kicking the boards behind her and stood for moment. Although her eyes had adjusted to the low light, she knew it would not be long before the shadows in the shed turned completely dark.

"Moisture. We need to find any really wet spot," Elspeth said out loud. Jasmine stopped kicking to listen as the cousins discussed moisture.

Carmen said, "We've got to find where the wood touches the dirt or where there might be a leak."

"There!" said Jasmine. "Beyond the mattress, I saw a water stain."

The women crowded around the mattress and Elspeth leaned against the wall to bring her heel down hard on the stained board. The board vibrated and her heel sank into the board.

"Yes!" Carmen looked to Jasmine. "Can you drop your hands and wiggle your rear end through your arms? This will be a lot easier if your hands are in front."

"Right." Jasmine knelt down on the floor and made quick work of bringing her hands to the front. "That's not so hard."

"I think I hate you," Carmen said. She turned to her cousin and said, "Can you step through your cuffs?"

"I don't know," Elspeth replied. "Remember, I couldn't do it when we tried it with Uncle Duane."

"You came close. Try."

Elspeth knelt down near the soft board and pushed her hands down, straining to bring the handcuffs around her bottom. The metal rings bit into her wrists. "Ow."

Jasmine began working on the soft board with her fingernails. The board crumbled slowly into small fragments. "Brown rot," she said. "Huh. As wet as this board is, I would have thought white rot to be more likely. Smells like licorice. No fruiting bodies, but I think this must be that *Neolentinus* fungus."

"Not the time, Jasmine! Faster!" Carmen said.

Jasmine continued to tear at the board while Elspeth tried again to bring her cuffed hands to the front. This time she could feel the handcuffs gouging into her wrists. She was close to putting her rear through the loop of her arms. Again she failed as the pain of the handcuffs on her wrists and the ache of her shoulders screamed through her system.

Outside, in the gloaming, Henry Fickham waited in an arbor of evergreen huckleberry and arching Indian plum. His eyes caught a flicker of action near one corner of the shed. Something was moving near the ground level. Henry craned left to get a better look. He could see small pale fingers tearing at a gap at the bottom of a vertical board.

Henry raised an eyebrow. At least one of the women was fighting back. She might actually be able to tear her way out of the old shed.

He found he approved of this development. How much more fitting it would be for his father and half-brother and miserable nephews to be brought down by a girl. He had some photos. He would use them if need be. If the girl escaped, then it would be best if he were far from here.

Henry looked at the mobile home and checked his watch. It would be closer to nine before his father had enough food and liquor to come back to the women. His father, brutal as he was, still had a consistency about him. Nine to ten was his most rapacious hour.

It was best to go. Henry stood up and stepped out of the undergrowth. He silently crossed the rutted parking lot to stand by the shed. He could hear some muffled kicking and then he saw small fingers again prying bits off at the base of a board. Another rotten sliver split loose and fell.

The girl could use some tools. Henry smiled at the thought. He reached into his back pants pocket and retrieved the screwdriver he had liberated from Sutherland's garage. He leaned forward and dropped the screwdriver next to the small fingers.

He stepped back and soft footed away. It was time to go. He needed to be with Lucinda.

The Sutherland Home

Richard Sutherland scowled. It wasn't fair. The power would be out for an hour or more. He was hungry. He needed his meds. Where was Lucinda?

It was his work that had paid for this house. He had given her shelter for years. He had allowed her a lover — more than once. The least she could do is make sure his health needs were met. He hated the weakness in his legs. At the moment he hated his wife even more.

Seething, he picked up the receiver to the landline phone. He stabbed out the sequence to Lucinda's cell phone and irritably shifted his aching body as he waited for her to answer. There were times when no position was comfortable. The deep cushion pad on the wheelchair was cutting off his circulation. His back hurt.

"Hello, dear," she said.

"Where are you?" Richard snarled.

"Finishing some work," she said. "I'm at a coffee house. Spreadsheets are impossible without coffee."

"The power is out. Another squirrel in the transformer."

"Oh. Well, I should stay here then."

"What about dinner?"

"Could you make yourself some soup?"

"We had soup at lunch," Richard shouted. "I am God Damned tired of soup!"

"Richard, you really need to learn to manage some of these things yourself." Lucinda sighed, adding a small tone of disappointment.

Her tone, no doubt, was meant to make him angry. It was time to remind her of who was boss.

"I could sink you," Richard told her. "You and that Henry. You could go to jail for years. I'd get a good attorney and the jury would see that you manipulated me. I'm helpless and you used me. Think on that, Lucinda."

"Don't get upset," Lucinda said. "I'm sure we can work this out. Tell you what — why don't you have a little snack and I'll finish here. I'll pick up some Thai food on the way home. I think you'd manage the red curry if we cut the chicken pieces a bit smaller."

Richard thought a moment. Red curry sounded delicious. "How long will it take you?"

"Oh, a bit. I'll be there by nine. I'm sure you can find a nibble to help you last until then. In fact, if you look around, you'll see I left you some chocolate pudding."

"Where is it?"

"In the fridge. A nice bowl of pudding."

"All right then."

"See you in a bit," Lucinda said. "I promise."

"Every man is the architect of his own future."
Sallust (86- 35 BCE)

Chapter Thirty-Three

Sunday, 8:35 p.m.
The Shed

"I have a screwdriver!" Jasmine called. "There was a clunk and there it was."

Carmen knelt beside Jasmine and whistled. "Someone wants to help us."

"Help us!" Elspeth shouted. "Anyone out there? Help us!"

The women fell silent and heard only the wind in the firs. Jasmine picked up the screwdriver and attacked the rotten board. Her second blow drove the tip of the screwdriver half an inch into the wood, which let her pry off a large sliver. "I'm making progress now."

Elspeth knelt on Jasmine's left and said, "We might be able to push the board with our feet."

"Let me," Carmen said. "I've got the strongest thighs."

"What about your ankle?" Elspeth asked.

"It's alright." Carmen wiggled herself in front of the rotten board until her rear almost touched the wall before lying down on the dirty floor. "I'm going to put my feet on the board and push into a leg extension," she said. "You two put your knees behind my shoulders so I don't slide. We want all the force going out."

Once in position, Carmen inhaled and pushed. She could feel where the softness of the board changed to solid wood, so she shifted her feet to just below the solidness. She exhaled, inhaled deeply and pushed.

The board bottom bent and splintered.

Jasmine scrambled over to the gap and cheered. "Almost enough!"

"You can get through that space?" Elspeth asked.

"I think so. I'll do it like childbirth," Jasmine said as she stabbed the next board to widen the gap. "My head, one shoulder, then the other shoulder. If I can get that far, the rest of me can slip out. My shoulders are the widest part of my body."

"I think I hate you," Elspeth and Carmen said in unison.

Jasmine's next blow on the second board again penetrated deeply. She leaned on the handle and pried off another wide sliver.

Elspeth tried again to bring her cuffed hands around her bottom. Again the metal rings bit viciously into her wrists.

The women heard a distant creak as the door on the mobile home opened and Russell's voice came booming through the dusk. "Tate! Besides the beer, fetch that lubricant tube from the truck and check on the girls."

Jasmine used her handcuffed hands to drive the screwdriver into the wood with the fury of a starving sapsucker.

Elspeth muttered, "lubrication." She stood up, walked across the flexing plywood floor to step onto the mattress. She took a deep breath and lay down on the bed of glowing mushrooms.

"What are you doing?" Carmen struggled to her feet and watched her cousin squirm in the oozing swath of mushrooms.

"Getting slimed," Elspeth said. "I need some slickness to get my hands to the front. I may have to get out of here fast. But right now we need to sit together in front of the hole." Elspeth rolled to her knees and staggered to a stand. "We need to be sitting like we're too scared to fight when Tate opens the door."

"I'd rather kick his ass!" Carmen argued.

"No!" Elspeth hissed. "We pick a fight with Tate and the others will be out here. It's better if Tate checks on us and goes away. But we do need to be ready to move fast once Tate is gone. We're running out of time."

Jasmine had her face next to the hole in the board and said, "Elspeth's right. Hurry. He's on his way here." She rocked back on her heels and scrambled into a cross-legged sit.

"Fix your hands. Move over. My ass is a bigger screen." Carmen sat down with her back to the hole as Jasmine slid her cuffed hands around her feet and around her hips.

"God, you are gross, Elspeth," Carmen complained as Elspeth took position next to her.

"You could try and be a little nicer," Elspeth grumbled. "If being slimy gets my hands to the front, then rolling in the mushrooms was a piece of brilliance."

Carmen snorted.

"Shhush!" Jasmine said as they heard the iron spike being lifted from the door hasp.

Tate Fickham pulled the door open. He had a cardboard twelve pack of beer dangling from one hand and a headlamp on. He swung his head from right to left with a dancing arc of light before seeing the women crouched together by the south wall. "Huh. Why are you over there?"

"I'm so c-c-c- cold," Jasmine whimpered.

"We'll come warm you up after a while," Tate grinned. He retreated, pulling the door shut and dropping the spike back into the hasp.

The women waited in silence as his footsteps receded.

Jasmine said, "And the Oscar for best actress goes to Ms. Jasmine Oh."

"Right, " Carmen said. "Let's move."

* * *

Sunday, 8:35 p.m.
On the road

Nico glanced at Duane as they walked down the long drive. Duane moved down the road with an easy, ground eating stride. The only signs of distress Nico could see were an occasional bulge in the muscles along Duane's jawline and the occasional flexing of fingers. An early rising moon provided moments of illumination as they passed towering firs. Duane's contracting jaw muscles were almost invisible, but Nico caught the tension when the group halted at the bend in the road that led into the Fickham compound.

Zoom chose this moment to hit the end of the leash with enthusiasm. Nico scrambled to keep her under control.

"Keep her still," Raposo growled.

"She may be smelling Elspeth," Nico said.

"Alright then," Raposo said. "Here's what we'll do. We'll advance together. When we get to the open area where the cars are parked, I'll give a shout identifying ourselves. It will be best if we can talk our way in. If we're not making progress, let the dog loose. You can make it look accidental. Nico, you and Jed follow the dog. Dwerryhouse, you stick with McRae and me. Everybody be alert and keep a thought out of where you're going to leap for cover if this gets interesting."

"Mr. Dwerryhouse," Nico said, "Are you okay?"

"Yes, sir," Duane replied. He inhaled and carefully said, "I am ready."

* * *

In the Shed

Russell's shouted instructions saved Henry. He was next to a large cedar and about to step onto the long dirt driveway when he heard his father's bellow directions at Tate. Henry stepped behind the cedar and crouched behind the trunk to the embrace of the undergrowth.

He peered through the fronds of a sword fern to see that Tate was headed to the Suburban. He rotated his head and shifted to look down the long dirt road. He saw a group of men and a dog in the distance. The wind was at their backs. The breeze came whistling through the understory to caress his face. The dog had not scented him yet and the wind was unlikely to change direction quickly. Henry sat very still. The early rising moon cast enough light to reflect off the badge on Don McRae's chest. Henry blinked. The law was here already.

Henry studied the rest of the group as they moved through a slice of moonlight. In addition to the lean man in uniform, there were two older men, one tall, the other middle height, both muscular, and two young men who did not look like law enforcement but still represented trouble. The dog looked to be an Irish setter who might be friendly enough. The dog, however was the biggest threat to his secrecy.

Henry contemplated his boot knife. Could he kill the dog quickly? Not likely.

It was best to remain still and hope the breeze persisted. As long as he stayed quiet and downwind, he might remain undetected. Intuitively, he knew the men were not after him. They were hunting for the girls.

Henry thought about the cream Lexus. It was just off the asphalt at the perimeter of the property. If the men had come from the east on Bloomfield Road, then they probably had left their vehicles at the start of the Fickham's road, perhaps blocking the road. They would not have seen the Lexus

That made sense. This exit was blocked, but his Lexus was further west. If he could reach the Lexus, he could drive out to Kamilche Road and make for the highway.

Henry made up his mind. He would sit still and let the men and dog pass. If he was lucky, they would soon be involved with his family and that's when he would sprint for his car.

Do not be too timid and squeamish about your actions.
All life is an experiment.
Ralph Waldo Emerson (1803-1882)

Chapter Thirty-Four

Sunday, 8:40 p.m.
The Shed

Elspeth struggled to keep from throwing up. Her mind had been busy with getting Jasmine warm and finding an escape point but now the horror of Troy and Russell Fickham returning had her swallowing hard.

"I'm sorry," she said to her cousin.

"For what?"

"I'm the reason we're here. Troy wanted me."

"So he's a goober, a shithead and a man with excellent tastes."

Elspeth was surprised by the laugh that burst from her lips. "Thanks."

"Let's get going," Carmen commanded, rolling to her knees.

Jasmine easily brought her hands around her bottom a second time. She scrambled across the dipping floor and found her shoes. She slipped on her shoes quickly, but struggled to tie the laces with her hands cuffed. "I'm ready," she said finally.

"Great," replied Elspeth. "Take a good look before you go across the parking area. It's rough all the way to the drive. You might want to circle around the parking area. The dirt road will bend right and eventually it takes you out to a paved road." She paused, trying to remember the drive in. "You'll want to go right, or east, on the asphalt. Look for a light."

"I'll jump up and down on the road if I see a car," Jasmine said. "Most people will stop for a girl in her underwear."

Jasmine knelt down at the hole in the wall, slipped her head through the gap and began to squirm. A section of the next board began to give. It crumbled as Jasmine dug into the floor with her toes and shoved.

A moment later she had one shoulder through and the rest of her soon followed.

She scrambled to her feet and looked around. The buildings and vehicles loomed as black shapes in a dark gray landscape. A light glowed from inside the mobile home, illuminating the head and shoulders of Ricky Lee Fickham as he watched television. A feeble porch light shone on the sagging wooden steps and front door.

Bats crisscrossed overhead.

Jasmine bent down and whispered through the hole, "I'll get help as fast as I can."

Carmen turned to her cousin. "The hole is a little bigger. Can you get through?"

"Maybe. I've got to get my hands to the front first." Elspeth stood up and shuffled away from Carmen. "I think I need more mushroom goo."

"Gross."

Elspeth's foot hit the edge of the mattress. "It's all organic."

"Very funny."

"Ugh. I agree. This is gross." Elspeth laid full length on the mattress and writhed. She did her best to make her outer thighs and inner arms make contact with the viscous mushroom caps.

"Here goes." Elspeth threw her head back into the mushrooms and pushed her cuffed hands down around her bottom. She strained as the cuffs bit into her wrists. She thought of Troy coming back and forcing sex on her on the remains of this mattress. That image made her dig in her heels and push.

The moment of victory was distinct. One second her shoulders and wrists were on fire and then, with a sticky slide, her bottom was through the loop of her arms. She curled up and brought her handcuffed hands around her feet and to her front.

"Did it!"

Carmen's teeth flashed in the dark. "You rock!"

Sunday, 8:42 p.m.
In the mobile home

Troy finished his beer and felt the warm satisfaction of the third beer buzz. He studied his father. Ricky Lee was watching a game show with the eagerness of a child. Ricky Lee thought he was a genius if he could get one answer right.

His father was a disappointment. Now, his Uncle Henry had spine. Henry had cold nerve. Henry came up short with women, Troy decided. He didn't have an appetite for dominance. No one was going to respect a man who didn't insist on respect.

Ricky Lee, now there was someone who craved respect and had no talent for getting it. His brother, Tate, was the same.

His grandfather was the full package. Russell was currently a six-pack into relaxing and power oozed from every pore. His grandfather terrified the hell out of Troy. You had to respect that.

Russell shifted in the recliner and reached for the beer, asking, "Tate, how were the girls?"

"Cold."

"They sittin' in the same place?"

"Nah. They were over on the south side. One of them had already been on the mattress. Can you believe it? Troy's girl had bits of mushrooms in her hair. Smashed the hell out of the mushrooms too."

Troy smiled. Elspeth had given in. She had already tried the mattress. He felt his prick swell. It was going to be a fine night.

Russell didn't see it the same. He set down his beer. "I'm not liking the sound of that. Gimme that head lamp. Troy, you and me need to go take a look."

Sunday, 8:44 p.m.
The Shed

Elspeth pulled on the rotten board. Her shoulders rejoiced with the opportunity to move forward. The handcuffs still were a misery with an intermediate stinging as the metal rings shifted in and out of contact with the gouges on her wrists.

The board gave a bit.

She said, "I don't think the rot goes any higher. It's nailed about a foot up. I think I can yank on the board and get it to split at the nails."

"Go for it," Carmen said.

Elspeth braced her feet and pulled on the board. It bent slightly.

"I need to find my shoes. I need more traction."

"Over here," Carmen said. "Can you help me get mine on too?"

Elspeth knelt and helped Carmen guide her toes into the sneakers. Pulling up the slack in the laces, she said, "I still don't get why there's brown rot when the wood is so damp."

"The board is probably a softwood," Carmen grunted as she shifted to relieve the ache in her shoulders. "An evergreen with needles, like a pine or Douglas fir. The brown rot fungus can de-methylate the lignins but it leaves most of the lignin in place."

"Taking methyls group out?"

"Yep. If it were white rot, then we'd suspect the board was a hardwood from a deciduous tree like maple. The fungal path matches the growth structure of the tree. Wood from deciduous trees get white rot, evergreens get brown rot."

"I am so taking chemistry and botany this fall," Elspeth said. She rose and moved back to the rotting board. "In fact, I think I'll earn a God-damned Ph.D. Maybe two of them. Mycology and nutrition." She yanked on the board. It bent slightly.

"Dr. Dwerryhouse. Sounds good." Carmen struggled to her feet. "Or Dr. Elspeth Pavlopoulos. That works too. I can be the maid of honor."

"Works for me. I'll let Nico know. First step is getting the hell out of here." Elspeth anchored her feet. She brought her cuffed hands to the rim of the rotten board and heaved.

The board bent, quivered and then snapped with a loud crack.

Russell and Troy Fickham were at the bottom of the mobile home stairs when they heard the board crack. Russell shouted, "Ricky Lee! Get out here! The girls are getting out!" as he sprinted for shed.

Inside the shed, Elspeth heard the shout. She dove for the gap in the wall, saying, "Oh, my God! I'm not sure I'll fit!"

"Go!" Carmen directed. "Turn around. For you, feet first. Boobs push up better than down."

Elspeth squirmed through the gap, rapidly wiggling her hips through. She stuck at the chest level.

Carmen ran over, turned her back to Elspeth and shoved her handcuffed hands next to Elspeth's spine. Carmen dug her fingers into the next board and pulled. A two-inch wide strip cracked off and Elspeth slid through the hole just as they heard the rasp of the iron spike being lifted out of the door hasp.

Sunday, 8:48 p.m.
Outside the Shed

Jasmine spent several minutes stuck in an agony of indecision. She had moved away from the shed with speed only to pause at the edge of the rough parking area. She decided it was wiser to circle the open patch and take to the road once beyond the view from the mobile home's rickety porch.

She picked her way around the perimeter, carefully stepping over the tongue of a boat trailer right into a tangle of Himalayan blackberry vines. The vines caught her bare legs, inflicting stinging slices around her ankles. She bit her lower lip to keep from crying out.

A steady breeze raised goose bumps on her bare legs. Jasmine clenched her jaw to keep teeth chattering at bay. As soon as she reached the long dirt road she could run. That would help.

When Jasmine finally navigated a semi-circle around the parking area she froze. Just ahead of her, the shadow of a man moved toward a large tree. He rounded the tree and disappeared into the salal. With some squinting, Jasmine picked out the shape of his head jutting just above the salal.

It was impossible to tell if he were friend or foe. Why would he be a friend? It was bizarre that a screwdriver had shown up near her fingers just when she needed a tool, but if this man had helped her, why hadn't he just opened the shed door?

Jasmine crouched behind the remains of an ancient enamel tub that had once been part of a wringer washer. A lonely snow-white trillium bobbed in the evening breeze next to the washer barrel.

She would wait and watch the man before trying to move past him.

The door to the mobile home opened and two of the captors emerged into the dim light of a single bulb porch light. She saw the large old man turn on his headlamp and the young man with the red ball cap followed with a long black flashlight in his hand. The long flashlight looked as long and heavy as a cop's baton.

The sound of a splintering board sliced through the night, followed by Russell's shouting and rambling run. Jasmine flattened onto the ground, her heart thudding like an engine. Russell and his grandson were to her right. The unknown man was to her left. The dark woods were behind her, the high branches of the towering firs showing as inky lace against the moonlit sky as the ground shrubs fused into a bank of blackness. She drew in a shaky breath.

She had no idea which way to run.

Sunday, 8:50 p.m.
On the Road

Zoom pulled strenuously at the leash, dragging Nico behind her on an ankle-twisting ski down the last of the driveway.

Henry concentrated on sitting still. He worked to keep his breathing quiet and measured.

At Russell's shout, one of the men said, "Let's go!" They surged forward at a run. Zoom yanked to right as they passed the large cedar tree. Nico unsnapped her lead and said, "Elspeth! Find Elspeth!"

The big red setter raced through the salal to far side of the cedar tree. Nico swore and shouted, "Come on, girl! Find Elspeth!"

Zoom gave Henry Fickham's face a lick before she darted away to obey.

Henry smiled as the big dog crashed through the salal and ferns. Only he and the dog would ever know how close he had just come to being under the big feet of the law.

He slid around the base of the cedar and crawled under an evergreen huckleberry bush to reach the edge of the dirt road. Henry emerged from the arboreal shadows and began to run.

We will either find a way or make one.
Hannibal (247- 182 BCE)

Chapter Thirty-Five

Sunday, 9 p.m.
The Shed

Carmen threw a quick look at the gap in the shed wall. Elspeth had barely made it through. There was no way her bigger body was going through that narrow slot. Carmen turned to face the shed door, rapidly running through her assets. No pants. She had her shoes on. Her hands were still stuck behind her back.

She would have to use her head. Not to think but as a weapon.

Russell Fickham's giant bulk appeared in silhouette as he pulled the shed door open.

Carmen swallowed, hard. The old man was over a foot taller than she. As big as she felt she was, Russell outweighed her by a hundred pounds or more.

"Troy!" he boomed. "There's a hole in the wall. Two of them are gone! Get around back! Find them."

Carmen heard Nico's shouted command to Zoom. So did Russell Fickham.

Russell leapt into the darkness of the shed. He swung the door shut and pulled out his knife. He turned to locate Carmen and then he smiled at her as he reached up and turned off his headlamp.

Carmen stood frozen with terror as Russell spoke to her. He said, "Be a smart girl. Come to me. Come to me now and I won't hurt you. If I have to find you, girlie, I'm gonna hurt you bad."

His voice was mesmerizing. Russell had a compelling voice with a seductive tone. Against her will, Carmen could feel part of her psyche wanting to please him. Her brain action was flat-lined with fear. Alternatives that should be presenting themselves hovered outside her mental grasp.

The interior of the shed was now pitch black. The mattress was obscured by shadows as the high dingy windows brought in only a little moonlight. The waxy yellow mushrooms glowed in the darkness. Carmen barely made out the silhouette of Russell's head as he stood between her and the door.

"Be smart, girlie," Russell crooned. "Come to me now."

Carmen was saved by a spasm that started in her arms and coursed through her body with a tooth-rattling wave. She instantly was reminded that she had missed her six p.m. prescription medication. The powerful drug that had caused her so much misery was not one that could be abandoned 'cold turkey.' It had to be stepped down gradually over weeks with full doses tapering to half-doses and half-doses moving to quarter-doses. Her body responded with spasms when the progression was interrupted.

The brutal spasm pissed her off. She was thirty pounds overweight, standing bare legged in underwear, handcuffed and facing an enormous, knife-wielding psychopath in a gloomy shed. She hadn't had a chance to meet with Jed and her biology project was going to be late. A second spasm rolled up her body. It was about time she got a fucking break.

She did the one thing Russell did not expect.

Carmen attacked.

She ran across the open floor of the shed, lowering her head to ram Russell in the stomach. He careened back and slammed into the wall, slashing with his knife as he crashed.

The knife skittered off Carmen's shoulder as she leapt back into the darkness.

Russell jumped up with a startling speed and stood in front of the door. "You can't get out past me. You're being foolish and now I'm gonna hurt you bad."

"You can't get away," Carmen shouted. "Give up already!"

Russell's stained teeth flickered in the dark. He crooned, "I can make a deal, baby. You are my ticket out of here. We just need to get to know each other a little better."

Sunday 9:02 p.m.
The Parking Area

Raposo did a quick scan of the parking area and saw that the door to the mobile home was open.

Zoom went charging around the gray barn to the right of the mobile home. Nico and Jed ran after the dog. That worked for the detective. The two young men would be out of harm's way, he hoped, as he and McRae checked out the Fickhams.

McRae was already charging up the steps of the mobile home as the door swung open further, revealing the beer bleary face of Ricky Lee who was holding a shotgun. McRae stiff-armed the door as Ricky Lee blinked and shifted to shut the door. McRae shot out his hands to grab Ricky Lee's shoulders and he spun the drunk around, slamming Ricky Lee's face into the faux wood paneling. McRae kept the pressure on as he reached around and took the shotgun from Ricky Lee's right hand.

Detective Raposo stepped in and took the shotgun from McRae

"You have the right to remain silent," McRae began as he wrested Ricky Lee's hands into handcuffs.

Duane came up the steps and moved into the shabby living room. He moved next to Tate Fickham who was flat out in a recliner with earphones on and his eyes closed. Duane took up a stance that was both still and ominous as Tate brought a smoking spliff to his lips, eyes still closed.

Raposo set the shotgun into a wall rack before stepping forward to gently tap Tate on the shoulder. Tate's eyes flew open and he focused with horror on Raposo's hound-dog face. Raposo crooked a finger and Tate swung the foot piece of the recliner down before gingerly standing up. Raposo reached over and pulled off the headphones.

"Set down the smoke," Raposo ordered. "You know the drill."

Tate looked over Raposo's shoulder and saw Duane Dwerryhouse's taut, dangerous face. Tate looked back at the detective and said, "You bet. No problem."

"Son," Raposo said, "I'm calling in for some backup. This place is about to be swarming with the law. I want you to start thinking hard about your future."

Sunday, 9:04 p.m.
On the road

Jasmine flattened into the ankle-high plants that grew behind the old washing machine drum. The unfrozen part of her brain told her the plants were the tri-lobed vanilla leaf, *Achlys triphylla*. Her analysis skittered back from the other common name for the plant, which was "sweet after death."

She heard the rush of feet and someone command, "Find Elspeth!" but she wasn't sure who was calling. She had heard of gangs of people who sold women into sexual slavery, keeping the women brainwashed and brutalized through drugs, rape and intimidation. She didn't know how many people were part of the Fickham gang. It was best to stay hidden.

She heard the whap of the mobile home door open. By the time Jasmine cautiously raised her head to peer through the darkness, McRae was already inside. She only saw the civilian backside of blue-jeaned and golf-shirted Duane

Dwerryhouse as he entered the home, poorly lit by a weak porch light.

Jasmine looked to her left. The man who had been hiding behind the cedar was rising. He went slinking around the tree trunk before disappearing into the murky brush. Jasmine crept to her left, moving as quietly as she could before crawling forward a few feet. She saw the shadow of Henry Fickham as he emerged from the undergrowth. She watched as he glanced toward the mobile home and then pivoted to run down the long dirt drive.

That looked like a wise choice. Jasmine shivered. The April night was morphing from cool to cold. If she didn't start moving, the horrible shivering of hypothermia would begin again. Jasmine made up her mind. She would stick to their original plan and try and find the next house where someone was home. She rose from her hiding place, stepped carefully around the junk pile and began to run after Henry Fickham.

Sunday, 9:04 p.m.
The Bog

Elspeth winced. The scrapes from shoving herself through the gap in the shed wall ran the length of her body. Despite the stinging skin, she needed to move. Now. She had told Jasmine to scout out the parking area and then circle around the vehicles before making for the dirt road. That had been her plan as well.

Russell's shout changed her plans. She scurried around the back of the shed. The rising moon cast a watery light on a footpath that led into a swath of sword ferns. Elspeth fled down the path, hoping she could find a place to hide.

A large, mossy log beckoned with its six-foot circle of roots sticking up like a plate jammed sideways in a dishwashing rack.

She wasn't very far from the shed. She could hear Russell's shouted directions to Troy. Chest heaving, Elspeth plunged on.

The path was barely a foot wide and was slick with wet moss. She heard a chorus of frogs. There had to be a stream or pond nearby.

Elspeth stopped, a stitch in her side triggering spasms of pain. She had to be careful now. If the frogs fell silent with her approach, it could tip off her followers as to her location.

She took three deep, steadying breathes and took two small steps forward.

Suddenly the ground became soggy. Moments later the trail turned left before a sheen of black water. The trail wandered in an S-curve and disappeared into ranks of spiky sedges.

Elspeth came to a halt. Going into the water would be a bad idea. Although she was a strong swimmer, there was no way she could count on her ability to kick to keep her afloat with her hands still cuffed. She also would not be able to discern the depth of the water. All around her, silence descended. The frogs had noted her arrival.

She turned and raced back down the trail until she was next to the fallen tree. She saw Troy's bobbing headlamp coming down the trail as she dove behind the upended root ball. She nearly brained herself on a tough projection from the log.

"Shelf fungus," she thought as she dropped behind the root ball and wriggled up against the log. She rolled over and could see the black shadow of a salad plate-sized *Ganoderma oregonense* above her, outlined against the night sky. The tough polypore was as hard as a horse's hoof and its edge had sliced into her forehead, causing a trickle of blood to start down one side of her face.

Elspeth tried to still her breathing. Her system was starving for oxygen. Her entire body was quivering and her breath came in ragged heaves as Troy drew nearer. Despite mashing herself against the log, she could see her long white legs gleaming in the moonlight. She would be safe only if Troy moved forward without looking back.

Troy Fickham ran down the trail past the log, the long flashlight bobbing on his shoulder as he moved. It was a policeman's light, over a foot long and weighing more than a pound that made as good a cudgel as a light.

The frogs stayed quiet. Moments later Troy used the light to survey the water. No sound.

Elspeth huddled under the log, praying furiously that Troy would move on. She watched as he studied the trail where it bent and rounded the water.

Troy turned and jogged back down the trail, scanning for any indications of a turn off. He smiled when he reached the log.

Elspeth did not have air to scream. She recognized the flashlight he had next to his face. It was a five-D cell battery monster that Uncle Duane had on clearance two shows ago, sold complete with a demonstration on how to disable an opponent by using the heavy light with a smashing or ramming stroke.

Now Troy loomed over her, grinning. "Hi, sweetheart," he said. "Why don't you just come on out from under that log and let's get warmed up together?"

"Leave me alone!"

"Nope. I'm not going to do that." Troy reached down with his left hand and grabbed Elspeth's braid, yanking her to her feet.

She screamed and struggled to hit Troy with her handcuffed hands laced together as he pulled her toward the trail.

Out of the darkness a rocket of fur blasted into Troy's chest. He staggered back, letting go of Elspeth. She dropped to the ground.

Zoom planted herself between Troy and Elspeth and began to bark. WOOF. WOOF. WOOF. WOOF.

"Leave her alone!" shouted Nico.

Troy looked down the trail and saw Nico charging down the trail. Snarling, Troy turned and lashed out with the long flashlight, smashing Zoom's left front leg, which buckled with an audible snap.

The screech owl, with ill aboding cry, portends strange things."
Lady Mary Wortley Montagu (1689-1762)

Chapter Thirty-Six

Sunday, 9:05 p.m.
The Shed

Russell and Carmen were at an impasse. He blocked the door, but the shed was large enough that he could not move forward to grab her without creating an opportunity for her to exit.

Carmen jogged in place, trying to keep warm. The movement of her pale legs had to be showing Russell where she was. The darkness in the shed was incomplete. The corners were opaque but moonlight came through a grimy upper window and the mushrooms on the mattress glowed in their slick yellow and brown shades.

She kept jogging. It was more important right now to be ready to move. She'd heard Nico yelling "Find Elspeth." Help was close. She had to survive until then and that meant she had to stay warm. Her stomach growled and another spasm rippled up her body.

Russell was in no hurry. "See those mushrooms?"

Carmen thought about staying silent. She decided to play for time. "Yeah. Very weird."

"This mattress here is special, little girl," he said. "Both my sons were conceived on this mattress." He laughed. "Well, all four of my sons were conceived on this mattress. Ricky Lee thinks those two boys are his but I know better."

Carmen shuttered as he continued. "Henry's mama was a local gal. Smart as a whip, that one. She tried every day for three years to get away from me. Never did learn that I keep what I want. She tried to poison me once."

It dawned on Carmen that she could play for time by keeping the story going. "She use rat poison?" she asked.
"Because you are a hell of a big rat."

Russell chuckled. "Nope. Mushrooms. She said they were shaggy parasols."

"*Chlorophyllum olivieri.*"

"Do what?"

"That's the scientific name. *Chlorophyllum olivieri.*"

"If you say so. She made a mistake though."

"What?" Carmen danced up and down, trying to keep the blood flowing. Her right ankle was pinging a complaint but there were no sharp pains yet. She inhaled and asked again. "What mistake?"

"She wouldn't give little Henry any of the stew. She said the meat was too big. So I cut up some small pieces and she still said no. Got me thinking."

Silence stretched out for a moment as Russell shifted his vast weight from one foot to another. Finally he said, "I got up from the table and went and found her mushroom basket. No shaggy parasols. Those are dry and kinda striped. What she had was yellow, slimy mushrooms."

"Oh, my God. The ones on the mattress?"

Russell's teeth flashed like tainted ivory in the dark as he grinned. "Yeah! She was trying to poison me."

"These might be edible," Carmen protested.

"Nope, but I fixed her." Russell swung his arms, knife blade flashing in a beam of moonlight. "I brought her and her mushrooms out here. Chained her like a dog. Fed her dog food too. Raped her like a bitch." His teeth flashed again. "I put her body in the pond. Henry saw me do it and I never had a peep of trouble from that boy. I got soft with the rest of them. They don't understand what I can do. Henry does."

Russell's voice was imminently reasonable. "You're a smart girl. Smart as my Henry. Read the tea leaves, sugar. You ain't gettin' out of here. You belong to me. The sooner you get that in your head, the better for all of us."

Carmen continued to jog as she said, "My cousin escaped. Our friend escaped. Other people are out there. If you're smart, you'll run now. My dad is coming and he will not be happy."

A bark of laughter came from Russell. "I do respect your daddy. He's a tough man. He's not as tough as me."

"We'll see." That wasn't much of a rejoinder. It was the best Carmen could do given her brain was still semi-frozen. She continued to jog and moved over to the hole in the wall where Jasmine and Elspeth had escaped. No matter how she studied it, it was still too narrow for her. To her surprise, a hand reached through the gap and tapped her ankle. Someone was out there.

Carmen stood in front of the hole and raised her voice. "You are really tough. And that's a big knife you are holding. It looks like a sharp knife. And you are so tall that you have a long reach."

"Now you're talking some sense." Russell said. "Or are you talking to someone outside?"

"Who would that be?" Carmen asked with great innocence as she inwardly swore. She had to remember that Russell was as cunning as a man could be. His lack of sophistication was uncorrelated to his mental speed.

Russell turned his headlamp back on just as Jed came sliding through the gap.

* * *

Sunday, 9:08 p.m.
In the mobile home

"I want my attorney!" Ricky Lee insisted. "You cain't come barging in here without a warrant. I want my attorney. Tate, you want an attorney too."

Tate Fickham's watery eyes strained with the effort of taking in the people in his living room. Detective Raposo loomed large like a determined giant and Deputy McRae's lean face held hard gray eyes. But it was Duane Dwerryhouse who radiated the most dangerous air. He thrummed with tight tension kept on a short leash. Tate's buzzed mind registered all three as unfriendly.

Raposo spoke mildly to McRae. "Of course we need to contact Mr. Fickham's attorney before we question him further. I sure hope Tate understands that first degree kidnapping is a Class A felony."

McRae nodded and said, "That could mean a life sentence. We're missing three young women. I don't think a judge or jury would be very merciful."

Raposo said, "Three young women. You know we're not going to stop looking. We're going to keep looking until we find them. It'd be really, really smart to be the guy who helps us find them fast."

"I want a deal!" Tate said. "Make me a deal!"

"Doesn't work that way," Raposo said. "You deliver and then we evaluate. It's a one time opportunity that will expire in about thirty seconds."

"Shut up!" roared Ricky Lee. "Shut up, Tate!"

McRae pushed Ricky Lee's face back into the plasticized paneling. McRae said, "Another word from you, sir, and the detective and I will be stepping out side leaving Mr. Dwerryhouse to supervise this situation while we search the grounds. We have three women in imminent danger, so we can spend a lot of time looking."

"They're in the shed next to the boat," Tate said. He licked his lips and said, "Grandpa and Troy went out awhile ago to check on them."

Duane wheeled and charged out the door. Raposo stepped in to take charge of Ricky Lee, saying "Go!" to McRae.

McRae sprinted after Duane.

Sunday, 9:08 p.m.
The Shed

Carmen felt rather than saw Jed's arrival through the gap in the wall. She had danced around in front of the gap trying to keep Russell engaged ever since she'd felt that tap on her ankle.

Russell smiled as he watched Jed's slender form slide through the narrow hole. "Aw. You got your reinforcements. How cute. Come on, buddy, show me what you got."

"Sheriff's deputies are outside," Jed said steadily. "It'll go best for you to go quietly now."

"I don't think so, sonny," Russell replied. "They aren't getting you unless I get to walk. I'll be dead before they take me. You will be too." Russell turned toward the door, perhaps thinking to look outside just as Duane Dwerryhouse yanked the door open. Russell's knife hand came slicing forward, catching air as Duane dodged back.

Carmen and Jed surged forward, racing across the spongy floor of the shed to slam into Russell's back. They bounced back like tennis balls hitting a brick wall.

They rallied and ran in again. Jed swarmed up Russell's back, endeavoring to get his forearm around Russell's neck. Carmen stuck out her left foot and hooked one of Russell's feet as Duane darted in and grabbed Russell's knife hand while elbowing Russell in the face. Carmen's right ankle pinged another protest but she ignored the stab of pain to put her left foot out again.

McRae dove in through the door, grabbing for Russell's knife hand from an outside angle, roaring, "You're under arrest!"

It was Carmen's determined foot-hooking that brought Russell crashing down like a mighty cedar. Jed slithered out and knelt on Russell's left arm as McRae and Duane wrestled Russell's knife arm flat.

Russell bucked and thrashed until Carmen knelt on the back of his neck, smashing his face to the flooring.

"Be smart," McRae yelled. "I can shoot you blind. I can kneecap you. Let go of the knife."

Somehow McRae's threat of disability registered more than the threat of death. Russell released the knife.

"Don't let him up," Duane said. "Everybody stay on him."

"God damn it," McRae swore. "My handcuffs are on Ricky Lee."

"If you've got a handcuff key," Jed said, "We could recycle the cuffs that are on Carmen."

Duane flipped the knife away as McRae used one hand to extract his keys and unlock Carmen's hands. She handed the handcuffs to McRae and watched as he snapped one cuff on Russell's right hand and pulled the hand back behind Russell's back. She held her knee on Russell's neck until his left hand was handcuffed. Carmen stood up and began to weep. Great sobs shook her body. "I knew you'd come," she said to her father.

Duane stood up and enveloped her in a hug. "You betcha, baby. Come hell or high water, I was going to find you. Dwerryhouses don't quit. We overcome."

Tears streamed down Carmen's face. "I didn't know if you were going to get here in time but I knew you were going to find me."

"Shh." Duane stroked his daughter's hair. "Let's not think about me not getting here in time. That kinda thinking is going to give us both nightmares."

Carmen laughed. "Too late. I'll be dreaming this stuff for years."

Duane patted her back. "Yeah. I know."

Carmen scrubbed her eyes and sniffed. "Where's Elspeth?"

"Nico and the dog went down the trail in back. I think the dog was on her scent. I'll go check on them."

McRae cleared his throat. "And where is Jasmine?"

"She's not outside?" Carmen asked. "She got out first. She should be on the road looking for help."

"Let's get Russell here over to Detective Raposo," McRae said. "We'll spread out and look."

"We should hurry," Carmen said earnestly. "If Jasmine is lost, she could be in trouble fast. She has no body fat. She can't handle the cold."

Sunday, 9:12 p.m.
On the road

Jasmine watched as Henry Fickham reached the end of the long dirt drive. She saw him slow to a walk and skirt the front of McRae's parked patrol car before stepping out onto the asphalt surface of Bloomfield Road. He turned left and walked rapidly down the road.

A watery bright moon sat low in the sky. The clouds had dissipated, revealing spring star constellations. The clearing skies correlated with plummeting temperatures, which didn't help Jasmine as she trailed behind.

The hoot of an owl echoed through the forest. Jasmine sniffed and whispered, "*Strix varia,* an invasive species." Her eyes flooded with tears as she thought of her grandfather. He had to okay. He just had to be.

Jasmine kept to the darker half of the road. She still wasn't sure if the man she was following was friend or foe. She closed the gap between them and crept just thirty yards behind him when he disappeared into the bushes. She slowed to a stop and watched. When he didn't reappear, she crept closer.

Henry was behind a cream Lexus with the trunk lid up. Jasmine tiptoed within a dozen feet and moved right to crouch at the base of a bushy evergreen huckleberry.

"My family completely fucked up," Henry said into his cell phone. "The law is already here. I got some pictures. Not good enough to nail my dad, but I don't think that's a concern anymore."

Jasmine's eyes widened. This man was related to her captors. Foe, not friend. This had to be Henry Fickham.

"Where are you?" Henry asked. "That sounds good. The red curry is really nice. Listen, I need to get out of town. Tonight. I should get rid of this car too. My truck too."

There was motion to the right and Troy Fickham stepped out from a deer trail. "Uncle Henry?"

Henry whirled and saw Troy. "What are you doing here?" he barked.

"Getting away. There's law at the house. I need a ride to town."

"Fuck off," Henry snarled. "You wanted the girls, you deal with the mess you made."

"I know about you and that pharmaceutical guy," Troy said. "You killed him and left him in a gully."

Jasmine stayed low underneath the huckleberry as Henry's eyes darted left and then right. Suddenly he smiled. He said, "Let me finish this call." Into the cell phone he said, "Lucinda, I think my nephew Troy is interested in the Lexus. What if I let him have it and I take the old roadster? Yeah. Great."

Henry tapped off the phone. "Not a problem, Troy," he said smoothly. "I'm headed into town to pick up a car I've had my eye on. It's an old classic. When we get there, I'll give you the keys to this car. You tell me where you heard that crazy story and we'll be good."

Troy hesitated.

"Or I can just go," Henry said.

"You got a deal," Troy said.

Jasmine did her best to remain absolutely still as the two men got into the Lexus and Henry drove out onto the asphalt. The headlights came on and blinded her momentarily. Blinking in surprise, she thought she saw Henry lift his left hand and waggle his fingers "good bye" as the Lexus surged past her.

She waited until the taillights of the Lexus disappeared before standing up and exhaling. She was shivering again. Jasmine wobbled up onto the paved road and saw a porch light off in the distance. She pulled her handcuffed hands in against her belly and began to run to the light.

"I'm going to make it," she gasped as a stitch built in her right side. "Grandpa, just don't eat the cupcake. Please, please be sleeping in front of the TV."

"What is done in love is done well."
Vincent Van Gogh (1853 -1890)

Chapter Thirty-Seven

Sunday, 9:18 p.m.
The Fickham Compound

Nico staggered down the path with Elspeth closely following. He was carrying Zoom over his shoulders. The dog whined softly as Elspeth crooned, "Hang in there, girl. We're going to get help."

To Nico, she said, "As soon as I get these handcuffs off and my pants back on, I am going to hunt Troy Fickham to the ends of the earth and murder the S.O.B."

"Works for me," Nico grunted as they reached the rough parking area near the yellow mobile home.

Carmen came limping out of the house with her jeans on, her face radiant with relief. "There you are!" Her face quickly clouded. "What's wrong with Zoom?"

"Troy hit her with a flashlight. One of those security models we had on sale."

"Oh, my God. Those are heavy."

"Yeah. We think it broke her leg. We need to get her to a vet."

Carmen said, "Let me go get one of the officers. They can get the handcuffs off you and I'll go grab your pants."

Jed stepped out of the shadows. He offered to take Zoom but Nico shook his head. "Thanks but it's better not to hand her off."

"Where's Jasmine?" Elspeth asked.

"Unknown, but they're working on that." Jed answered

The group moved toward the mobile home and saw that Detective Raposo had Ricky Lee Fickham and Tate Fickham sitting on the ground outside the mobile home with their hands cuffed behind them as McRae escorted Russell Fickham from the shed.

"It's cold out here," Ricky Lee whined. "Why can't we sit inside?"

"Because I don't know where you have weapons stashed," Raposo said pleasantly. "You thought this was a good temperature for women, so a manly sort like yourself should do just fine."

He turned to see Nico and Elspeth. Raposo quickly released Elspeth from her handcuffs.

"We need to get Zoom to a vet. She's going into shock," Nico said.

"Go," Raposo replied. "Back up is on the way. Any idea where Jasmine Oh might have gone?"

McRae stopped next to Elspeth, ready to hear the reply. Elspeth said, "I think she'd make herself known by now if she was close by. She was going to run down the road for help."

Raposo addressed McRae. "Why don't you grab her britches and catch a lift with Nico and Elspeth out to the patrol car? Start a sweep east because I think that's where you'll find the closest house. Duane and I will wait here for the backup. If you haven't found her by the time they arrive, we'll call in Search and Rescue."

Duane said, "Nico, you've got the keys to the Civic. Give them to us and we'll get that car moved."

"I could do that," Jed offered.

Carmen said, "I'll walk out with you."

"Don't you need your medicine?" Duane asked. He fished out a pill bottle from his pants pocket.

Carmen eyed it. "I think I am past the worst of the withdrawals." She checked her body. Even her ankle seemed happy. She stepped toward the road. "Dad," she called over her shoulder, "I'll be walking in the moonlight with Jed. I'll be fine!" She linked hands with Jed and the two began the walk out to the Civic.

Nico's Jeep still sat in the rutted parking area. It took several minutes to arrange Zoom and Elspeth in the back. Zoom whined softly when Nico let the clutch out and rolled over a rut in reverse.

From the passenger seat, McRae asked, "How is the dog?"

"I suspect she has a broken humerus." He looked at McRae's confused face and translated, "Broken front leg. The long upper bone."

"That's fixable, right?"

"Theoretically. It will depend on whether it's a break or a shattering. We need to get her into the vet tonight." Nico did his best to navigate the rutted road gently. He came to a complete stop before a particularly deep pothole and before continuing, he reached into his back pocket for his cell phone. "Elspeth," he said, "Will you call my parents and let them know we're on the way to the vet emergency clinic? And that I'm about to max out my credit card?"

"Oh, Nico!"

He laughed as he carefully navigated the pothole. "No worries. They'll take the news fine from you. Once you tell them that Zoom saved your life, they'll keep her in chewy treats for life."

"You and Zoom together saved me."

"They'll like that version even better."

* * *

Moments later Nico pulled the Jeep up at McRae's patrol car. He tapped his cell phone and called Elspeth's number. McRae stepped out of the Jeep and followed the chiming to a rose gold phone sitting in a mound of fir needle duff. He delivered the phone to Elspeth and made his way to the patrol car. He waved as Nico eased the Jeep onto the asphalt and turned toward Olympia.

The evening was turning colder. A brisk breeze sent a chill around his ears. Where was Jasmine?

McRae opened his car door and sat down. The smart thing to do was to keep all lines of communication going. He'd let dispatch know he was back in his unit.

Cheryl, the night dispatcher, responded with, "Be advised that a young woman is waiting for your contact. She is at the following address . . ."

McRae sagged against the seatback. Jasmine. She was alright.

He found Jasmine at the home of one Mr. and Mrs. Dabrowski. She was bundled in a quilt on a loveseat and sipping hot chocolate under the worried eyes of the graying couple dressed in flannel pajamas and matching quilted bathrobes. An elderly dachshund and a silver-muzzled Labrador snoozed in dog baskets near a roaring wood stove. The dogs had greeted McRae and quickly retired. He had the impression this was a household that went to bed early.

"Roxie, our dachshund, started barking," the man said. "I went to look and there was Ms. Oh, running up the driveway."

"I got the handcuffs off her using a bobby pin," his wife said. "We looked it up on YouTube." She paused. "We may have messed up any fingerprints."

"You did the right thing," McRae assured her. "We have the men responsible in custody."

"All of them?" Jasmine asked. "Because I saw the guy with the red baseball cap get into a car with a man I think was Henry Fickham."

"When was this?"

"When I got out of the shed, I saw a man hiding behind a tree. I followed him down the dirt road to the asphalt road. He kept going to a nice car that was parked behind some bushes. Then the young guy – the one with the red ball cap – came out of the woods. He called the first guy "Uncle Henry" and said he knew about the murder in the woods."

"Really?" McRae's fingers danced on his knees as he digested this news. "Did Henry acknowledge this?"

"Not really. He said he had another car he wanted and that . . . Troy — it was 'Troy' — could have the nice car. It was a light colored Lexus."

"Where were you?"

"In the bushes, being as still as a mouse."

"Did they see you?"

Jasmine hesitated. "I'm not sure. Maybe Henry did see me. He gave this funny hand wave in my direction when they drove off."

"Let me go radio this in. I've got your jeans in the patrol car. Are you ready to go home?"

"Big time!"

A few minutes later McRae came back in and handed her the jeans. She smiled at him as she slipped off her shoes and slid her legs into the pants, hoisting them up with grin. "Wow. That is so much better."

She thanked her hosts with a hug apiece. "I am so glad you were home," she said. "Thanks for the hot chocolate, the bobby pin and the use of your phone."

"Anytime," the man said. "Come back and see us. We will make you a proper Polish meal. Bring your Grandfather."

"I hope he doesn't have any more ants," the woman said. "I'm glad he didn't eat the bad cupcake!"

"He says he's fine. I'm going home right now and will make sure," Jasmine replied.

Out in the patrol car McRae contacted Raposo and got approval to take Jasmine home. Duty done, he pulled the patrol car out onto Bloomfield Road and spoke to Jasmine. "What's going on with your Grandfather?"

"Oh, Don. God. I didn't tell you that part. There is something majorly strange going on. My grandfather is fine but I think a woman tried to poison him this afternoon. And I think it may be related to Henry Fickham and the man we found in the woods."

She added, "Let me start by saying I don't totally understand who those creeps were that kidnapped Carmen and me." Jasmine said, "They seemed to want Carmen and her father, but Elspeth was important too."

"There was an incident at a trade show yesterday," McRae told her. "Troy Fickham has had a crush on Elspeth. Duane Dwerryhouse hit one of the Fickhams and the kidnapping was a revenge move. You just got swept up in the action."

"But these Fickhams are related to Henry Fickham who we think hammered the man in the woods?"

"The old man, Russell, is Henry's father. Ricky Lee is a half-brother. Troy and Tate are Ricky Lee's sons. That would make them nephews to Henry."

"That's not so confusing then."

"Not by backwoods family standards. Not confusing at all." McRae navigated the country road with ease, keeping a steady speed as he scanned for eye shine that might indicate a deer about to step out onto the road. "In fact, we find much of law enforcement and social services often revolves around just a few families." His eyes slanted to her face. "So what happened with your grandfather?"

"Nothing, Thank God. This afternoon he went to play cards with some retired professors — the home of a Dr. Sutherland. I dropped him off. While he was there, Grandfather went to get some beer from a refrigerator in the garage and he saw the tools were marked like the hammer in the woods. He asked Dr. Sutherland about it and got told that the hired help must have stolen things."

"Always the fault of the hired help," McRae said.

"Right. When Carmen and I were bouncing around in the back of that totally gross Suburban, my grandfather called my cell phone and Tate answered. Tate said he'd take a message for me and that's when my grandfather said something about food. Maybe he was trying to say he wasn't going to wait for me, but the message was that he had a snack—a cupcake- delivered by Mrs. Sutherland."

Jasmine inhaled and went on. "After Tate hung up, the old man, Russell, started talking about Henry's 'cold stone bitch' of a girlfriend who is collecting thousands of dollars from an online video site. Russell has a friend at the bank who told him so. And Henry's girlfriend is supposed to be Mrs. Sutherland. They talked about how maybe she was poisoning people with Henry Fickham's fentanyl."

Jasmine took a second breath and continued, "As soon as I got to the Dabrowski's house I asked to use their telephone. I called Grandfather and he said he did get a cupcake but he went for a walk to collect licorice ferns and ended up going out to dinner with a neighbor. He got home and found a line of ants on the cupcake, so he dumped the cupcake down the disposal. He's never been much for sweets."

"Damn. So the cupcake is gone?"

"I asked Grandfather not to use that sink until I got home. I was thinking maybe we could detach the garbage disposal unit and see if there were any leftovers."

McRae shook his head. "It might be interesting but it wouldn't hold up in court. Say there was poison and it was your standard rat poison. That's warfarin, which is often prescribed as a blood thinner for people with heart conditions. The defense would argue that someone in your house had been cleaning out the medicine cabinet or cleaning out old rat killer from the garage. It'd be impossible to connect to Mrs. Sutherland."

"What if it was a different poison? The old man Fickham mentioned fentanyl."

"Just how much expensive testing is the district attorney going to have done on a bunch of slime from a household where no one suffered injury?" McRae tilted his head in another small headshake. "No way. The DA is going to have a full plate prosecuting the Fickhams we've got."

He tapped the steering wheel as he thought. "The fentanyl angle is interesting. We already suspect Henry of being in fentanyl distribution. I don't know, Jasmine. I still think getting the garbage disposal slime tested is a long shot. There's not a way to verify the chain of transit from Mrs. Sutherland to pipe sludge."

"What about the videos? It might be porn."

McRae snorted. "Porn isn't illegal. Although if she's making big money with it, maybe it's got animals. We could sic the ASPCA on her."

"Oh. Yuck. I hadn't even thought that."

"Welcome to the wonderful world of law enforcement. It might be child porn. That's a money maker too."

"Ugh. I feel sick."

"But your grandfather is definitely alright?"

"Yes. He said he was going to bed. I didn't tell him about my evening. I just said I was with friends. Hey, please stop when we get to the top of this hill," Jasmine requested.

When the patrol neared the crest, Jasmine said, "Here! Stop just for a second. Can you douse the headlights?"

McRae brought the patrol car to a halt. He kept his foot on the brake pedal and turned off the lights.

Jasmine craned her neck to look through the windshield and up to the stars. "As I was freezing my tuckus off tonight I kept thinking that the dropping temperatures came from clearing skies. We don't get enough spring nights without cloud cover. Leo is one of my favorite constellations."

"I know that one. Looks like a question mark."

"Very good Deputy McRae."

"Do you think there is anything to the horoscope stuff?"

Jasmine laughed. "I used to think it was totally stupid. My grandfather and I would read all the daily horoscopes in the newspaper and pick the best one for the day. Then I learned that infants typically have one of three different types of gut flora."

"Ah. What?" McRae looked at her.

"Gut flora is bacteria and fungi in the intestines. We each have several hundred species of bacteria and fungi in our guts. Some of the species train our immune system and let us know what our bodies should fight. Babies that don't pick up the right collection of bacteria and fungi tend to become toddlers with asthma and allergies. Babies that grow up on farms tend to have less allergies."

Jasmine shrugged. "So maybe the babies who are the right age to take on a picnic in the summer pick up different bacteria than the babies who are inside all winter. It could affect our personalities based on how we're feeling." She smiled. "So I'm a Taurus. The bull. We get the job done. Made possible by my inner life!"

That makes sense." McRae hesitated. "When I filled out the report on the body you found, I looked your record up. That's standard when we have a body. I . . . noticed . . . You've got a birthday soon."

"This Friday." She paused. "I'll be nineteen."

"That's really young," McRae said.

"But it's not eighteen."

"Is that a hint?"

"It's a fact," Jasmine said, sitting back. She turned to stare at him, a challenge in her dark eyes that reflected in the moonlight.

McRae studied her eyes and the elegant swoop of her neck and delicate jaw line. He said, "Jasmine. You and me. We don't work."

"How do you know that?"

"You're going to go to Columbia and studying science. I'm staying here and catching bad guys."

"That doesn't mean we can't go to a show or eat a meal together."

McRae thought about that. Finally he said, "If we survive the week and catch Troy and Henry and God Knows Who Else, do you suppose you'd like to go see a movie with me to celebrate your birthday?"

"Yes. I'd love to."

"Good." McRae turned the headlights on and put his foot down on the accelerator. "All we have to do now is find the rest of the bad guys."

The Thai Palace Restaurant, Olympia

Henry was already pulling into the parking lot of the Thai Palace restaurant. He parked and said, "This car is yours, Troy, with one condition."

Troy ran his hand over the beautiful paneling and said, "Yeah?"

"You forget you ever knew me. I mean it. Forget what you heard about me and this car, me and anybody, anywhere, ever. I'm leaving the state. If I ever hear you mentioned my name to anyone, ever, then I'll reach out to my friends and tell them I'll pay ten grand to collect your ears and thirty thousand for your dick mailed to me on ice. Savvy?"

His nephew swallowed and nodded. "Anybody looking for this car?" he asked.

"Yeah, but I swapped out plates and shielded the GPS. If you don't drive stupid, you should be fine for a while. Here." Henry leaned over and opened the glove box. He took out a pistol and an envelope. From the envelope he took out a bundle of hundreds and counted off twenty. "Get the car repainted. You know where to go. Then you'll be solid and off the radar."

Henry doubted that his nephew had the discipline or the smarts to see the wisdom in spending the money on paint, but the pile of hundreds made Troy immensely agreeable.

"Can I have the pistol too?" Troy asked.

Henry narrowed his eyes. "Who are you thinking about shooting?"

Troy shrugged. "Nobody. I just know where Elspeth Dwerryhouse is staying. I thought I'd drop by later tonight. Even up the score some."

Henry leaned back into the luxurious leather of the Lexus as his mind raced through the details. He'd liberated this pistol from a kid who had been one of his fentanyl distributors. It wasn't traceable to him. If Troy fucked up his payback, which was highly likely, then Troy would be picked up with Jeffrey Zhang's Lexus, sucking the attention of law enforcement away from Henry. That could work.

He popped open the storage bin between the front armrests and pulled out a lens cleaning cloth and a small spray bottle. "Yeah. You can have it. I'm getting my fingerprints off it, so if you do stupid and get caught, it's all on you."

"No problem!" Troy grinned. "I won't get caught." Casually, Troy tipped back his baseball cap and asked, "Where are you going next?"

"Out of town," his uncle replied.

"Any place particular?"

"Not sure yet. Got a mail order business in mind." Henry winked at his nephew. "I am going to help people in need."

"With your girlfriend?"

Henry kept polishing the pistol and managed a shrug. "Nah. I'm done with her. Time for a fresh start." It was interesting that his heart rate had spiked with his lie. Henry gave the pistol barrel a final buffing and realized that Lucinda made life worth living. She was fierce, she was ruthless and she was his soul mate.

Troy didn't need to know that. Henry leaned over to slide the pistol back into the glove box. He ran the wipe over the dashboard. "There," he said. "All tidy."

Henry climbed out of the car. He could see Lucinda waiting at a table inside the restaurant. He smiled. She'd like the coast. No hospice, no Richard — just a little home with him and their new business.

There were a few more details to manage.

Leaning into the vehicle, Henry passed the keys to Troy, saying, "Have fun."

"A man's character is his fate."
Heraclitus (540-480 BCE)

Chapter Thirty-Eight

The Thai Palace Restaurant
10:00 p.m.

Henry strode across the sparsely populated restaurant to Lucinda's table. Her smile lit up his heart. Her soft gray hair framed a face with alert, shining eyes. Henry loved her eyes. Somewhere between gray and blue, they reflected as violet when Lucinda wore light purple. Tonight her lavender camisole and sweater set off her eyes to perfection.

"You are beautiful," he said as he slid into the chair opposite hers.

"I may just be free," she said. "I am thinking that Richard may have eaten the snack I left." Her eyes danced merrily. "Of course, I may get home and find that he is only sleeping. But he hasn't texted or called and I am most hopeful. I've also had a powerful idea."

"Let me order and then tell me."

A waitress appeared, consternation on her face, saying, "Sir, our kitchen is closing. Can I get you something to go?"

Henry thought a moment. He reached into his pocket and pulled out a hundred dollar bill that he passed to the waitress, saying, "I would really like to eat something now. What if you bring me a plate of whatever the cook has and I'll eat it quickly."

"Of course, sir!" she said cheerfully. "I'll have something right out."

"And now," Henry reached across the table and took Lucinda's hand. "Tell me."

"I was thinking about what would happen if I do go home and find Richard's body. I have a 'Do not resuscitate' bracelet in my purse. I've been carrying it around for months, and I have the correct paperwork, but, Henry, these are all features we could add to our on-line business."

"I'm not sure I follow you." Henry unfolded a napkin and placed it in his lap as the waitress appeared with a plate of yellow curry.

Lucinda waited until the young woman stepped back before leaning in to say, "When paramedics arrive at a home, they are required, by law, to attempt to resuscitate even a very dead body. Unless, of course, there is a Do Not Resuscitate device on the body supported by specific paperwork in the home called the 'Physician's Order for Life-Sustaining Treatment' or 'POLST'. We routinely have these forms filled out when someone comes into the hospice. They are on lime green heavy paper and they are to be filled out by a doctor and witnessed. I've got one ready for Richard."

"Does he know that?" Henry asked with a leer.

"Of course not!" Lucinda smiled. "The point is that I've set things up so this will look like an expected death and his body should not be flagged for the coroner. If all goes well, he'll be at the crematoria tomorrow."

Lucinda leaned in closer and whispered, "We should set up a deluxe package. Customized fentanyl pills, Do Not Resuscitate bracelet and completed POLST form so the buyer is truly all set."

"Wow." Henry grinned like a child. "We could charge a grand, easy."

"I was thinking fifteen hundred." Lucinda folded her hands on the tabletop. "Each state has slightly different criteria. We could start with our Washington expertise and expand from there."

"How do we get the doctor's signature?"

"Please!" Lucinda waved a hand. "We need to ask the name of the patient's doctor from the buyer and we just squiggle something along those lines."

"Right." Henry shoveled in curry and swallowed before saying, "My love, I do need to leave tonight. How about some place on the coast?"

Lucinda nodded. "Perfect. I finished cleaning the hospice files and I have the pill press in the trunk of my car. Do you need things from your apartment?"

"A few things, yes. I'll take the boxes from your garage too. You aren't going to want that sitting out if you're calling an ambulance." Henry ate quickly and added, "A suitcase plus the pill press and the boxes of powder will be a full load for the roadster."

"Yes. The Z3 is flashy too. Please drive well below the speed limit."

Henry finished the curry. He said, "It would be best if I'm out of town by midnight."

"Do you anticipate more challenges from your family?"

"Most of them are in jail tonight. Troy, I think, will be joining them shortly." Henry rejoiced as he helped Lucinda into her smoke purple overcoat. It was a long time in coming but he was finally rid of his kin. "Troy has Zhang's Lexus and he's about to go do something stupid."

"Oh, Henry. You are such a brilliant man." Lucinda put her arm through his and let him guide her into the night.

Monday, 2 A.M.
The Lowenstein Home

Elspeth was beyond exhausted as Nico pulled the Jeep into the driveway at Mrs. Lowenstein's home. Zoom was stretched out in the back, profoundly stoned with painkillers and with her left front leg encased in plaster.

"That was so much money," Elspeth whispered. "My God, that was as much as a full semester at the community college."

"Surgery is expensive," Nico said. "Emergency surgery even more so." He looked at her. "I'm keeping Zoom. After all of this, there's no way I'm giving her up to Mitzi."

"I'll bet Mrs. Lowenstein will be on your side," Elspeth said. "I am! Is it against the law to hide a dog until the owner gets another whim?"

Nico chuckled. "We could find out. Meanwhile, let's send lots of texts about how hard it is to nurse a dog back to health."

"Is it going to be hard?" Elspeth shot a worried look to the back where Zoom lay.

"You heard the vet. We've got to keep her gently moving and the really hard part will be when she starts feeling great but the bone isn't completely healed. We'll have our hands full. For Mitzi, it'd be, I'm guessing, impossible." Nico smiled at Elspeth. "But for us? We'll manage. My folks will help."

"Your parents are the nicest people on the planet," Elspeth said sincerely. "I can't believe they came out in the middle of the night and held my hand for two hours."

"Yeah. They're good that way." Nico yawned. "Come on. Let's get Zoom inside."

Nico lifted Zoom onto his shoulders and carried her inside. She slept through the transfer. He gently laid her down in the living room while Elspeth gave Mr. Midnight a very late dinner. Mr. Midnight sat on the kitchen counter and lashed his tail as he bolted down the last of the Azul Kitchen's shredded chicken.

"Go ahead," Elspeth told the cat. "You deserve it. We should have fed you dinner hours ago."

Nico called from the living room. "If you're going to talk to the cat, be sure to tell him that you were tied up. Really tied up." Nico stretched out on the floor next to Zoom and closed his eyes. "I think I can sleep right here."

It was Mr. Midnight who noticed the front door opening. The cat stopped sniffing the empty bowl and raised his head to direct his bright yellow eyes on the swinging door.

Elspeth looked up in horror as Troy Fickham walked in, large black pistol in hand.

"Hello, Elspeth," he said.

'However long the night, the dawn will break.
African proverb

Chapter Thirty-nine

The Lowenstein Home
2:20 a.m.

Elspeth felt her skin sprout with sweat. She tried to croak a protest but nothing emerged from her mouth. Nico sat up. He froze as Troy turned the pistol to point his way.

Troy said, "Don't do anything stupid, lover boy." He swayed silently and struggled to enunciate his words.

"You're drunk," Elspeth finally managed.

"So? Just had a little something. It's a cold night and I needed warming up." Troy smiled at Elspeth as his right hand kept the pistol on Nico. "Oh," Troy laughed. "Poor doggy. Got hurt, huh?"

"Maybe we could all party together," Elspeth said carefully. "I wouldn't mind a drink." She needed something, anything, to change the layout. Nico was on the floor and she was at the kitchen counter. Neither one of them could possibly dodge a bullet.

"Yeah," Nico said from the floor. "A few drinks would be great."

Troy shook his head. "Nope. Not you. Just me. Me and Elspeth." He waved the pistol and used it to point down the hallway. "Go on. To the bedroom. We're gonna party on a mattress. You thought you were gonna get away from me, but when I say we're gonna party on a mattress, by God, we're gonna party on a mattress."

It was as if Russell Fickham were standing in the doorway. Troy suddenly had the same ominous air. Elspeth's eyes darted around the kitchen counter. There were no knives out and no heavy crockery.

Nico was slowly drawing his legs up. Elspeth knew that he wanted to launch himself at Troy. It was too far. Troy could get a shot off and might not miss.

Zoom slept on.

Mr. Midnight leapt off the kitchen counter and ran down the hall.

Troy laughed. He took two steps into the living room and turned to take aim at the cat. His arm waved as he closed one eye to focus.

A slight breeze came from the front door.

And Troy was beaned in the back of the head with a baseball-sized bronze statue of Buddha.

Troy went down in a heap. Nico scrambled across the floor to wrest the pistol from Troy's hand as a diminutive white-haired lady in coral polyester slacks and a coral floral sweater rushed in to land swift kicks to Troy's kidneys. Troy howled in pain and tried to use his hands to shield his lower back.

"Here." The little lady thrust a coral and cream silk scarf at Nico. "Tie him up!"

Nico parked the pistol on the sofa and grabbed the scarf. He did his best to tie Troy's hands together and then repeated the process when Elspeth brought over a ball of twine from a kitchen drawer.

Elspeth said, "Nico, this is Mrs. Lowenstein." She found she was grinning as Nico pushed Troy's face into the carpet.

"Nice to meet you," Nico said.

"You're the young man who has been training Mitzi's dog, aren't you?" Mrs. Lowenstein looked over at the sleeping Zoom with her bright white cast. "Did she get hit by a car?"

"No. This son-of-a-bitch hit her." Nico said. "He's been stalking Elspeth."

"And trying to shoot cats." Mrs. Lowenstein glowered down at Troy. "You had best lay still until the police come because otherwise my next kick is going to be straight at your snozzola!"

Elspeth tried not to giggle as she dialed 911. Her hands were shaking but she felt just fine.

Moments later she joined Mrs. Lowenstein on the sofa. "The police are on their way. I'm so glad you came home early."

"I had to." Mrs. Lowenstein sighed. "I thought I'd like a cruise to Acapulco. What a dumb bunny I am! There was so much food and so many young people on spring break. Honestly, it was boring as hell. It wasn't anything like my trip to the Galapagos or the ship around Tierra del Fuego. No bird watching. No wildlife sightings. And the food was terrible. So much sugar. Nothing yummy and fun like on my trip to Phuket."

She grimaced. "When some of the kids came down with a norovirus, I was ready to jump ship. Then I got a text from Mitzi." Mrs. Lowenstein looked down at Nico, who was sitting on the floor, keeping a hand on Troy. "Do you want a dog?" she asked. "Mitzi is in love. She met a guy and they are getting married next weekend in Paris. I'm supposed fly out on Thursday. I told Mitzi I would find a good home for the dog as a wedding present."

Elspeth grinned down at Nico, who laughed back up at her. He said, "You bet. Mrs. Lowenstein, I would be delighted to have this dog."

* * *

Tuesday, May 2
Mason County Sheriff's Office

"Boss, come look at this." McRae was at his computer as Raposo wandered back from the coffee urn. "Jasmine told me that Mrs. Dwerryhouse had passed. Here's the obituary."

Raposo leaned over McRae's shoulder and scanned the screen.

Obituaries

Yera Marie (Meso-Landa) Dwerryhouse, passed away on April 25 after a long illness. She is survived by her husband, Duane, her daughter, Carmen and her niece, Elspeth. Yera was a loving mother and an avid cook and had a great love for her family. She was cherished for her impish sense of humor. Her family takes comfort that she is no longer in pain. There will be a celebration of her life on May 5 at 2 p.m. at Funeral Associates of Olympia.

"We should pass the hat and send some flowers," Raposo said. "After the Dwerryhouses delivered the Fickhams to us, everybody's had a smile on their face."

"No kidding. I'll bet chainsaw thefts will be down across the county. We might even be able to keep some big-leaf maple growing."

"I'm sure somebody else will become the next dealer in dubious saws, but it'd be nice to have it quiet for a bit."

"And look at this." McRae pointed at the screen.

Richard Adam Sutherland, 64, beloved spouse of Lucinda Sutherland, passed away at home April 23. Dr. Sutherland was a professor of communications and philosophy who taught at regional community colleges over many decades. He served as a Board Member for the University Union of Professionals and as a volunteer for Neighborhood

Security. Although never a father, Richard had a lifetime love for children. His ashes will be scattered near Hood Canal.

"She had him cremated," McRae said. "No remains to be examined."

"Interesting. Do we have a file on her?"

"I don't think so."

"Why don't you start one?" Detective Raposo smiled. "You could interview Ms. Oh and her grandfather for background information."

"Totally on it, boss." McRae laughed but then sobered. "You think we're going to be seeing Mrs. Sutherland again?"

"Her and Henry? You bet we are. Cats like that don't change their spots."

Mason County Journal 'What's Happening' Column
Monday, June 19

Brooke Louise Peters married Rodger James Raposo on Saturday afternoon at the Hood Canal home of the bride's parents, Edward and Betty Peters. The bride, a popular second grade teacher at Twin Cedars Elementary School, wore an ivory gown with a beaded lace overlay and a family heirloom veil. She carried a bouquet of sunrise sweetheart roses and was attended by her twin nieces, Bethany and Annalee Peters, who wore satin Grecian gowns in a deep horizon blue accented with lemon and apricot ribbons. The groom is a detective at the Mason County Sheriff's office.

Summit College Alumni Newsletter
June Issue

A trio of freshmen biology students is drawing international attention for their work on identifying a natural lubricant produced by local fungi. "We had several topics under consideration and it was hard to choose a direction at first. We were drawn to the extreme slipperiness of a waxy cap mushroom and wondered about its function and structure," said Team Leader Taz Candelaria who worked with Jasmine Oh and Carmen Dwerryhouse.

Candelaria says, "We worked with a retired botanist and a graduate student in mycology to determine the mushroom's ooze slip coefficient and expanded from there to look at possible applications in industry. We are also working with a DNA laboratory to ascertain if this is a new species of fungus."

The students will be traveling to Chicago in August for the National *Lubricants* and Sealants convention.

Rural Mason County,
July 28

"Are we close?" Elspeth peered out the window of the Jeep at the rows of Noble firs that stretched out for half a mile. She shifted in the seat, feeling anxious and a bit sweaty.

"You are as bad as Zoom!" Nico teased. "But, yes, we're almost there. Look up on the right."

"What sort of trees are those?"

"Hazelnut trees. Planted about ten years ago on top of an old hay field. You can't grow truffles well in an area that already has competing ectomycorrhizal fungi, so truffle farmers look for a place where crops have been grown. Those hazel nut trees had their roots inoculated with spores from the French black truffle, *Tuber melanosporum*."

"And Zoom can find them."

"Absolutely. That's why we've been working with the scent for the last week and she's a natural."

"And when do I hear about your surprise?"

"Patience! You'll know it when you hear it. Just be cool, calm and collected. It'll work." Nico turned the Jeep down a long lane that led to a sprawling complex of buildings.

"It's so clean," Elspeth marveled.

"Vannock and Bopha have been working very hard. The building on the left is the lecture hall and guest quarters. Straight ahead is the dining hall and office."

"So it's more than a Christmas tree farm."

"Oh, yeah. They are hosting seminars on the slow food movement, on sustainable micro agriculture and, of course, gourmet fungi and wine tasting. Very upscale."

Zoom leaned in from the back seat and licked Elspeth's face. "Down, silly." Elspeth reached over her shoulder with her left hand to scratch Zoom's long ears. "We'll get out in just a minute."

Nico parked the Jeep and clipped a long leash onto Zoom's collar. "Showtime. She's looking pretty mellow."

"A five mile run tends to do that for her."

Nico's friends emerged from the office just as Zoom jumped down from the rear of the Jeep. Nico chirped at her and Zoom gazed up at him with adoration in her eyes. She fell in beside his left leg and kept pace with him as he moved to the front of the vehicle.

Elspeth stepped down from the Jeep and smoothed the front of her new olive vest. The patch on the left front read "Olympic Mycological Services" in a black arc. Carmen had pronounced the vest and red-checked shirt a dynamite combination with her dark hair. It was easy to add a large smile to meet Nico's friends, Bopha and Vannock.

"We've been looking forward to this," Bopha said. "You could add an exciting event to our fall weekends."

"Yes," Vannock said. "It would be something not every foodie retreat has to offer. Very special."

Elspeth kept her bright smile in place, as Nico said, "As I mentioned, Elspeth has long experience in sales and product placement. I'm sure she would know your gift store inventory in no time."

"And Zoom is so gorgeous! What a beautiful dog!" Bopha leaned down to pat Zoom, who managed to wiggle enthusiastically without careening into the woman's legs.

"I'll be surprised if she can find anything today," Bopha said. "It's been a cool summer so far but it is summer."

"One way to find out." Nico handed the long leash to Elspeth. "Showtime," he said.

Elspeth took a deep breath and addressed the dog. "Zoom!"

The big red dog perked up and put a laser focus on Elspeth's face.

"Find Truffle!"

Zoom scampered toward the rows of hazelnut trees with Elspeth at a run beside her. Zoom halted by the third tree and barked. She began to dig on the south side of the tree until Elspeth pulled her back.

Vannock came jogging up from the parking lot with a garden trowel in his hand. "Let's see what she's found." He gently inserted the trowel into Zoom's scratching and soon unearthed a trio of dark blobs.

"Excellent!" he said. "That's actually surprising as our results with these inoculated hazel trees has been underwhelming so far." He stood up, pocketing the two truffles.

"Let's try the woods. It's a bit of a hike."

"Zoom and I are ready!" Elspeth said.

Vannock led the way across two fallow fields to rural road. Elspeth brought Zoom into a heel position and the dog proudly paraded down the gravel road at a sedate pace.

Eventually they reached a stand of Douglas fir. "We're looking for the spring Oregon white truffle here. *Tuber gibbosum.*"

Again Elspeth directed Zoom to look for truffles. The dog bounded forward, legs moving smoothly under her rippling red coat. Elspeth followed her into the woods until

Zoom stuck her nose into the duff at the base of a large Douglas fir.

Vannock came forward and scratched down into the dirt. He paused, and then began gently digging with his fingers. "Whoa." His fingers swept dirt aside. "Look at this!" He pried up a tennis ball sized black lump. "Normally we look for these in the fall. My God, Bopha! What a prize!"

Bopha was grinning hugely. "Outstanding!"

Elspeth shot a questioning look at Nico, who smoothly said, "Oregon black truffle! *Leucangium carthusianum.* That's a monster."

"This one truffle will pay our power bill this month," Vannock said. He asked, "Can Zoom be trained to find non-truffle species? Like Matsutake?"

"Very likely," Nico said. "I think Zoom has a strong ability that can grow from here."

"Ms. Dwerryhouse," Bopha said formally, "We'd like to offer you a job. I understand that Zoom belongs to Nico but that you are the one available to bring Zoom out this fall to hunt truffles for our guests."

"I am interested," Elspeth said, trying to stay calm even as her inner eye was visualizing a happy rhumba away from her table-bussing job. Nico winked at her.

"Let's see," Bopha mused. "We start events on the Labor Day weekend and go to the second weekend in December. Are you available?"

"Yes! I'll have some classes during the week but I am absolutely available to work weekends this fall."

"Lovely. Let's say a base pay of six hundred dollars a weekend?"

Elspeth blinked.

Vannock added, "Plus tips. I suspect many of our visitors will tip generously if you turn up more truffles like the one we found just now." He smiled at his wife. "The Beijing delegation would go nuts."

Bopha smiled back. "Hong Kong and Macau clubs too. Absolutely bonkers." She said to Elspeth, "We do plan a spring season as well. Meanwhile we would want you working in the gift shop too. We have a full line of truffle products from around the world. They are expensive, so our sales people need to know the product line thoroughly. From what Nico tells us, that would not be hard for you. If we can link the field finds to our gift store shopping, well, that could go together nicely. We could designate a percentage of the truffle product sales go to you on the days you are selling. Say, 10%?"

Nico arched an eyebrow at Elspeth. "What do you think?"

It took two tries to move past the lump in her throat before she croaked out, "I'd be delighted to be in the mushroom business."

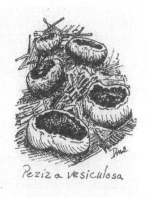

Peziza vesiculosa

Interested in reading another mushroom thriller by Ellen King Rice? The next page has the opening chapter of *The EvoAngel*— or check out www.ellenkingrice.com

"Once the mushroom has sprouted from the earth, there is no turning back." Luo proverb from Kenya

Chapter One

Tuesday morning, September 15,
Kamilche Peninsula, Shelton, Washington

She could poison the doctor.

Edna's hands trembled slightly as she lifted the latch on the door to her cabin. There was no lock. There had never been a need for one. Edna entered and hung her purse and jacket on the peg row by the front door. She desperately needed a cup of chamomile tea.

Oh, she knew which mushrooms to use. She could kill the doctor dead, dead, dead and, if she was careful, no one would connect the death to her.

Edna crossed her narrow living room, navigating carefully around the edge of the rug. At her age, she didn't need a fall.

She knew where to collect the Death Angel mushroom. There was a disturbed site behind the school bus barn that produced *Amanitas*. Even if the species she needed happened to be growing in a mixture of other fungi, as mushrooms often do, the Death Angel would stand out to her. She would know, instantly, when she had found any specimen of the Death Angels group. Eighty years of mushroom hunting was good for something. She knew her fungi.

Edna made it to her kitchen and rested her hands on the deep enamel sink. She remembered the day her husband had installed it. There was a chip near the drain hole. The geraniums on the windowsill needed watering. Edna blinked back tears. She had bigger challenges now. Her hands continued to tremble as she filled the teakettle.

She knew a Death Angel signaled its presence with a bright white stem erupting from an egg shaped sac. Then there was the white ring on the stalk, the white spores, the unattached white gills, and the elegant profile that all said *Amanita phalloides* just as clearly as a nametag.

She would have preferred the prettier *Amanita ocreata,* with its brighter cap, but that was a spring Death Angel. She was going to have to make do with the fall alternative.

As the flames of the propane burner licked the bottom of the teakettle, Edna's nerves steadied. She should think this through.

Amatoxins were not affected by heat. Cooked or raw, they poisoned. Surely a casserole would be a better vector than a salad. Who gave a gift salad?

Edna's mind skittered through the details. It would take several hours for the mushrooms in the dish to begin their poisoning of Dr. Band. The vomiting and diarrhea might not be connected with her offering. A day of intestinal agony might be attributed to a passing virus. She could hope. That weasel of a woman deserved all the agony the planet could deliver.

There would be a rebound day. Her victim would feel much better. It would be on the third or fourth day when the kidneys and liver began to fail.

Edna lifted the squealing kettle off the fire and poured the boiling water over a teabag. She made her mind take a step back from thoughts of murder.

She trusted Dr. Patel. He was a sweet man. None of this was his fault. She had made the appointment with him, trusting that her odd condition would be discretely discussed. And, no, she hadn't been naïve. It was time to tell someone about her changing body.

She had not known there was a visiting doctor at the clinic, an intense, scary woman with a tiny body and ferocious eyes. Dr. Band was a witch of the worst possible sort.

Edna grimaced, a sour taste in her mouth despite sipping the mild tea.

"These days it is 'witch' with a B," she muttered.

Dr. Band was trouble.

As she sipped her tea, Edna considered her options. She could get a dog. A large dog with large teeth. And a *No Trespassing* sign. Her daughter would think her aging poorly, with the fears of old age sprouting like mushrooms after fall rains.

Edna's mind veered back to murder. Weasels sometimes had to be killed to protect a flock. No matter what, she should protect her daughter and granddaughter.

What she had, they might have next.

Feathers. An old woman should be sprouting chin hairs, not feathers. And a feather had emerged on her sternum a month ago and now that odd emergence was adding little friends. Dr. Patel had been kind and soothing. Dr. Band had been . . . fascinated.

Edna had seen the rectangle of a smartphone in the pocket of Dr. Band's white coat. When Dr. Band's hand went snaking into that pocket, Edna had leapt off the examination table and she had fled the clinic. There would be no photographs of her chest. Not if she could help it.

Edna picked up a frame from a kitchen shelf and studied the picture of herself as a bride. Marrying a cousin had not seemed so bad as they had no plans of children. She had been a fifty-year-old bride, for heaven's sake.

"*Well, 'oops', as they say.*" Edna replaced her bridal picture on the shelf and took down a framed photo of Lena. Edna hugged the picture frame to her sagging chest. Her daughter Lena was so much more than they could have ever hoped for. More marvelous, more flawed and in so much danger from the modern world. Thank goodness Lena's husband was such a good man. And their daughter, Piper, had the family cunning to go with the family oddities.

Edna kissed the glass of the picture frame, steering her lips to the glowing halo of bright hair surrounding her daughter's perfect oval face. Edna's stomach swooped down with a wave of worry, then stabilized as the chamomile did its magic.

Edna's jangled thoughts began to settle. There was a better way.

She would protect Lena. She would protect her granddaughter. She would forge a back up plan in case she needed a speedy exit for Dr. Band. Forget the mushrooms that had sustained and enchanted her all these many years. She needed to get out of the cabin and into the woods. She would collect some water hemlock.

How to help an author

In these times of online algorithms, authors sink or swim by online reviews. Reviews on Amazon.com and GoodReads. com let an author know what worked and tells other readers what is worth their time and money.

Please talk about what you read, whether it is online or in person. Your words shape the market and help an author grow or retrench. Your opinion matters!

Find out more about Ellen's books at:
www.ellenkingrice.com

And join in on Facebook at: https://tinyurl.com/y7k4w6gu

Thank You!

Thank you, friends and family who have supported these mycological adventures. I am grateful for the assistance of Duncan Sheffels, Gloria Temple, Sally and Gregg Bennett, Steve Ness, Cindy Levy, Chris Herrera, Melodie Gates, Greg Falxa, Janet Brislawn, Teri Brown, Hilary Lewis, Lee French, Connie Jasperson and the many friends at the Olympia Writers Group, the Oyster Bay Book Club and the South Sound Mushroom Club.

Most of all, I send my thanks and love to Cliff, Paxton and Forrest Rice.

Made in the USA
San Bernardino, CA
27 July 2018